Needle In A Haystack

CHAPTER 1

Her mind was wandering. She was mentally checking off all the things she still had left to do. She really needed to bounce, but, Mr. Gore was going on and on. She glanced impatiently at her watch. *Aaaaaahhh! If this fool don't shut up! I've got fifty-leven things I need to be doing and he calls an impromptu meeting! I knew I should have just kept the party at Marvelious like we did every year, but noooo, I just had to have this hotel's huge ballroom with that fly VIP area and the huge glass window overlooking the ballroom. This is my fifth and last year doing the B93 Biggest Baddest Birthday Bash and I want to go out in style! And, from the looks of it, it's going to be huge! Let's see, all of our performing artists are here and accounted for, and I've even secured that super-fine sing-his-butt-off Giovanni Lay as the headliner. Advance tickets and the hotel are sold out. So, I really don't feel like listening to this right now. I'll just have to let him ramble on a little longer and help this man understand that not all black people are going to shoot up his dern hotel!*

"...So, that's why I was thinking maybe we should put metal detectors at the doors," said Mr. Joshua Gore, the middle aged portly General Manager of the Grand Omni Hotel and current pain in her booty.

Skerrrrt... In the words of Whitney Houston, aw HELLS to the NAW! I know he is not trying to flip the script! And on the day of the event!

Brooklyn Bridges cleared her throat and smiled calmly. Her leg bouncing a mile a minute under the table was the only clue that she was upset.

"Mr. Gore, you and I want the same thing, to have a nice and safe event tonight. In the previous four years that my radio station has done this event, not once has there been an incident. In fact, none of our station events have ever had a shooting, not even a fist fight to break out. Not once! That is not who my audience is. Now, I can sit here and go over Radio 101 with you and explain the difference between radio station listeners, but really, I don't have the time," she stated, starting to get frustrated. "The event is tonight and I am not going to sit here making changes on something that was done over nine months ago! Now, didn't we sell out your hotel… all the rooms are booked?"

He stammered and stuttered, "Yes, but..."

"No buts, Mr. Gore. My listening audience are professionals. And frankly, we're going to be looking too good to be messing up our beautiful and much too expensive outfits," Brook joked with a smile, somewhat easing the tension in the room.

From working on the event they had a mutual, professional respect for each other. He had been very helpful and accommodating throughout the planning and execution, that's why Brooklyn didn't understand why he was trying to switch it up on her, today, the day of the event. He knew legally there was nothing he could do, but, he was still trying her. And she knew that to make her event as successful as she wanted it to be, she needed him to be 100% on board.

"Mr. Gore, can I talk openly with you? Now, we've had this event planned for almost a year, and tonight is the big night. Instead of making sure everything else is going according to plan, I'm in here with you, discussing things that we've already finalized."

Mr. Gore cleared his throat, turning slightly red, and stated, "Well, Ms. Bridges, people were saying they had a big shootout over at *Marvelious* when that other radio station had their big party, so we just want to take precautions."

"Mr. Gore," Brook sighed, "let me give you a quick rundown, and it will have to be quick because I really have a lot to do. What kind of music do you listen to?"

He looked at her like she was straight trippin', but said, "Well, I like news talk myself, but if I'm in the mood to listen to music, then I'll listen to soft rock."

"Okay, now if you were going to have a nice evening out with the wife and were going to listen to live music, would you go listen to a heavy metal band?"

"Of course not! I don't listen to that crap," he said indignantly.

"Well, you're white and if you're white, then you must go to those concerts and break things, and tattoo and pierce all kinds of unspeakable parts of your body," she said with a smile, dimples deepening both of her cheeks. "My point is, you're an adult and you do adult things and listen to adult music. The same goes for the people that will be attending the event tonight. They're no more interested in fighting than you are interested in getting a tattoo... on your face." Brook laughed.

"Point taken, Ms. Bridges," he conceded with a grin, nodding his head.

"Thank you, Mr. Gore. This is going to be a great event. Your hotel is sold out. Advance tickets are sold out. I just need you to make sure your people are on top of things. Now, is everything set with the top shelf drinks in VIP?"

"Yes, it will be handled, Ms. Bridges. Have a great evening, and I'll see you tonight."

And that's why Brooklyn Bridges was one of the baddest Promotion Directors in the Midwest. She got the job done!

CHAPTER 2

"Hey, Mr. Toby, you have everything in order for me?" Brooklyn asked the ever-present front desk manager at the Grand Omni.

She had come to really care about the old man. He reminded her of old Negro spirituals and marching with Dr. King. He wasn't very tall, probably about five-seven, but was strong as an ox and stood erect, like he was proud, and was anywhere from age sixty to ninety years old. He'd told Brook that he'd been working at that hotel for over forty years, way before the renovation. He lost his wife of "forever" about three years ago. "She's gone on to glory," he had woefully exclaimed. He had two grown daughters, Courtney and Brittany, with three grandsons, Tayveon, Taron, and Tyler. Courtney, her husband, and Tayveon lived in town and Mr. Toby went to dinner there every Sunday. Brittany, her husband, and two sons, Taron and Tyler, lived in Georgia and her husband was a retired Army Vet. "My grandboys love me to death," Mr. Toby said proudly. Yep, over the past nine months, Mr. Toby had told Brooklyn all about his life.

"Yes ma'am, Ms. Bridges, got everything ready just like you asked. I've got the welcome baskets in all the rooms. Giovanni Lay's suite is at the end of the hallway and his security has the room next to it. You have the whole fifteenth floor for all the artists and their party. Man, they sure travel with a lot of people." Mr. Toby laughed, looking up from his clipboard.

"That's why the radio station is only paying for the artists' rooms. They can pay for their own entourage if they want them to come. And no gratuities! Please make sure of that, Mr. Toby. I remember my first year doing this I got stuck with a $2000 gratuities bill!"

"Already taken care of, Ms. Bridges."

"And, Mr. Toby, for the hundredth time, will you please call me Brook like all my friends do?"

"Will do, Ms. Bridges." Mr. Toby smiled.

"Divvvaaaaa!" Brook heard the screech all the way across the room. It was her favorite record rep and good friend, Pamela Saunders.

They'd done so many of these events together. She'd bring in whatever artist was hot at the time, to whatever event the radio station happened to be doing. She and Brook had become great friends. Pam always showed Brook the best time when Brook was in Atlanta. In fact, she was one of the main reasons Brook had the new job in Hotlanta. Pam had given her a wonderful reference and Brook was making the move from Promotions to Sales.

"Divvvaaalicious," Brook screeched back, probably frightening the people in the posh hotel. The ladies always attracted attention whenever they were together. Both were approximately the same size, 5'5, weighing in at around one hundred forty pounds. They weren't skin and bones, but shapely, with womanly curves in all the right places. They both wore a size eight in clothing and in shoes and really tripped when out shopping they discovered they even wore the same bra size, 34C. The craziest part was they both had deep dimples. However, their looks were totally different. Brook had a bronzed penny complexion with slanted almond-shaped eyes and while she had always worn her hair long, down past her shoulders, she had recently gotten it cut. Pam was light skinned with what they called 'good hair', always rocked a bangin' short cut, and had the cutest round eyes.

With hugs and air kisses, Pam squealed, "You cut your hair!"

"Yeah, you like?"

"I love it! It's just so, so.... sassy! And it looks fierce, girl."

"Thanks, sweetie, my head feels so much lighter with short hair, should have done it a long time ago."

"And, check you out! You are wearing that suit, girl. Aren't you kinda dressed up to be having a party tonight?"

"Had a meeting with the general manager of this hotel, girl, talking about we need metal detectors," Brook said, rolling her eyes. They both burst out laughing, never getting over how much white America truly didn't understand the sophistication of the adult urban radio listener. They were running their mouths so much that Brook didn't even notice when they walked up behind her.

Ump, he's even finer in person, Brook thought when she turned around.

Pam said, "Gio, this is my girl Brooklyn Bridges, the Promotions Director at B93 and the person who put this gig together. Brook, this is Giovanni Lay and his bodyguard, Tha Dogg."

Now that is the perfect name for him. He looked like he's tear somebody apart, Brook thought. She felt safe just being near him.

"Hello, Giovanni, Tha Dogg. Welcome to Louisville, the city of fast horses and fine women, or fine horses and fast women, depending on how lucky you are." Brook winked and everyone chuckled. As Gio shook her hand she looked into his eyes. *Yep, a sista could get lost in those. What are they? Gray? Green? Brown? Just exactly what color is that?* Brook wondered.

He really did look better in person, and that was saying a lot because he was hella fine on television. And that smile, those teeth. Okay, Brook knew she had to get a grip! She'd been around some of the hottest acts around and hadn't had that reaction. Of course, there were some she was attracted to, a few that she wouldn't mind getting hot and sweaty with, but she always remained professional. She'd seen it happen too many times. Established, professional woman gets busy with an artist, next thing you knew, the word got out and she was reduced to somebody's latest conquest. Not happening to her! She'd worked too dern hard to get where she was. But, he was indeed foine. Standing about 6'2', he was lean, yet muscular, as you could see from those hot videos he made. He was a nice shade of chocolate, which was what really made his eyes stand out, and had his hair cut in a nice, low cut. *Mm, mm, good. Yes sir, just mm, mm, good.*

"I hope your ride was nice from the airport," Brook stated, her professional side taking back over. "Here's Mr. Toby now. He'll take good care of you. And I know what y'all are thinking," Brook whispered to the three as they watched Mr. Toby approach "Why his name gotta be Toby?" exclaimed Brook. They all broke out laughing, remembering the slave named Toby from the movie *Roots* who had to change his name from Kunta Kinte.

"You crazy, Ms. Bridges," stated Tha Dogg, chuckling.

"Hey, that's Brook! Ms. Bridges is my mama," grinned Brook, this time showing off her deep dimples.

"Hey, Mr. Toby, this is Mr. Giovanni Lay and his body guard, Tha Dogg," introduced Brook.

"Well, that's a good name for ya, Tha Dogg, 'cause you sure do look vicious," laughed Mr. Toby, not one to be tactful.

They all laughed, because even though Mr. Toby wasn't being very tactful, mean was another thing he wasn't. He was just funny, in a grandpa kind of way.

"And, this is Pamela Saunders, Mr. Toby, the one who will be handling the business part of it."

Mr. Toby, with a huge smile on his face, asked Pam to follow him, talking the whole way.

Old flirt, Brook thought, chuckling at how Mr. Toby seemed to even stand taller.

"Let me grab your room keys, and you two can go on up," Brook said, noticing the crowd of people standing around whispering and staring.

Better hurry this up, she thought. She hurried over to the desk and grabbed the keys while Pam finished up the paperwork. Brook gave Tha Dogg both key cards, showing him the room numbers that were written on the envelope. She gave them both her business card and told them to call her if they needed anything. She also gave them a copy of the itinerary for Giovanni Lay.

"Radio station at 4pm, sound check at 7pm, then performing at midnight, otherwise, the limo is yours to do as you want." Brook thanked Gio again for coming and headed over to Chris, the limo driver. "Here's the itinerary, Chris, you know the dealio."

"Not a problem, Ms. Bridges. You know I never let you down."

"I know, Chris, but I'm just a little stressed on this one, just making sure everything is everything."

"I feel ya, Ms. Bridges. This is your last gig, you trying to go out with a bang. I just don't know what I'm gonna do when you leave. You have definitely showed a brotha love on these gigs."

"I've given you a great reference, so I'm sure whoever takes my place will continue to request you as a driver. You earned it, Chris. I wasn't giving you a hook up, because you know one slip up and your behind would not have been driving," she teased.

"That I know, Ms. Bridges," Chris said seriously, "that I do know."

CHAPTER 3

Thank goodness Brook had checked into her room at the hotel and dropped off her clothes earlier. At least coming to the hotel to meet with Mr. Gore wasn't a total waste of time. She was back at the office tying up a few loose ends. As she strolled through the radio station, Justin and the Crazy Crew, B93's hilarious hometown morning show, were in the conference room. She went in to make sure all was set.

"Hey, fellas, how did the on air interviews go?" she asked Justin, her boss and Program Director of the Urban stations. Justin was one of the best programmers period. He'd taken their stations from little, black, hometown radio stations to revenue making, award winning stations. The big wigs just loved him. He was another person that helped her get hired in Atlanta.

"Everything is smooth sailing. You know how I do." He grinned cockily.

Justin was fine. Light-skinned, curly hair fine with a bangin' body, drove a Porsche, single, no kids, and just a straight up ho. Really, how much punani could one man get? And the ladies just loved him! Truth was, Justin hadn't been right since his divorce. Supposedly, his ex-wife did him super wrong. The story went he thought they were trying to have a family, only to find out she had gotten pregnant and had an abortion. And, he only found out about it because a friend of a friend was there at the clinic and told. He never talked about it and unless you knew him back then, you'd never even know he'd been married. Well, he'd been a ho ever since, and that was nearly five years ago. Men just never knew how to get past heartbreak, yet, women did it every day.

"The last interview is Giovanni Lay, he'll be here at 4pm," Brook reminded.

"We know. We got that from the itinerary, the email, and the meeting. You stressing, sis? I know this is your last hoorah, but I don't remember ever seeing you doubting your execution."

"Yeah, just a little bit," Brook admitted.

Although she'd probably done this almost one hundred times, she still got those jitters the day of the event. Normally, they didn't really get to her, but this was the big one... the biggest event they'd had so far and the event everyone would remember her by. It didn't matter that she'd done those events successfully over the past five years. People would remember a mess up. Plus, the fact that she was a Virgo, the perfectionist, she really needed to de-stress.

"Had a crazy meeting with Mr. Gore about metal detectors at the doors tonight. That man was on my last one!"

"What? I know he ain't trippin' 'bout the event that is tonight," he exploded. "I know he don't want me to crack the mic on his ass! I'll have the whole city boycotting that hotel!"

"Pump your brakes, bruh, it's all good. I handled him... 'cause you know how *I* do." Brook grinned, dimples beaming and all.

Brook walked into her office and shut the door. Well, her little piece of an office. It wasn't that big, had a window, but not a real view. She could look down and see traffic since they were on the 5th floor and she could see other buildings, but that was it. That didn't matter to her. She still liked her little space. She sat behind her desk, picked up the phone, and hit speed dial #2.

The phone barely rang when she heard, "You know it's going to go fine, everything is on time and everything is in order. You got that organizational part from me," laughed Brook's mother, Frances.

"Hey, Mama, how did you know I was stressing?"

"Well, this is the big finale. And I know my baby girl. You want to make sure everything is perfect. Don't worry. It will go as smoothly as always. Do you have your list?"

"Yes, ma'am. And almost everything is checked off."

"Then everything is going according to plan. Now, quit worrying before you get an ulcer and go on out there and do your thing."

"Yes, ma'am." Brook laughed. "Thank you, Mama, I love you."

"I love you too, baby girl."

As always, after talking to her mother, Brook felt better. She changed into jeans and her station tee, threw on her Peppermint Crème Pastries, and left. She really loved the cute little gym shoes that the Simmons sisters had come out with. And she loved her some *Run's House*. She even liked their spin off, *Daddy's Girls,* and was glad there was finally a program showing positive young ladies and not just dirty dancing all over the videos. Brook slid into her Mercedes and tuned in to finish listening to the interview with Giovanni Lay. They had arrived at the radio station not long ago and did the customary picture taking and autograph signing for the employees. The interview was going great when she left. He and Katelyn-J, the afternoon drive jock, were really vibing.

"Not only is he fine, ladies," Katelyn-J was winding down the interview, "but he smells hella good, too. And you know Katelyn-J loves her a man that smells good," she flirted.

"And, I loves me a woman who loves her a man that smells good,"

Gio joked right back.

"Well then, let's smell good together," she said seductively.

"Well, alright now!"

"Oh yeah, we are live on the air," she laughed. "Okay, forreal forreal, are those contacts?"

Gio laughed "No, they're the real thing."

"So, exactly what color are your eyes?"

"Sepia is the actual name of the color."

"You know what, sepia is my new favorite color!" she said. They both laughed. "I'd like to thank Mr. Giovanni Lay for coming to our fine city and helping us to celebrate our Fifth Annual B93 Baddest Birthday Bash going down tonight at the new location, the Grand Omni, downtown Louisville. This is Katelyn-J, and I'll see y'all tonight after I go get beautified and smelling good." She laughed.

Brook stopped at the party supply store to pick up some little champagne glass confetti she forgot to pick up on one of her many trips to the store. She wanted to add them to the tables in VIP. She had little birthday cake confetti for the regular tables. She finished her last minute errands and headed to the hotel. She was getting out of her car when she heard it again.

"Diiivvaaa!" Brook grinned at her crazy friend.

"Heeeey, Divaaalicious!" she screamed back.

As they got out of the limo, Brook told Gio how great she thought the interview went. Gio laughed and said that Katelyn-J was off the chain. Brook grabbed her Nextel and chirped Candi, her life-saver assistant.

"Hey, Boss Lady," came Candi's reply.

"Hey, Candi, Mr. Lay is here and ready for sound check. Are we ready in there?"

"We're good to go. We finished up the last sound check about ten minutes ago. Is Giovanni Lay as fine as he is on TV?" whispered Candi, not knowing he was right there and could hear her.

Brook gave the phone to Gio and he said, "I don't know about all that, but I'm really cool peoples."

They all fell out laughing while Candi stuttered and stammered, and finally hung up the phone. They laughed even harder.

As they walked into the hotel, Brook saw Tiffany, the party decorator she had been using at their events for the past three years.

"Hey, girl, you got it looking good as always," Brook said.

And it was. The balloon arch was beautiful in the colors of the radio station logo, sage and mauve.

"Thanks, Brook. It's your vision that's coming alive. And, you must be Mr. Giovanni Lay." Tiffany smiled, reaching out to give him a handshake.

"Yes, ma'am," grinned Gio.

"Hi, I'm Tiffany, Tiffany Bennett and decorator to the stars. You need someone to decorate something, I'm your girl," she winked. "Bam!" she hollered, scaring the crap out of all of them and about to get a big karate chop from Tha Dogg as she pulled out her business card. "Just in case you need a decorator... or something. Holla at cha girl."

Shame, shame, shame. Just no shame at all, Brook thought. "Okay," Brook said, "we'll let you get back to work."

Tiffany sashayed herself back over to the balloons, ba-dunk-a-dunking all the way. She knew she had a certified sistagirl booty, and knew they would look. Of course, Gio and Tha Dogg did with boyish grins on their faces.

As they all trooped into the ballroom, Tha Dogg let out a whistle. "This is nice, real nice," he said, with his best Bernie Mac impression. They all laughed.

Brook noticed a huge portable stage some workers were moving out of the ballroom. "Excuse me." Brook hurried over. "Where are you going with that stage? Is someone else using it?"

"Nope. We're just taking it to storage," answered one of the workers, "since you all are using the big stage."

Brooke had an idea. "Let me ask you something. Do you think you can wheel that stage over in front of the VIP door? We can use portable stairs to get up and down. We'll have somewhere for the artists to sit inside the party instead of just being in a separate room."

She knew through experience that people loved having the celebrities in the party with them. And, the stage was big enough to comfortably allow for a good five round tables with six chairs at each.

"Sure, we can do that. And, we have portable steps in the back. We have them in three steps and five steps. We'll see which works best."

"Are you all coming to the event tonight?" asked Brook.

"Well, we were planning on it, but I heard the tickets are sold out."

"I tell you what, you two hook this up for me, make this stage an extension of the VIP room, and I'll give you a pair of tickets each. Can you make that happen?"

"That's a bet," the tall one said.

"We got your back," said the short one.

That's another thing Brook knew, people loved freebies. And for freebies, they *would* have your back. Those guys were over there humping, putting the stage in place. She knew when they were done, her vision would be there. And what a great idea! The VIP area was now bigger with an inside and an outside. *Man, I'm good,* thought Brook with a smile. And for the finishing touch, she'd have an intern hang a couple of station banners on front of the stage and put reserved name cards on the tables for the artists. She chirped Candi so she could get the interns to make it happen.

Gio was still doing his sound check and was up there blowing! That boy knew he could sang. Not sing, but sang. He hit the highs, the lows, and the in betweens. She turned around to check him out and saw he was already checking her out. She smiled and gave him the thumbs up signal and left. She still had thangs to do.

CHAPTER 4

Brook was finished getting ready. The party started at 9pm and it was almost 9:30. She had just gotten her hair hooked up by her girl, Lorri, and it was fly. Lorri knew she could lay some hair. Brook was rockin' a beautiful, gold beaded Chanel halter dress that fell just below her thighs, so it wasn't an ultra mini, but also wasn't above the knee. It was more like above the above the knee mark, if there was such a thing. The halter showed the small tattoo on her shoulder of an angel with *Grammie* written under it in cursive. Her shoes were Prada… gold, strappy, and bangin'. She just hoped they didn't start to hurt later.

It was time to roll out. Checking herself out in the mirror and satisfied that nothing was out of place and no little unfriendlies were hanging out of her nose, she grabbed her cute, little, gold beaded handbag and headed on down to the party. She knew the party was going to be off the chain. That was the thing she loved about the radio station listeners, give them a chance to dress up and they would show out! From minis to gowns, and suits to tuxedos, they would wear it all and that's just the way Brook liked it. Their parties were always dressy events unless they did a theme, like their Funky Fresh Throw Back Jam when they dressed in the 80s, or their Pajama Jam when they dressed in their nightclothes. She figured as long as they kept the music old school, the kids would stay away. Added with an enforced dress code and a twenty-five and older requirement, they were sure to have an adult event. It was time the grown folks had somewhere to go without worrying about getting shot or a fight breaking out. Her listeners knew that if they were coming to a B93 event, then it was gonna be on point.

Brook took the elevator and headed down to the main ballroom, and it was a beautiful sight! Tiffany knew she had it going on. The decorations were impeccable, the balloon arch festive without being kiddy and sprays of sage and mauve flowers everywhere. There was a long line to get in, Brook noted, and the interns looked like they were stressing. People hated to wait in line. Heck, she hated to wait in line! Brook headed to the front door to see what the hold up was. They had four people there, one collecting money, one checking IDs, and two putting on the entry bracelets since that took the longest.

"Good evening, good peoples," Brook greeted.

"Hey, Brook," they greeted a little nervously.

"Looks like the line is backed up. Why don't we do this, I need one person checking IDs, and all you have to do is look at the year and keep it moving, one person taking tickets, and two lines of people collecting money. Just give them their bracelet instead of putting it on them."

Brook then asked the line of people to separate. "If you have advanced tickets, come to the far left line, if you still need to purchase tickets, then these two lines are selling tickets." As they split into the separate lines, there was a huge sigh of relief from those waiting. "This is how you work more effectively," she told the interns with a smile.

Brook walked around the huge ballroom, stopping briefly to talk to friends and acquaintances. Candi and her trusted interns executed every detail and had even done some things she hadn't asked for. From the banners to the table of souvenir glasses, every detail she had planned was executed perfectly. Candi knew her so well. *Now this is how things run smoothly,* thought Brook. She walked over to the table where the commemorative souvenir glasses were being sold.

"Hey, Jayla, how's it going?" Brook asked.

"Pretty slow," Brook's favorite intern replied.

"Yeah, it should start out pretty slow, which is why you're here alone. You all will do the one hour shifts and then one hour before we close, I'll have all five of you here. That's when the big crowd will come to buy glasses. No one really wants to carry glasses around with them. Awww, that's my jam!" Brook said as Kid Capri played *Tootsie Roll,* the old jam by 95South. The dance floor instantly got packed, everybody breaking out in the tootsie roll.

Brook made her way into VIP where the powers that be hung around talking, laughing, and enjoying the fact that they were VIP. As Brook walked through the room, she shook hands and gave out hugs to some of Louisville's most prominent African Americans. That was the fun part, because even though Brook was pretty down to earth, it was nice knowing Louisville's important people. And even better was Louisville's important people knew her. She really was going to miss that. And there was Mr. Gore, smiling and grinning all over the place.

"Ms. Bridges," Mr. Gore greeted happily. "A wonderful party you have here. And, I just want to apologize again for giving you such a hard time."

"No problem, Mr. Gore, it just takes some people longer to understand some things than others," Brook said with a smile, rubbing it in a bit.

Brook made her way onto the stage/VIP area inside the party. *Man, this was really a good idea,* she thought. She saw Tiffany and Candi's touch there as well. Tiffany had added two beautiful balloon bouquets at each end of the stage and little planters of sage and mauve flowers across the front of the stage. *Yep, one of them babies is coming home with me tonight,* she thought. Mama would love it. Candi had added reserved signs with nice candle centerpieces on each table. Candi had come such a long way. Brook was so proud of her and knew she was going to make a great Promotions Director. They were even able to add more tables for the air personalities and there was still room enough to get around. Brook made her way over to her Station Manager and good friend, Dominique Ochoa, to see how she was enjoying herself.

"Brook, this ballroom is absolutely beautiful. You really outdid yourself this time," said Dominique, a beauty from Trinidad you wouldn't even think was the Station Manager and definitely wouldn't guess she was in her fifties. She looked like a thirty year old exotic model. "And, where the heck did this little area come from?" Dominique asked.

"It's a portable stage," Brook whispered. They both fell out laughing.

"Girl, you know you will find an idea from anything!"

"Come on, honey. Hey, Brook," shouted Ralph, Dominique's husband, "that is my song!"

As they made their way to the dance floor to the sounds of *Doing Da Butt*, Brook could only laugh at some of these people really thinking they were looking good doing da butt.

It was about time for the artists' performances to start, so Brook headed back stage to make sure everyone was ready to get it started. The first person Brook spotted was Candi, clearing people out of the path so the artists could get through easily. That was Brook's #1 pet peeve, people back stage. Either go in the party or in VIP, there was absolutely nothing back stage to do but be in the way.

"Excuse me! I need everyone to go out front. This is not part of the party area and is hazardous for the artist. So, can everyone please move it out front so you can enjoy the concert?" Brook said firmly, but kindly.

Everyone started moving out the door to get the best spot in front of the stage. Candi looked at Brook in amazement.

"How do you do that?" Candi asked. "I've been asking them to move for the longest!"

"You don't ask them, you tell them in a way that's firm, but doesn't piss anyone off. And, they have to know that you will throw their behinds out of the party if they even think about showing out. It just comes with time. Next year when you're doing your own event, you'll see."

Candi held up her hand, fingers crossed.

"You have done a wonderful job as usual. What in the world would I have done without you?" asked Brook, giving Candi a hug.

"Die, just die and throw the worst possible events in Louisville's history." She laughed.

"I really do appreciate you, girl," Brook said, getting sentimental.

"I know," Candi said with a big smile, blinking back tears. "Now let's get these groups on stage. These may be Louisville's sophisticated adults, but they will act a complete fool if this concert doesn't start on time!" Brook couldn't argue with that.

CHAPTER 5

Brook and Candi met up and were making their way throughout the party, checking on the food table and making sure everything was in order. "Oooh, I just can't wait for Giovanni Lay to perform, you know he is too fine for his own good," laughed Candi.

Three groups had performed and they had one more to go before Gio did his performance. Brook noticed that having multiple bars was a good idea because although all of them had a line, it wasn't too much of a line that would make you impatient.

"Girl, haven't you seen him perform on television a hundred times?"

"But this is the live, in person, throw some sweat on me performance," laughed Candi.

"Well, I'm just glad these performances are about over. I just had to have five performers for our five years. But they all have done good. Three down, two to go."

"You did a wonderful job, Brook. This is a memorable event and I'm going to miss you entirely too much. Even if I do get your position at the radio station, you have taught me what it is to have a great event and I will have awfully big shoes to fill," Candi said, getting misty eyed again.

"Girl, don't you start. You're gonna make me mess up my makeup. I taught you what you wanted to learn. You have been my assistant for what, two years, and you have done more in that two years than any assistant I've ever had. You think about what I'd like before I do, which means you know what is needed. You are going to be a great Promotions Director," Brook said, giving Candi a hug.

"Thank you, sweetie. Now you go back in VIP and make those people feel important. I got it out here."

"Alright, boo. I'll holla at you later. Just don't jump on stage with Gio while he's performing and start hoochie dancing all over him."

Candi laughed and headed through the party, making sure there was nothing left undone.

Brook really did want to see Giovanni Lay perform, too, but didn't want to act like a groupie. That was #2 on her pet peeve list... groupies! So when he went on stage, she would have to find a nice little spot to peep him.

CHAPTER 6

"Wanna dance?" the fine brotha rocking a nice crème colored suit asked Brook.

"No, thank you. I'm still working. But, I will take a rain check," Brook flirted.

"I'm gonna hold you to that, too," he flirted back.

Gio was to go on in about a half hour. Brook wandered backstage again to check on the progress, and there was Candi, making sure it was clear. No groupies and no people were standing around. That was one of the great things about her, you told her something once and she was like a sponge, she soaked it up.

"Hey, girl. I see we're all set back here."

"Yep! No groupies, no crowds, just waiting for His Fineness to make his appearance," laughed Candi.

As Brook made her way back toward VIP, she noticed how pretty the new VIP area looked. It stood out with the tables glowing from the candle centerpieces and all the artists sitting and standing around. It was high enough that the people couldn't climb up on it without being noticed, but it was still low enough so people could see who was sitting up there, which was a bonus. Brook made her rounds, talking to the artists and thanking them for coming.

"Heeeeyy, Diva," Brook heard, turning around to see her friend and soon to be homegirl making her way onto the VIP stage.

"Heeey, Pam! You're looking as fly as usual."

"Fly ain't even the word for you! You know you are wearing that dress!"

"Can't go wrong with Chanel," dimpled Brook.

"I take it Gio is ready to go on?"

"But of course. I don't care how big the artist is, you know I don't play. Although with him, he is totally professional and no problem, thank goodness. He asked me if you were married." She grinned.

"What!? Girl, you know I don't mess around with the help."

"And that's just what I told him, you were not the one. So, are you really ready to give up all of this? You're going to into a field of cutthroats and back stabbers in sales. You know it's about the commission. But, you will make good money. I can't believe you're finally making the move."

"I'm so ready. Although I love my city, I'm ready to get away for a while. I went to high school here and went to college at the University of

Louisville. I just want a change. My best friend, Debra, moved there two years ago and she loves it. And the great part is, I'm still close enough to come see my parents whenever I want. But to be honest, I'm a little nervous about the career change. Everyone says I'll be great, but I'm still a little nervous."

"Well, that's normal. Of course you'll be a little nervous, but we tell you you're going to do well because we know you. You won't rest until you're the top seller in the station." Pam laughed.

"You do know me. In one month, I'll be starting a new career in a new city."

"But, you'll have old friends and definitely some new ones. You know you *gots* to remember to watch out for the down-lows! You know Atlanta is the new San Francisco... they're everywhere!"

"Girl, I'm trying to get my grind on with this sales thing first and foremost. I'm focusing on my career. The men, that'll be my bonus. And if I have that itch, you know I can always come back home and get a round with old trusty Roman, bless his heart," Brook said.

"Why do you always say bless his heart when you speak of him?"

"Do I? I never even noticed I did that. Probably because I feel guilty 'cause I feel like I'm using him. He really does deserve a good woman, it's just that I'm not that one. I'm not ready to settle down and have 2.5 kids. Hopefully when I'm gone, he'll find the one."

"Girl, please, you're only doing what he allows you to do. He's reaping the benefits, too. You're giving him the goods, right? And you're not asking him for a commitment, so he should be happy."

"That's just the thing, he wants more and I'm happy just giving him the goods. That's why I'm deciding right now I will not make booty calls to Roman when I'm gone. He's never gonna find somebody if I keep coming back confusing him. So, I figure I'll have three months to get this sales thing together, then it's on in Atlanta, 'cause after six months of no sex, my disposition starts to change!"

"Six months?" screeched Pam. "Psssh, make that one."

CHAPTER 7

Brook's feet hurt. The shoes were definitely not meant to be walked on for four hours. Gio, their final act, had finished about fifteen minutes prior and the party was in full swing. She had another hour and then it would be over. Brook walked into VIP, got a glass of wine, and grabbed a seat in the back of the room. She really didn't feel like socializing anymore because she was tired and ready for the night to end. She had just sent the interns back to the souvenir table to finish selling the commemorative glasses. The rest of the night would be smooth sailing.

"You look tired," Brook heard. She looked up and there was Gio in all of his fineness.

"That's not exactly a compliment."

"Oh, no, I didn't mean it like that."

"I know, just thought I'd mess with you." She laughed. "I am tired and my really cute shoes are hurting my feet."

"Would you like a foot massage?"

Brook chuckled. "No thanks, I'm good."

"I'm just saying, a brotha's got some skills in the feet department," Gio flirted, wiggling his fingers.

"I'm sure you do," laughed Brook.

"You mind if I sit?" he asked.

"No problem. Have a seat."

"This was a very nice event. I've been to some radio events and you would not believe what they do, and don't do."

"One thing my GM always said is we would not have chitlin' radio. Just because we're a black station doesn't mean we have to be ghetto."

"True that."

"So, I see the new album is doing well. It sounds like you've got another hit on your hands."

"Thank you. I'm just doing what I love to do, and that's sing. The fact that I get paid to do it is a bonus."

"I hear you. Well, if you weren't singing, what would you be doing?"

"Hmmmm, probably something in the business while trying to get on *Wheel of Fortune*."

"What? You are not a *Wheel of Fortune* fan!"

"Why, do I look stupid or something?" He laughed.

"No, there's just not that many of us."

"You a Wheel fan, too?"

"Yes, sir! Got my Spin ID and everything."

"Me too! The only problem is when I'm on the road. I still tape it though, and hope I'm not too late if my number comes up."

"So from now on when I'm watching, if the spin ID starts with GL, I'll know it may be you."

"I'll do you one even better. How about I give you my phone number? That way, you can call me and tell me when a GL number comes up."

Think he's slick, Brook thought. She heard the DJ say it was the last song. "Okay, Mr. *Wheel of Fortune*. I'll call you if I ever see a Spin ID that starts with GL."

Gio happily jotted down his phone number, knowing she'd probably call him in a few days.

CHAPTER 8

Brook couldn't believe it was really time to go to Atlanta. The last month seemed to fly by with packing up her house and making sure the movers got all of her stuff in storage with no mishaps. She had gotten a realty company to handle the screening of potential tenants and to rent out her house and they were good. There was already a nice family that was due to move in. Brook moved back home with her parents her last weeks in Louisville. She was excited and scared at the same time. She had never failed at anything she put her mind to and knew that eventually, she'd get the hang of the sales thing. Brook had talked to Rose and a few of the other sales people at her station and had gotten a lot of good advice.

"The main thing," Rose Lyons, one of the most successful salespeople and good friend of Brook's explained, "is to make sure they understand that your station is a commodity. You are not going to ask them to buy advertising from you so you can make your budget. You are helping their company increase revenue by reaching thousands of potential buyers through your radio station. Word of mouth is fine. But, how many people can you actually reach through word of mouth? Maybe fifty, I'll even say one hundred on the high side. Your station will reach thousands!" Brook hugged and thanked her. She had never heard it broken down so simply before and it made so much sense.

Atlanta has too much dern traffic! You needed a flying car to get around here, Brook thought. She finally reached her hotel, the Crowne Plaza in Buckhead. The radio station had put her up for two weeks and she started work in one week. She had two weeks to find a place to stay, otherwise, she'd move in with Debra until she found something.

It was Saturday and Debra had taken off work for the next few days to show her around town. Debra, never to be called Debbie Williams, was her childhood home girl from Louisville who talked her into moving to Atlanta in the first place. They met in the second grade and had been best friends ever since. Debra transferred to Atlanta two years prior when her bank opened a new huge branch downtown. She was a Senior Loan Officer in Louisville and went to try out the market in Atlanta. When Debra moved, Louisville had gotten so boring. Brook missed her friend. People always thought Debra was a model because she was tall. The thing was, she wasn't really model tall, but when you were a woman and stood 5'7 and wore three to six inch heels, that was tall enough. Her looks were exotic due to the fact that her mom was Black and her dad was Hawaiian. She kinda favored Chili from the group TLC, minus the slicked down baby hair, and her eyes were more slanted. While Brook worked out and prided her body, Debra never worked out and had a body women envied and men craved. Debra lived in Marietta, one of the many suburbs of Atlanta. So, they were going to start looking there first. Brook had planned on finding an apartment complex that would give her a six month lease, and then she could figure out if and where she wanted to buy her home.

As Brook was unpacking her stuff, her phone rang. Grabbing her phone out of her purse, she answered screaming, "I'm here!"

Brook heard a big scream on the other end of the phone "Girl, about damn time, too," Debra screamed. "Are you finished unpacking?"

"Not quite, but I'm getting there."

"By the time I get to that side of town you'll be finished."

"Ain't that it! I sure hope I get used to this traffic."

"You will. You just learn to use the traffic time wisely. I was going to take you to show you all the different areas of town today, but, girl, guess what? My girl, Carmen Stewart, she's a Realtor. She told me about a house right here in my neighborhood, a good three minutes away! I know you said you wanted to rent for a while first, but, girl, with the way the economy is going, the house is a steal."

"For real? Tell me more."

"It's only like four or five years old, three bedroom, two and a half bath, two-story, nice sized eat in kitchen, separate living and dining rooms, and the master bedroom has a garden tub. The back yard is really small, but you do have a small patio outside the kitchen."

"How much are they asking?"

"That's the great part, for you anyway. It really sucks for the sellers. They've lowered the price to $135,000."

"You're kidding me. Okay, something must really be wrong with it. Is your friend straight up or is she just trying to sell a house and make a commission?"

"No, my girl is straight up. She's cool peoples. Carmen will walk away before she makes a bad deal. She said that's what has made her so successful. Now, you know I rode by the house to take a peek and it looks nice from the outside, and Carmen can show us the inside. She said she'll be free after five, so let's go grab some grub. By the time we finish eating, she'll be ready. And for $135k, it's definitely worth a look."

"You know that's right. That's cheaper than my house at home!"

Brook didn't get too excited because although Debra lived in a nice neighborhood, she also knew that like in any city, you could turn a corner and end up in the hood. And for $135k, she was sure it had to be in a not so desirable area, had rats, something was wrong.

"This really *is* a nice house!" Brook said incredulously.

She just couldn't believe that it was only $135k. She almost felt like she was taking advantage and needed to offer more. That was almost, she wasn't crazy. The bedrooms were a little small, but they weren't that bad. And the backyard was tiny, but that was okay, too. It was still a really cute house. The upgrades were wonderful, like the wooden shutters and the crown molding.

"Why is the price so low? I'm afraid there's some underlying problem that we don't know about," Brook said to Carmen.

Carmen was really cool and had the whole professional thing going on, which Brook appreciated. There was nothing worse than someone not knowing when to be professional. Carmen Stewart was sharp from her beautiful weave to her navy Prada pumps. She stood about five six, a pretty brown complexion with a cute, little button nose. She was wearing the heck out of a navy St. John suit, short skirt, but not too short, more like professionally short, and a nice, expensive, leather briefbag. She was definitely a walking picture of success.

"Unfortunately, this house has been on the market for almost two years. It started out at $175k and now the owners have to sell it. It's really sad for them, and a lot of other families that are going through the same thing. People are giving so many perks to sell their homes. It's definitely a buyer's market right now," explained Carmen. "The house has been appraised at $190k due to the upgrades and has already been inspected. If there was anything wrong, it would have come up in the inspection. My personal opinion, it's a steal."

"Wow," Brook said, "this is just so unbelievable that I would find a house on the day I move here."

"I'll tell you what, take a week or two, look around and see what's out there. Look at different areas and apartments since Debra said you wanted to rent first. I can also put together some potential homes for you whenever you're ready to buy if you want to check out other options," Carmen said.

"That sounds good to me, and I'd definitely like you as my realtor when I do buy. I can tell you're good at what you do."

"Most even say the best," bragged Carmen with a laugh.

And, Carmen was absolutely right. It took Brook all of one week to figure out that the house Carmen showed her was a steal. The rent in the apartments she looked at was more than the mortgage would be for the house. Brook grabbed Carmen's card and gave her a call.

"Carmen Stewart speaking."

"Hey, girl, it's Brook, Debra's friend from Louisville."

"Hey, girl, it hasn't been two weeks yet," Carmen said.

"That's because it didn't take two weeks to figure out that the house is definitely a steal."

"So, I take it you're interested in purchasing it?"

"Yes, ma'am, let's do this. How long do you think it will take to get this wrapped up?"

"Have you thought about financing?"

"I'll get financing through Debra's bank, you know, throw ole girl some business," laughed Brook.

"Hey, we're all benefiting on this deal."

"I'm so excited. I can't believe I found a house. I'm starting to feel like I really live here."

"Welcome to Atlanta." Carmen laughed.

CHAPTER 9

Brook was excited, yet nervous, about her first day at work, almost like your first day of high school. Her Sales Manager, Jeremy Fisher, introduced her to everyone. Brook would be selling advertising for the Adult Urban Contemporary station, Love101.1, and their Hip Hop station, The Beat 100.7. There were eight other salespeople, three women and five men. They were all black, except for one white male and one Hispanic female. Brook would be getting to know them all very well over the next couple of months as she would do ride-alongs with them to see how they handled their business.

Because Brook had already worked in radio promotions, the sales part was easy to understand. Local clients owned businesses like Jeremiah's Auto Shop or Danitra's Soul Food. National clients, McDonalds, Walmarts, and Targets were huge and went through Advertising Agencies. Advertising Agencies were the middle man for the big clients. They negotiated the deals, got better rates, and did all the work for them. On top of that, they charged the radio station fifteen percent for giving them the business. Brook understood all of that. What she needed to do was get from understanding how it worked to actually selling advertising. Luckily, she was on a six month guarantee, meaning she earned a salary for six months. After six months, then she would be on commission. So, she wasn't stressed about not making money, she just hated not knowing what to do.

By the time Friday rolled around, Brook was sick of watching videos. If she watched one more video telling her how to sell advertising she was going to scream. It was already hard enough keeping her eyes open.

Jermaine, one of the sales guys, poked his head into the conference room. "Hey, Brooklyn, you want to ride with me to one of my appointments?" he asked.

"Yes," Brook said quickly.

Jermaine laughed. "Tired of watching those videos, huh?"

"Yes! I'm ready to get my feet wet. I'm ready to see you guys in action."

"Well, you're getting ready to see a pro at work." Jermaine laughed.

They went to a Honda dealership, one of Jermaine's regular clients. Jermaine had come up with an idea to simply place one of their cars at an upcoming concert so people would see the car when they went to the concert. That simple! Brook watched in awe as they hung on every word Jermaine said about how to mention in their commercials that the car would be at the concert and to encourage them to check it out. Then, show their concert stub at the dealership and receive $10,000 off the price of the car. They thought it was a wonderful idea and signed on the dotted line. When they got back in the car, Jermaine explained that the concert promoter was also a client of his. It was called a cross promotion. He got the concert promoter to buy extra advertising as well asking the concert goers to check out the car and save their ticket stuff for a $10,000 discount. In essence, he sold the same thing to two different clients, and they were both benefiting from the deal. Brook didn't know if she'd ever even think of something like that. Jermaine assured her she would since she had a background doing just that.

"Instead of having to ask salespeople to get things for you to give away, you think of clients who have product that compliment each other. Then, you put them together and give them something that will benefit them both, and they both buy advertising," Jermaine explained.

"That sounds simple," Brook said.

"It is. And with your background, once you start, you'll get the hang of it. Just don't get in your own way by over thinking it, Brooklyn."

"Thanks, Jermaine. It really was good seeing a pro at work. And, please, no one calls me Brooklyn. Please, call me Brook."

"Okay, Brook. I hope you enjoyed your first week, even though most of it was spent watching videos."

"Well, hopefully next week I'll be able to go out more often."

"Fo sho." Jermaine laughed.

Ewwww! Fo sho, how country, Brook thought with a giggle.

CHAPTER 10

Things were definitely looking up at work. Brook had gone out with everyone except two of the guys and was checking out everyone's style. Mia Rosario was bad, and she had them excited about everything she said. In her cute accent, she would explain the need for advertising, or a special package, or whatever she was selling to that particular client, and would get so excited, the clients would get excited, too. Brook definitely liked her style. She had spent the day with Mia and it was four o'clock. Mia said she was feeling good because she closed two nice deals and signed up a new client. So, they were going to check out early and head over to happy hour. Brook asked if that was going to be okay.

"Chica, in sales, you spend probably only about five hours a day actually selling. Now, sometimes those five hours may fall after hours or before hours, but you always have flexible time, which is one of the reasons I love it! Now let's go get us a well deserved drink." She laughed.

They were in Jordan's, another one of Mia's clients, and happy hour was off the chain. It was a smaller club, but the drinks were great and the men were even better. There was a live band jamming, total adult crowd, and it was business casual. Also, you could drop your business card in the fish bowl and every half hour, they'd raffle off a free drink. They'd call the name, business and job title. It was way for everyone to get to know each other. Mia said it had started off as a promotion she did for them. She had tied it in with Crown Royal to give away the free drinks and after the promotion was over, the club continued doing it. Brook thought it was a cute idea and was really starting to understand how to build more business. By the time Debra had gotten there, Brook was feeling pretty good. She'd had a couple of Mojitos, danced with a few guys, and was having a good time.

"Heeey, Debra, what took you so long?" Brook asked happily.

"Look at your drunk ass. Unfortunately, I don't have the luxury of leaving work when I want to. Hmm, I have never been here, this is a nice little spot," Debra said, looking around.

Jaelyn, their waitress, came over to their table. "Hey, Jaelyn, this is my girl, Debra, hook her up. Debra, tell Jaelyn what you're drinking. Heck, Jaelyn, bring her two of whatever it is. She needs to catch up," giggled Brook.

"I'll have one Screwdriver because it looks like I'll be driving," Debra told Jaelyn.

Mia half stumbled to the table. "Hey, chica, you having a good time?"

she slurred.

Mia was definitely drunk. While Brook had a drink or two, it looked like Mia had five or six.

"Hey, Mia, this is my girl Debra I was telling you about. Debra Williams, Mia Rosario," Brook introduced.

"Heeeey, chica. How you doin'?" Mia slurred.

"Hey," Debra said, eyebrows arched.

Oh boy, Brook knew she'd better keep the two of them apart because Debra would definitely say something inappropriate and she didn't really know Mia like that. All she knew was that she was a heck of a salesperson. She also learned that she was also a heck of a drinker.

"Girl, them bitches over there looking at me crazy. They don't wanna see me act a fool up in here. I will kick all they asses! I know y'all got my back," Mia said, pointing across the room. A table of girls were laughing and talking to each other, not even looking in Mia's direction. Brook sobered up real quick. She and Debra looked at each other with a "What the heck" look on their faces.

"Are you okay to drive?" Brook asked, trying to change the subject.

"Drive! Girl, I'm not about to leave. I know you're not ready to go, your friend just got here."

"Oh yeah, she just came to pick me up. I still have to pick up my car from the station and I forgot I had promised her I would ride with her."

"Well, where y'all going? I could go somewhere else."

"Oh, I have to pick up my niece and we're taking her to Chuck E. Cheese," Debra said, jumping right into the lie. "I know you're not trying to run around with a bunch of kids."

"Oh no, Mia does not do kids," Mia said.

"Alright, girl, thank you for today. I'll see you at work tomorrow," Brook said. Debra waved and they both left.

"Brook, that girl is a trip! Not only was she sloppy drunk, but she was ready to fight those girls who weren't even paying attention to her! She's one of those get-drunk-I'm-ready-to-fight type chicks. You know that means she's on some white liquor! Heck, she puts you in the mind of Frankie, Keyshia Cole's mama, when she's been drinking." Debra laughed.

"The crazy part is she is totally opposite in business. She really has it together," Brook said.

"Well, you know you can take the chick out the hood, but you can't take...," Debra started to say and Brook finished it with her, "...the hood out the chick!" The both laughed and went on to the next happy hour spot.

CHAPTER 11

Brook was really feeling a lot more comfortable about Atlanta, her job, her life in general, and had moved into her house. She couldn't believe they turned it around so quickly, but the owners were desperate. The husband was in the military and had gotten stationed in Virginia. They thought they'd be able to quickly sell their home and buy a new one, but not with today's market. So, they were stuck with the house that Brook was buying, still paying the monthly mortgage and had to move into an apartment, so they were paying rent as well. And, Carmen was the bomb. She really was about her business. In a little over three weeks, they were pretty much squared away. Brook hired movers to get her stuff from storage in Louisville to bring it to Atlanta. It was expensive, but a whole lot better than her having to drive all the way there, get the stuff and drive all the way back, plus set it up. And, she was really getting the hang of sales. She'd been there over a month, had gone out with each of the salespeople a few times to see how they sell, and came up with a technique of her own. She had even talked Carmen into putting her house listings on their website to try and sell houses. Carmen thought it was a great idea and jumped at it. Internet advertising was a whole lot cheaper than advertising on the radio, so she was getting a lot for a little.

It was Friday and they were meeting up at yet another happy hour. There were so many clubs in Atlanta. Anything you wanted to do, it was there to do it. Brook was just getting ready to leave when Debra called her.

"Giiirrrl, I got some VIP tickets to this gig tonight that Diddy is having!"

"Diddy, as in P. Diddy, Puff Daddy, Sean Combs?" Brook asked.

"Well damn, girl, you know his middle name, too?" laughed Debra. "And, yes, that Diddy. So, bump happy hour, we're going to a classy, yet slutty, event. You're gonna see it all, from dressy to sexy to down right tacky. The really funny part is the tacky part is his mama!" Debra hooted.

"Girl, don't be talking about that man's mama, that's just wrong."

"If she'd take that damn golden wig off her head and get something to match her complexion and quit wearing size eight clothes when she knows she's a size twelve, then I wouldn't have nothing to say," Debra said, cracking her own self up.

"Shame on you! That's still his mama, leave her alone. Now, let's talk about something more important, like what are you wearing?" Brook asked.

"Hmmm, haven't really thought too hard about it, but it will definitely be dressy classy."

"Okay, cool. What time are we leaving and are you driving?"

"Let's head out around nine, and yes, I'll drive. You'll have us lost somewhere," Debra cracked.

Brook was feeling good. She had grabbed a Chicken BLT salad from Wendy's on the way home, ate that, and took a long, leisurely soak in her garden tub. Knowing Debra was going to be fly, Brook knew she had to come correct so they could turn the heads when they walked in the room. One of the biggest things Brook and Debra had in common was they loved show-stopping. So, Brook wore a black, silk Donna Karan strappy mini dress with her black four inch strappy Prada sandals. She always had called the dress strappy because it had lots of little straps crisscrossing across the back. It was a bad dress and she knew she was wearing the heck out of it, too. Putting her necessities in her little black Prada purse, Brook was ready to go.

CHAPTER 12

Debra was not lying, people were dressed in everything from gowns to jeans. "How'd you get these tickets?" Brook screamed over the loud music.

"One of Diddy's people was in the bank today and gave them to me. Diddy has several accounts there. I've met him a few times. What you see on television is not the way he is in everyday life. You'd expect him to come walking up in the bank waving his hands in the air, waving them like he just didn't care. Nope, he's really cool. And most of all, he's a businessman." Brook laughed at the visual of Diddy walking in the bank, doing his little dance that he was famous for doing.

"Well this is a great hookup," Brook said.

"Let's go see who's in VIP," Debra suggested.

They walked over to the roped off area. Debra waved at someone and he came out.

"Hey, what's up, money lady? You sure do look different than you do at the bank," he said, eying Debra up and down.

Debra knew she was fly. She had a Serena Williams type body… small waist and big butt, and she loved wearing different types of pants outfits. She was rockin' a bad Valentino silk purple jumper. It draped in the back, almost down to her butt. It flared out at the legs, was really cute and she was wearing it!

"I try to make it do what it do, baby," Debra said, copying Ray Charles' line that Jamie Foxx made famous all over again.

"Well, come on in here with your fine self," he said, telling the bouncer to move the rope.

"This is my girl, Brooklyn," Debra introduced. "Brook, this is Adam, one of Diddy's trusted accountants."

They shook hands and did the hellos. That showed that you definitely could not judge a book by its cover because he looked nothing like an accountant.

"Let's get you ladies a drink," Adam said as they followed him deeper inside.

Walking through, they were definitely turning some heads. Brook dimpled through the room and Debra smiled her *bad ass* smile as Brook liked to call it.

"You ladies want Dom?" Adam asked.

"Sure," they both agreed as Adam walked over to the bartender.

"You're just eating this attention up, aren't you," Brook laughed.

"I can't help it that I'm fabulous." Debra laughed.

"Girl, everybody is up in here. There's Keyshia Cole! That girl can sing! And look, there's a few of the Day 26 guys! You know I watched every season of *Making The Band*," Brook whispered excitedly.

"Now, don't get all groupie up in here," Debra teased.

"Psssh, yeah right! I'm just saying everybody is in here."

Adam came back and handed them their champagne flutes of Dom. The VIP rooms Brook had done back home had nothing on this one.

"Well, if it isn't Louisville's own, Ms. Brooklyn Bridges," Brook heard.

She and Debra turned around to see who could possibly know her in there, and there stood Giovanni Lay!

"Hey, Gio," Brook greeted with a smile and a hug. *Ump, he's fine*, Brook thought. "How it's going? This is my girl, Debra Williams. Debra, this is Giovanni Lay," Brook introduced.

They greeted each other and Gio asked, "What are you doing here?"

"I live here now. I moved here about a month ago."

"You mean to tell me we did all of that talking and you never once mentioned you were moving to Atlanta?"

"I didn't really think about it I guess. What are you doing here? Are you performing or just hanging out?"

At that point, Debra was looking back and forth between them like they were a tennis match.

"Just hanging out. I live here as well," Gio said.

"In Atlanta! Really!"

"Yeah, I live out in Alpharetta. Are you still in radio?"

"Yes, I'm still in radio, just not promotions. I'm in sales now. Hey, you wanna buy some advertising?" Brook joked.

Nosy was an understatement for Debra. That girl was so into their conversation, when they turned to look at her, she had to move back a little because her head was almost between them. They all laughed.

"So, how is it you two know each other?" Debra asked, pointing at each of them, eyebrows raised.

"Gio performed at one of our events. In fact, it was my last event. He was the headliner. Hey, where's Tha Dogg?" Brook asked and Debra looked even more puzzled.

"He's right over there," Gio pointed. Sure enough, there was Tha Dogg, taking up a huge part of the room.

"Oh my," Debra said. Gio and Brook cracked up.

Gio waved him over and he came and swallowed Brook in a big hug.

"Hey, Dogg," Brook dimpled.

"Ms. Brook! What are you doing here?"

"I was just telling Gio I live here now. Dogg, this is my girl Debra. Debra, this is Tha Dogg."

"Wow, you live here now? That's really interesting," Tha Dogg said, looking at Gio. "She lives here now, Gio."

Gio gave him a funny look and then said to Brook, "So, have you played any *Wheel of Fortune* lately?"

"Oh no, not you, too." Debra laughed.

"Shut up, Debra," laughed Brook. "Just watching it on television. It's really hard to get someone to play it with you," Brook said, eying Debra.

"So, we have to get together and play. I definitely can't seem to find anyone who even *likes Wheel of Fortune*," Gio said.

"I know what you mean. Okay, we can do that," Brook said.

Gio wrote down his number again and gave it to her, smiling. At that point, both Tha Dogg and Debra were looking back and forth between them with big smiles on their faces.

"What the heck are you two smiling for?" Brook asked them.

"Nothing," Tha Dogg grinned.

"'Cause I didn't even know anyone else besides you even liked *Wheel of Fortune*," joked Debra. They all fell out laughing.

"So, you *are* going to call me this time, right?" Gio asked.

"Sure. When is good for you?" Brook asked.

"Tomorrow," Gio smiled.

Tha Dogg and Debra gave each other a look, still grinning because they both could see that their friends liked each other. Tha Dogg was really pleased because Brook was definitely a step up from the groupies that were always around. Gio was *never* serious about a woman. Sure, he'd sleep with some of them, but he never brought them into his home and he never saw the same one more than once or twice. Gio used to date industry women, but said one of the reasons they wanted to go out with him was for their career. This one wanted to go to this event. That one wanted to go to that event. And, they always had to find the cameras. Gio said they were too much work and entirely too insecure, so he hardly ever dated them anymore. Brook was different. She seemed like a really classy lady. He also knew Gio talked about Brook when they left Louisville, something he never did. And, he and Brook had sat there and just talked for a long time. Tha Dogg was impressed. She definitely had his attention, and it wasn't just because she was fine. And, now Brook lived in Atlanta. He knew his boy was going to be all over that.

"Wow, tomorrow?" Brook said trying to think of a reason she couldn't.

Brook thought Gio was fine, super fine, especially with those pretty brown eyes, beautiful chocolate complexion, and could sing the panties off of you, but unt uh, she wasn't even trying to go there with him.

"Well, tomorrow may not be a good day. Let me call you and we'll set another day."

"Okay, whenever it works for you, pretty lady. I'm in the studio most nights, otherwise, I'm yours."

"Okay, cool. We're going to head back out to the party. I'll talk to you soon."

"That's a bet" Gio smiled that sexy smile of his and winked.

"Okay what was that all about! You never told me you knew him," Debra said excitedly.

"I haven't told you I met a whole lot of people. You know I met people all the time when I did my events. Heck, before you moved, you were there at every one of them," laughed Brook.

"But, you two seem awfully cozy. Did you do him?"

"Heckie naw!" screeched Brook. "You know I don't mess with the help."

"But, that's Giovanni Lay with his fine self. And those pretty eyes. Giiirrrl, have you seen his videos? Why are you brushing him off? What's up with that? One minute you two are all into each other, talking about nouns and verbs, and then when he asks to get together, you pump your brakes. What is *really* going on?"

"Unt uh, 'cause he is just too fine! You already know he has about fifty women, probably all in this club right now. I am not trying to be part of nobody's girlfriend club! He's cool and I really will call him to play *Wheel of Fortune*, but that's it! You know he is definitely a playa."

"True, somebody that fine and can sing like that, too! Aw heckie yeah, he's a playa."

"So, let's go get our dance on," Brook said to Debra as they headed out into the party straight to the dance floor where the music was pumping and the people were partying.

"What are you grinning for?" Gio asked Tha Dogg with a smile of his own.

"You know you feeling that girl. That's all you talked about when we left Louisville. Brook is cool peoples. Brook is fine. Brook's body is righteous. Brook likes *Wheel of Fortune*," teased Tha Dogg.

"Man, please. She a'ight. It was nice being able to hold an intelligent conversation with someone."

"Naw, she just ain't sweatin' you."

"And, that's the cool, too. It's good to have a chase once in a while. I haven't had to chase a girl in a really long time. I need a challenge to keep me up on my game," Gio bragged.

"Yeah, okay. This I can't wait to see. It's easy when them chicks are hanging on your every word, but Brook don't seem the type to be easily impressed."

"They all are, bruh. She slipped past me in Louisville, but she lives here now. Just watch me turn my swag on. Oh yeah, it ain't never off." Gio laughed confidently.

CHAPTER 13

Brook was hard at work. She had an important meeting with one of the Mercedes dealerships who had never advertised on urban radio before. She was excited and nervous at the same time. Her presentation was done, but it was her first big deal. She wore her red Jones New York power suit that she had gotten on sale at Macy's with red her pumps. Jeremy was going with her as back up and moral support.

Dionna, the receptionist, called her and said she had a package at the front desk. Brook headed up to the front, still going over her presentation in her head. They'd be leaving out in about an hour, but Brook wanted to be super prepared. If she could pull it off, it would be huge for her.

"Hey, Dionna, where is it?" Brook asked, looking for an overnight package. Dionna was grinning and pointed to a huge vase of three dozen red roses. "Wow!" Brook said, grinning. Debra was her girl with a capital G. She knew Brook had a big presentation and sent them.

"Umm hmm, and who are those from?" teased Dionna.

"Probably from my best friend, Debra. She knows I have this big presentation today," Brook said, taking the flowers back to her desk. She opened the card and her mouth fell open.

I'm really looking forward to playing Wheel of Fortune with you. Don't be afraid, I won't beat you too bad. It was signed *G.*

Brook could not believe it. How in the world did he even know where she worked? And then she thought it really wasn't that hard. All he had to do was check around at the radio stations and ask if she worked there. She had already decided that she wasn't even going to call him. Oh, he was smooth.

Brook called Debra. "See, I thought you were my girl," Brook said when Debra answered the phone, sniffing her roses.

"What? I am your girl. What happened?" Debra asked.

"Well, I got three dozen roses this morning and I just figured they'd be from you since you knew today was the big day, but guess what, they're not even from you."

"What! Who sent you three dozen roses?

"Girl, Giovanni Lay!"

"Shhhuuuttttuuuuppppp! Did you tell him where you work?"

"No. I guess he just called around to find out which radio station."

"That's what's up! That is hella fly! He just got ten cool points from me!"

"Girl, boo. He probably does stuff like this all the time. Ain't nobody falling for his little games."

"Whateva, girl. What time is your appointment?"

"We're leaving out in about a half hour, so let me get back to work."

"Good luck. Just go in there and do you. Heck, you drive a Benz! You're definitely their market," Debra said encouragingly.

"Thanks, girl, I'll let you know how it goes," Brook said, making note to herself to make sure she drove her car to the meeting.

Brook had just finished the PowerPoint presentation on her laptop with all the statistics of the power of the Black dollar and how those people with disposable income listened to her radio station. Elijah Bland was the General Manager and the man who had Brook's fate in his hands.

"Mr. Bland," Brook began, "you have an opportunity to be the first luxury car dealer to invite this African American audience to come shop with you, to let the African American community know that you want their business. None of the other luxury dealerships are inviting this market right now, which means it is wide open. Now, will they jump on the bandwagon once you've started the trend, I'm sure. But right now, it's all yours for the taking. You see we have the income to afford the Mercedes, heck, that's my Benz parked outside. My people love to do something affectionately called *showstop*. That means we love for people to see what we have. Do we invest our money? Not always. Do we own our homes? Sometimes. But, the first thing my people will do is to buy a nice car, a car that will make everyone think they have arrived. And with Mercedes, that is telling people you have arrived," Brook finished.

There was total silence for about five seconds in which Brook's heart dropped to her toes. Then, Mr. Bland said, "Ms. Bridges, I don't think an annual contract is feasible at this time. However, you're absolutely right. Your listeners are exactly who we need to attract. I love the promotional ideas you've come up with as well, especially since you've come up with one almost every month. Why don't we start off with a six month contract, and we love the Black History Month Title Sponsorship, so sign us up for that as well. After six months, we'll revisit and see where we want to go from that point on."

Brook was ready to jump up on that beautiful mahogany conference room table and start popping it. She simply smiled a really big smile, dimples almost glowing at that point, and said that they could make that work. Jeremy was really pleased. He really hadn't had to input much into her presentation at all. They all shook hands with Brook, promising to bring over a couple of sample commercials, and were out the door.

"You were smoking in there." Jeremy laughed.

"I started off so nervous! Then, it dawned on me, I was only speaking the truth and it got so much easier. I really didn't expect them to sign the annual contract, but like you said, you won't get it if you don't ask. I had actually thought that they may start off monthly or something like that." Brook let out a squeal, causing Jeremy to laugh at her. "I'm so happy he signed a six month deal and he's also doing the Title Sponsorship of the Black History Month package," Brook squealed again, clapping her hands.

"You did a really good job, Brook. You looked like you've been doing this for years. And, your promotions background is a real big plus for you, too. That was really smart to tie them in to a different promotion each month."

"Well, that part was pretty easy since that is what I did as a Promotions Director. The great part is it's his own commercials that are making him the sponsor. All I'm doing is specifying the different events each month. For instance, October is Breast Cancer Awareness month so his October commercials will reflect that."

"The typical K.I.S.S. Keep It Simple Stupid."

"Exactly," Brook agreed.

Brook got back to the office and first called her parents and got their answering machine. She left them a message to say hello and to tell her mom how great the meeting had gone. Next, she called Debra.

"Girl, I was smoking, okay! Had them eating out of my palm, talking about what my people do and don't like," Brook laughed. "That's one of the good things about White clientèle, you can tell them all kinds of what my people think stuff because they think we're in some exclusive race that they don't know about. So, I use it to my advantage."

"You go, super saleswoman. I knew you could do it. Now we gotta go to happy hour and celebrate," Debra said.

"Girl, if it was up to you, we'd be in happy hour every day."

"So does that mean you don't want to go?"

"Heckie naw that doesn't mean I don't want to go! Pssh, where we going?"

"I heard they have a new spot on Peachtree that has live music and the best wings around! We can go over there."

"You are gonna turn into a chicken as many chicken wings as you eat."

"Bwaawk, bwaawk" Debra laughed.

Brook took a deep breath, grabbed Gio's phone number, and called him. He answered his phone with a curt, "Yeah."

"Hey, Gio, this is Brook Bridges. I wanted to call and thank you for the roses. That was nice of you," Brook said, hoping she didn't sound nervous.

"Hey, Brook, I'm glad you liked them. I was assuming you'd like roses and hoping that you wouldn't be allergic or anything."

"No, I actually love roses, red, yellow, pink… all of them. But, I'm curious. How did you know where I worked?"

"Aw, that was easy, all I had to do was call Pam. You know she can't hold water!" They both laughed.

"So, can I take you out to dinner sometime?" Gio asked. "Or, if you prefer, we can do lunch. Maybe even breakfast."

"You are so crazy, Gio. Sure, we can do lunch sometime. I've been a little busy at work. In fact, I just closed a really big deal with Mercedes this morning," Brook bragged.

"Well, then we need to go and celebrate."

"I'll tell you what, how about we do lunch on Thursday?" Brook said.

"Hey, I'll take what I can get. Thursday will work for me. I'll come scoop you up and we can go wherever you want to go."

"No, I'll meet you. I'll be out and about doing my sales thing anyway." She definitely didn't want him coming to her job having everybody all up in her business.

"I'll call you Thursday around noon'ish and we'll decide then."

"That's a bet. I look forward to it."

"Talk to you soon," Brook said and hung up the phone. Gio seemed pretty cool, but she'd have to watch herself with him. He had smooth down to a science. The one thing that Brook loved was smooth and confident men.

Brook was getting ready to head out of the office. She was going to grab a sandwich and then head over to another appointment she had with one of the clients she inherited. The client at one time spent a lot of money with the station, but had been spending less and less. Brook was going to do a consult with them, find out what was going on, and try to help their business. Dionna, the receptionist, called her again.

"Hey, Brooklyn, you have another package up here," she laughed. Brook headed back up to the front desk. She knew Gio did not send her more flowers. As she rounded the corner, there were at least two dozen congratulations balloons of every shape and size. Brook cracked up. She knew those could be from no one but Debra's crazy behind!

CHAPTER 14

As promised, Brook called Gio at eleven o'clock to see if they were still on for lunch. She knew he had been asleep when he answered the phone. "Hey Gio, this is Brook. Did I wake you?"

"No, no, I'm up. Are we still on for lunch today?" he asked, trying to sound like he was awake.

Brook chuckled. "Sure, I was thinking about twelve-thirty. I should be done with my appointment by then."

"That works with me. Where would you like to go?"

"How 'bout Jason's Deli downtown off Piedmont Avenue? Do you think you'll be able to get there in time?"

"Wherever you want to meet, pretty lady, I'll be there. See you at twelve-thirty," Gio said.

Gio was there when Brook got there. *He must've been flying to have to wake up, shower, and get all the way downtown*, Brook thought. *Ewww, unless he didn't shower! Oh my gosh, suppose he didn't shower*? Brook panicked.

"Hey, dimples," Gio greeted as Brook walked up to his table. They gave each other a brief hug.

Brook did a little sniff to see if he was stank, but no, he smelled good. He smelled damn good. She also snuck a look at his fingernails. Dirty fingernails were a deal breaker for her and his were neatly trimmed and clean.

"So, did you have a good meeting?" Gio asked with a smile. *He really is entirely too fine*, Brook thought.

"Yes, it was good. Not as good as the one I was telling you about with the Mercedes dealership. They hadn't been advertising to the Urban market and I convinced them how great of an idea it would be."

"Well, you go, girl. I was actually thinking about getting a new Benz."

"Oh, wait until the commercials start." Brook laughed.

Brook and Gio ordered their sandwiches, headed to a table, and started eating, throwing small talk in between each swallow.

"Excuse me, but aren't you Giovanni Lay?" a college-aged girl asked with a huge smile on her face.

"Yes ma'am, that would be me." Gio smiled.

"I'm sorry to bother you, but do you think I can have your autograph?" She giggled.

"You sure can," Gio said, writing his autograph on a tablet she produced.

"Thank you so much. You have such a beautiful voice. I'm a huge fan. My mom is, too," she gushed.

"Well, thank you very much. And please, keep listening," Gio smiled.

"We will," she said, waving as she walked away.

"Wow, I forgot I was with a superstar," Brook teased.

Gio laughed "I can't forget my fans. If it wasn't for them, I'd still be singing in local night clubs and working a nine to five."

"So, is that what you used to do, sing in nightclubs?"

"Every one of them." He laughed. "And *every* talent show. I was always singing."

"So, how did it all happen?"

"I was working on my demo, saved every dime I could to make it. So DeVonte, who owned the studio, really thought I had what it took. He helped me out so much. One day, I got there and he said he wanted to let someone listen to one of my songs. At this point, my whole demo wasn't done yet. Cool, I told him. Not even a week later, Dee called and told me he had someone he wanted me to meet. I didn't even get excited because that had happened before. So, I get over there and you'd never guess who was in there." Brook shook her head no, wanting to know who was in there. "Jermaine Dupri! I stood there with my mouth open, no sound would even come out. But Jermaine was totally chill. He was like, 'what up, man, I heard your demo, and you got pipes'. After that, it was on and poppin'. DeVonte has been with me ever since. He's the one who saw an opportunity for me and grabbed it. For that, I'll always be grateful to him."

"Um, excuse me, Mr. Lay. I was wondering if me and my girl could get a picture with you. We don't mean to disturb you," said hoochie one with a Marge Simpson beehive with decorations in it.

"Yeah, we don't mean to interrupt or nothing, but we saw you over here and just had to ask if you'd, ummm, take a picture with us," said hoochie two with the two toned red and gold hair, insinuating that taking a picture was the least of what they wanted to do with him. Hoochie two looked at Brook and smirked "You don't mind, do you?"

"Of course not," Brook said with a smile. Brook took their disposable camera and took their picture. Gio had a strained smile on his face as the two hoodrats tried to drape themselves all over him. But, Gio stood in a way that made them only able to stand next to him.

"Thank you so much, Mr. Lay. We yo biggest fans," hoochie one flirted.

"Thank you very much, ladies. You all have a good day," Gio said graciously.

They waved goodbye and switched their asses on away.

"Well, I have to be getting back to work. This was nice," Brook said.

"Nice enough to do it again?"

"Sure, we can do it again."

"Well, how about tomorrow?"

"Well dern, you just come right out with it, huh?" Brook laughed.

"Dern? Is that a Louisville word?"

"I'm just trying not to cuss. So, I say dern instead of damn."

Gio nodded his head. "That's what's up."

"I'll tell you what, let me see how my week is going and I'll give you a call."

"That's not a brush off, is it?" He laughed, half playing, half serious.

"No, it's not a brush off."

"Then, how about dinner tomorrow night? You know if you have dinner plans, don't you?" he asked.

Brook laughed. She really wasn't feeling going to dinner with him. Dinner led to drinks and drinks led you down a whole 'nother avenue.

"Are you scared of me? I'm a nice guy. Ask my mom, I'll call her right now," he said, taking out his Sidekick.

"No! Don't you dare call your mother!" Brook laughed.

"I'll tell you what, how about I'll cook for you? I can grill a mean steak. You come over to my place and bring your *Wheel of Fortune* game, and I'll cook for you. We can eat and then play the game."

Brook gave him a 'Negro, please' look and Gio cracked up.

"No, I mean it. I'd love to play *Wheel of Fortune*. You know us word nerds need to stick together."

Brook laughed and agreed. "Okay. What time is dinner?" Brook asked.

"Let's say around midnight," Gio said, wiggling his eyebrows, then burst out laughing at Brook's expression. "I'm kidding! What about eight'ish? Will that work for you?"

"Sounds like a plan to me. I hope you can really cook. Don't be having some burnt food talking about you tried."

"My steaks will melt in your mouth!" he bragged.

Brook wrote down his address, figuring she'd put it in her GPS. They gave each other a brief hug, although Gio held on a little longer, and said their goodbyes. Brook snuck in another little sniff just to make sure he really wasn't hiding the funk. If there was one kind of man she absolutely would not date, no matter how nice and fine they were, that was a funky one!

CHAPTER 15

Brook could not believe Gio's house. It was in a gated community in Alpharetta, a suburb outside of Atlanta, and it was off the chain. Heck, all the houses in the neighborhood were off the chain! Brook pulled her Benz in his curved driveway and there was a black Escalade there as well as a beautiful, Champagne colored Benz, so Brook just parked behind the latter. She grabbed her *Wheel of Fortune* game and checked out the Benz as she got out of her car. *My Benz is gonna look just like that when it grows up*, Brook thought. She wondered if there would be more people there. The entrance was massive and the doors thick. Brook didn't know what she had expected, but this sure wasn't it. She rang the doorbell and got nervous. The door opened and Tha Dogg grabbed her in a big hug.

"Hey, Ms. Brook. How you been?" he asked with a big grin.

Tha Dogg knew his boy was really feeling her. He invited her to the crib already and he never invited women to the house. Dogg couldn't even remember the last time a woman had been to the house for a date.

"Hey, Dogg, how's life been treating you?"

She genuinely liked Tha Dogg. He was a really nice guy, like a big ole teddy bear, but she was sure he was mean when he needed to be.

"Life is good, Ms. Brook." She walked into a huge foyer, looking around impressively. "Let me take you to the backyard. You can get lost in this big house."

As they walked through the house, Brook checked out her surroundings. He had a wonderful decorator. The house was absolutely beautiful, and it was very classy. She definitely had expected something smaller. She had to remember he was a celebrity. He was so down to earth... just Gio. The backyard was also off the chain and she figured he had hired a landscaper.

"Welcome to Casa De Gio." Gio laughed.

He had on his apron that read, *When Bad Means Good*, and had a picture of a black man grilling. Brook had to admit, it was smelling good out there! There was a nice sized swimming pool, complete with Jacuzzi. Then, there was a path that led down to somewhere which was lit up down there.

"Gio, your home is beautiful," Brook said as they greeted with their customary hug.

"Thank you. This is one of the first things I bought when I got signed.

I've been living here about four years now. Everyone was buying cars and gold teeth. But my mama didn't raise no fool. I bought a home. I also paid off my parents' home and had an extension built on. They wouldn't allow me to buy them a new one. They love where they live and definitely were not moving. I'll give you a tour a little later. But now, the food is ready. It's a nice evening so I figured we'd eat out here."

They walked over to where Gio had a table set and a bottle of wine chilling in a wine bucket by the swimming pool. Real china, real silverware, nice wine glasses, Brook noted.

"It smells really good, and I'm starving," she said.

"Let me go grab the salad. The food is on the grill in the warmer."

Gio ran inside, grabbed the salad, and put that on the table next to some bread. Then, he took the plates to the grill and came back with two New York Strips and baked potatoes.

"Do you need anything?" he asked, looking over the table to see if there was anything he missed.

"I have A-1, Heinz 57, and ketchup. Although you really won't need any of them.

"I'm good," she said.

As Gio sat down, he bowed his head in prayer, earning mad cool points with Brook. Brook bowed her head as well and said her prayer, then snuck another look at his fingernails just to make sure his hands were clean. Yep, still neatly trimmed and clean.

The steak was delicious. He was not kidding, it was so tender it almost melted in her mouth.

"Ump, ump, ump," Brook grunted.

Gio nodded, smiling. "Umm hmm."

"Okay, this is really good. Keep it 100, you ordered this, didn't you?" Brook laughed.

"Now that is definitely a compliment," he grinned.

"So, where are you from originally?" Brook asked.

"A little small town called Midway, Georgia."

"Aw heck, that sounds like a place a black person could get hung, Midway, Georgia," laughed Brook. "Is it close to Atlanta?"

"Not that far, about four hours away, depends on how you're driving. I go home every few months. That's one place I can still get peace. Nobody there cares that I have a few of awards. They're more concerned with if you're living right. It's a great place to raise a family. One day, I'll probably even retire there. Most of my extended family lives there."

"Do you have a big family?"

"I'm from the country, of course I have a big family." He laughed. "Actually, my immediate family is relatively small compared to most of the families we grew up around. I have two older sisters and a younger brother, but I grew up with my cousins, second cousins, aunts, and uncles. That's how we do it in the South. Now my sisters, both of them are married. One still lives there in Midway and has twin girls, Kennedy and Kendyl, and the other lives in Ft. Lauderdale, Florida. They don't have kids yet."

"Awww, twin girls, how cute is that?" Brook gushed.

"You best believe they have me wrapped around their little fingers, too. They're only four years old and so cute. They're just so little and soft and girlie. I had only been used to having a little brother, so little girls were something new for me. I just sent them the cutest little doll house. It's little girl sized, so they can go inside and play. My sister threatened if I bought them one more thing, she'd send in the tape of me singing when I was five years old to one of the television stations." He laughed. "As for my little brother, he's a junior at the University of Georgia. He's a Music Major with a minor in Business Management. He thinks he's going to be my business manager." Gio laughed, clearly proud of his little brother. "And he sings, plays the piano, guitar, and drums."

"So, exactly how old are you Gio? I guess I should have Googled you before I came."

At this point, they had finished their meal and were sitting back sipping their wine.

"I'm twenty-eight years old, single, no children. I'm a Cancer, birthday July 10th. I like golfing, swimming, and playing *Wheel of Fortune*," he said like he was auditioning for a dating show.

Brook cracked up. "You are so crazy! And speaking of *Wheel of Fortune*, you ready to get beat?" Brook asked.

"Let's do this," Gio laughed, leading her in the house.

Gio gave her a tour of the house first. There were four bedrooms, five and a half bathrooms, and each room had a different theme. Gio's bedroom was beautifully decorated in earth tones. It was huge and had a sitting room with a fireplace. On the mantle sat his two Grammys. Brook picked one up and didn't realize it would be so heavy. His room was about the size of all three of her bedrooms put together. Thank goodness he didn't have a big, tacky, round bed with mirrors on the ceiling. Even his master bath was huge, about the size of her living and dining room together. Then, there was a study complete with a fireplace, desk, and book shelves that were filled with books, and a formal living and dining room. The kitchen was really big. Brook wished her kitchen was that big. It was spacious and had a sitting room on the other side of a bar that had a humongous television and sofas. Brook got to see pictures of his family. There were pictures of his parents, both of his sisters and their husbands, and quite a few of his nieces, who were the cutest little things. His younger brother was too cute. She knew he had all those little girls chasing him. All of them had those eyes. Brook saw that they had inherited them from their dad. Then, they went down to the basement and that was where the fun took place. He had a game room with arcade machines, a pool table, a big plasma television, and all the guy games - Xbox, Playstation, and Wii. There was a hallway that led to the media room where there was a humongous projector with sofas and recliners as well. There even was an old popcorn machine. It was a comfortable room that made you want to curl up and watch a movie. He had old movie posters decorating the walls, from *Guess Who's Coming To Dinner* with Sidney Poitier to *Set It Off* with Queen Latifah and Jada Pickett Smith. He also had his platinum albums on the wall and all of the awards he won in a beautiful glass enclosed cabinet. There was everything from MTV Awards, BET Awards, Soul Train Music Awards, and American Music Awards. They headed back out to the game room.

"So, that concludes the tour, except for the basketball court, which is down the path from the swimming pool."

"Wow. That's all I can say. You did a wonderful job on the decorating," Brook hinted.

"I hired a team and they decorated. I've also added on a lot as well. I bought the land next to me when that became available and added the basketball court. The backyard was horrible. I just had that done probably two years ago. It seems it took forever to get the house together. And, I'm sure I'm still not finished."

"I hear you. Heck, you make me want to go home and start redecorating my house."

"So, where do you live?"

"In Marietta. I had no intentions of buying when I first moved here, but came across a deal that I just couldn't walk away from."

"We're going to need a keyboard," Brook said as she handed Gio the DVD for the game. Gio left and came back with a keyboard, and went over to the television and fiddled for a few minutes.

"Okay, now how does it work or is it obvious?" he asked.

"Yep, just like the game on television, so let's do it!"

Brook was on her way home and she was smiling because she had a wonderful time with Gio. She didn't expect him to be so funny and down to earth. She went over there with her guard up, but came away with a better understanding of who Gio was as a person, not as a celebrity. And he was a really good opponent, although she still beat him. Of course, he said it was because he was rusty. They had a great time, joking, laughing, and playing *Wheel of Fortune*. She was reluctant to leave, but she knew she had to go. She didn't want to stay too late.

When she gave him a hug goodbye, he said, "Can I ask you

something? Am I falling into the friend zone?"

"No, crazy!" Brook laughed. "I'm having a good time with you. And yes, I consider you a friend. But no, not the let's go shoe shopping type of friend."

"Well, in that case." He softly grabbed her face and kissed her. Brook got the tingles just thinking about that kiss. It was nice, really nice. She had to stop because she knew she could get carried away.

"Thank you for a wonderful time," Brook dimpled.

"I look forward to doing it again. So, can a brotha get your phone number… please?" Gio asked.

Brook laughed, not even realizing she hadn't given him her number. She gave him her cell number.

Brook was on her way home, thinking, *Dangit, why did I kiss him?* His lips were so soft, his tongue nice and teasing. Brook would definitely have to keep her wits about her because he was dangerous!

Gio couldn't believe Brook had left. He just knew the nice, romantic, homemade dinner would have her panties on his floor. But instead, they talked, and that was cool. It was actually real cool. He didn't have to sex every female that he came across. He was actually a lot more selective than he used to be and was the one normally trying to get out of it.

Playing *Wheel of Fortune* with Brook had been a ball. He didn't normally have that kind of fun, except when he went home and he was with family and he could be himself. Something about her made him comfortable. He was more impressed with Ms. Brooklyn Bridges every time he saw her. And that kiss that he planted on her had him wanting more. He found himself excited at the prospect of the next step. He knew just what he'd do. The MTV Awards were coming up and he was performing. Now, that was a guaranteed panty getter. He'd invite her to go with him, take a few pictures with her on the red carpet, make her feel all important, and then they'd be playing the naked tango all night long. Gio felt himself harden and looked down in surprise. Brook was definitely getting under his skin.

CHAPTER 16

When Geo invited Brook to go to the MTV Music Awards with him, she declined. She saw pictures of him on the red carpet, but didn't see a date and didn't know if that meant he didn't take one or if she just wasn't on camera. She still hadn't slept with him yet, but she knew she would. She was truly intimidated by him, something she wasn't used to being. They'd been hanging out for the past few weeks and she really enjoyed him. They had a good time together. He was easy to talk to and really funny. They also had something else in common besides *Wheel of Fortune*. He also thought it was hilarious to scare people. One night, they laughed so hard watching the television show *Scare Tactics*, Brook thought she would pee her pants. They'd gone to lunch again and a few dinners. They'd even gone to the movies, Gio in his cap and shades. He came over to her house and they played *Wheel of Fortune* again. That time, he even won a few games, too. And, each time they parted, the kisses got longer and deeper. It had been quite a while since Brook had sex. She even fantasized about having sex with him, so she knew it was inevitable. He was cooking for her again on Saturday night, and she knew she was going to stay. She wanted to stay with him. Debra thought she was crazy. They were on their way to yet another happy hour and Brook's girl, Pam, the record rep was meeting them there.

"I still can't believe you haven't slept with him yet! What the heck are you waiting for? Your stuff is gonna close up," Debra teased.

"Girl, can you imagine how much stuff is just thrown at him? I just don't want to be one of those women."

"Hell, it's been about seventeen years already! You're definitely are not one of those women," Debra laughed.

"It has only been a little over a month since we saw him at the club. I'm just a little nervous. On one hand, we're together, we have fun, he's hella sexy, and those eyes, giiirrrl! Then, we go out in public and people are asking for autographs and pictures, and it brings it all back home for me."

"Well, you know he is a celebrity and it's his job," Debra reasoned.

"No, I totally understand that and really don't mind that aspect of it. I just step to the side and let him do him. But, when it's just the two of us, he's Gio, and when we're out, he's Gio the Superstar. Most of the celebrities I knew weren't about nothing. Heck, most of them tried to get with me, married or not. So, I just don't want to get too deep with him."

"You can't blame him for those dogs. If he makes you laugh and makes you smile like you've been smiling, then, girl, have fun. Just have fun for now and worry about later when later gets here."

"I know. You're right. I don't know why I'm holding back. I don't have much resistance left anyway. So, it's getting ready to be on!"

"Good, and make sure you call me with all the details, 'cause his body is bangin' in them damn videos," Debra teased.

"Shut up, girl." Brook laughed.

CHAPTER 17

Brook was nervous. She didn't know if she should bring an overnight bag or what. She didn't want to seem too presumptuous, but she didn't want to not have something if she did stay. So, she just put some clean underclothes in her gym bag that stayed in her trunk.

She had gotten a mani and pedi after work the day before, and that morning got a facial and her hair done, and had even gotten a Brazillian wax so she'd be all smooth and nice just in case. She wanted to make sure everything was just right. It was kind of intimidating knowing that the man you were about to sleep with probably had gotten some of the best punani around.

Two cars were in the driveway when Brook got there. The new Mercedes was Gio's. As promised, he had bought it after her commercials started airing on the radio, giving the impression that her commercials made him want to come in and buy it. The other was Tha Dogg's Escalade, he answered the door again.

"He's in the kitchen, Ms. Brook. Y'all have fun, I'm outtie," Tha Dogg said, leaving as she was coming.

"Dogg, can I ask you something?" Brook said.

"Of course, Ms. Brook, what's up?"

"How come you keep calling me Ms. Brook? I told you, plain ole Brook is fine."

"'Cause you're a lady, Ms. Brook. So, I call you Ms. When I was growing up, we always called the ladies Ms. This or Ms. That. It was a sign of respect. So, because I respect you, I call you Ms. Brook," Tha Dogg said with a smile.

Brook gave him the biggest smile. "Thank you, Dogg. That is really sweet of you."

"Just keeping it 100, Ms. Brook. You know, in this business, you don't run in to a lot of ladies. You may run into women and females, or even girls, but it's not often you find a lady. What can I say, it's a corrupt business."

"Ain't that it," Brook answered and headed back to the kitchen. "Man, it sure smells good in here," Brook said as she walked into the massive kitchen.

Gio smiled at her. This time he had on an apron that read, *Kiss The Chef... Please*. "Thank you. You know how I put it down." Gio laughed.

Brook thought, *Not yet, but I sure plan to*.

"Okay, so it's steak and baked potatoes again. But, you know that's my specialty. I also grilled some corn on the cob," Gio said.

"Hey, I can never get tired of grilled steak," Brook said.

"I know. Me either." They sat down and started eating. "You know I have my own *Wheel of Fortune* game now," Gio said

"Forreal! When did you get it?"

"I had Tha Dogg pick it up for me. So, you don't have to bring yours. Now when we're at your house we can play your game, and when we're here we can play my game."

"Sounds like a plan to me. Whichever game you need to get your butt kicked is alright by me."

"Well, why don't we do a little wager then?" he asked.

"Oh yeah? Bring it!"

"Whoever wins the best of seven games is the winner. And the loser has to do whatever the winner wants." He grinned.

"Oh yeah, let's do this."

They were in a dead tie, both winning three games. Brook won the first three and started to get cocky. Then, Gio came back to win three straight. Then, they went back and forth until the final game. It was the last round and Brook could not figure out what it was. She was almost there. It was a place and she was never good at places. It was Gio's turn and he had just given the letter L. Three Ls came up. She got it! The answer was Walt Disney World of Florida. Buzzer!

"Ha, ha, my turn," Brook shouted and spun the wheel. She landed on *Lose A Turn*!

"Your game is cheating," Brook said.

"How can a computer game cheat? Don't be mad. I'm gonna buy a vowel. Give me an E. That ought to clear it up for me," he said. The lone e came up. "Damn," Gio said. Buzzer!

Brook spun the wheel again, fingers crossed, and landed on $300. She jumped up and started doing the cabbage patch dance. "Ut oh, ut oh, go, Brook," she sang. "I'll take a D. And, I'll also guess the answer." Brook laughed as the three Ds came up.

"Noooo," Gio yelled as he realized what the answer was and wrestled her onto the sofa. He started tickling her.

"Stop it, Gio, you cheater," Brook screamed, laughing hysterically. She could not stand to be tickled. "You're a sore loser. The answer is Walt Disney World of Florida," Brook screamed hurriedly.

"It doesn't count unless you type the answer in, so technically you didn't win."

Brook tried to get up and hurry to type it in the computer, but Gio grabbed her around the waist and then the buzzer sounded.

"You little cheat," Brook laughed.

One minute they were laughing and wrestling, next minute they were tongue wrestling. Laughs slowly turned to moans. Gio was doing a slow grind into Brook's center and she was ready to explode.

"I want you, Brook. I want you so bad," Gio whispered as kisses trailed down her jaw to her neck.

"Um hmm," Brook agreed.

After a few more minutes of getting entirely too hot and heavy, Gio asked if she would come to his bedroom. Brook just shook her head yes, desire making her voice too hoarse to even speak.

Brook was nervous. How would she measure up? Gio must have felt her tension because he just continued to softly kiss her, not rushing her. They must have laid there kissing, exploring each other's mouth, for a good ten minutes. By then, Brook was so hot and bothered, she didn't care who he had slept with before. All she thought about was getting her fires put out. She started unbuttoning his shirt, letting him know it was okay to go further. He pulled her up off the bed and started to undress her, kissing each part that he took clothes off. First, he took off her blouse, and then softly kissed her shoulders. He unhooked her bra and slid it off, taking his time to suck each breast, making Brook shiver with excitement. He unbuckled her jeans and slid them down, kissing trailing down her stomach. He pulled her jeans off and started trailing kissing up the inside of her thighs. He pulled off her panties and softly kissed her center.

He stood up and looked at her naked body lying across his bed. "Wow," was all he said as he dropped his jeans, standing at attention.

That time it was Brook who said, "Wow."

He grabbed a condom, slid it on, and joined Brook on the bed. He lay next to her on the bed and started kissing her mouth, her neck, and her breasts while doing a slow grind. He got on top of her and slid into her hot wetness. Brook took a deep breath. He was hitting spots that hadn't been hit in a long time. He started a slow roll, watching her face as he went deeper inside. Brook grabbed his face and started kissing him deeply. She was having her first orgasm and couldn't stop it if she wanted to. Gio heard her moan and felt her body shiver with her orgasm and started working her faster. Brook flipped him over and rode him hard. He was hitting her spot and she came hard, that time groaning louder. Gio flipped her back over and turned her on her stomach. He pulled her up on her knees and slid inside her from behind. He started long stroking her and Brook felt her orgasm building. At that point, they were both sweating hard. She felt Gio swelling.

"Give it to me, baby," he groaned, and Brook rolled it back as he thrust it forward.

Gio was exploding.

Brook was exploding.

The room filled with moans and groans of their orgasms. They both flopped onto the bed, breathing hard. Neither said a word. They just laid there until their breathing became regular again.

"Damn!" Gio said, giving her a kiss.

"Ditto," Brook smiled.

Gio got up and wobbled to the bathroom to dispose of his condom. Brook lay there, thinking about how he had just turned her out. That was unbelievable, and she didn't know he was packing like that. Of course, she felt his hardness when they kissed good night, but she didn't know that was what was hidden inside his pants. That was definitely a sign of a man that was packing. He never bragged on it, just surprised you with it when he put it on you. Brook was dozing off. She felt Gio slide back into the bed, but she was almost gone.

"Don't get too comfortable," he said. "That was just round one."

Brook just smiled and drifted off to sleep.

CHAPTER 18

Brook woke up the next morning sore as heck. It really had been quite a while since she had sex so she was especially sore, and coupling that with the fact that they had gone three rounds didn't help either. Damn! Brook had to go to the bathroom, but she didn't want to get up and go naked. Although Gio was snoring, she didn't want to chance him waking up. Although she was proud of her body, she just wasn't used to him like that yet. But, her bladder was full. She grabbed her cami and panties and went to the bathroom to relieve herself as she tried to think of a clever way to get her stuff from her trunk. She wanted a bath in his huge jetted tub, but she didn't want him to know that she knew she was staying the night. *The games a single woman has to play*, Brook thought. She walked back in the room and Gio was awake. She was glad she had put on her underclothes.

"Good morning," he greeted. "You're not getting ready to leave are you?"

"Good morning to you, too," Brook blushed. "Well, I was thinking I need to get home and get a bath and clothes."

"Well, I have a bath here. You didn't bring clothes with you?"

"No, I didn't even know I was staying," Brook lied. "Hmmm, I probably have something in my gym bag that's in my trunk. I normally keep extras in there."

"Where are your keys? I'll go grab your bag."

Brook grabbed her purse and gave him the keys. He got out of the bed, went to his dresser, and threw on a pair of pajama pants, evidently not ashamed to walk naked in front of her. She hadn't expected the lovemaking to be that good. But then again, that was probably because she hadn't had any in so long. She'd give him another shot or two, or three she giggled. Gio came back in the room with her gym bag.

"Let me see," Brook said, knowing good and well she had just put her underclothes in there. "Yep, I have extras!"

"You want a bath or shower?" Gio asked, walking to the bathroom.

"Definitely bath."

Gio came back in the room and came over to her. He pulled her up off the bed and gave her a hug. She hugged him back, feeling so good in his arms.

"Last night was wonderful," he said.

"Yes, it was."

"You okay?"

"I'm fine. A little sore, but I'm good."

"You're not gonna run off on me are you?"

"No, why would you say that?"

"Umm, probably because you were getting ready to leave this morning! That isn't a good sign to wake up to the woman you just sexed all night to find her sneaking out of your house." He chuckled.

"I wasn't sneaking out of the house. I didn't think I had anything to put on, and you can't bathe and put back on the same underclothes. I wouldn't have left without saying goodbye."

"So, next time, you can bring an overnight bag with you and then you'll be good to go."

"So, you just know I'm going to spend a night with you again?" she teased.

"Weren't you in the bed with me last night? That was some lets-do-this-again type stuff," he teased.

Brook blushed. It was unbelievable. "And I still won *Wheel of Fortune* last night, so you owe me," she reminded him.

"Fine, I'll give you that. So, what is it I have to do?"

"No sweetie, I won that, so you're not giving me jack. Don't get it twisted, I whupped you!"

"Yeah, yeah, yeah! So what do I have to do, a foot massage, paint your toenails?"

"No. Go to bible study with me on Wednesday."

"Oh!" Gio said, stunned into silence. "Wow, never saw that one coming. Okay, we can do that. What time does it start?"

"Seven o'clock, and Pastor don't play, so you have to be on time. You can meet me there. It's a smaller church, located right between Alpharetta and Marietta, so it makes sense for us to meet there. I'll give you all the info on Wednesday."

"Cool. Now, let's get in this tub." He grinned.

Brook didn't know he was going to get in with her. She was still a little shy about being naked in front of him. When she got in the bathroom, he had candles lit around the bathtub.

"Oh, this is nice." She took off her underclothes and got in. Gio sat behind her and she lay back on his chest. "Ahhhh," Brook said.

"Mm hmmm," Gio agreed. "Now it's your turn. You hardly ever talk about yourself. Tell me all about Brooklyn Bridges. Where did you get your name from? I know it wasn't from the actual bridge."

"My parents have a warped sense of humor." She laughed. "Umm, okay, I have one older brother, Brandon, who just happens to be perfect. He graduated Summa Cum Laude from Loyola Law School in New Orleans. He was Valedictorian in high school. He married his high school sweetheart, who is also an attorney. They don't have kids yet. And, although I love my brother to death and am proud of his accomplishments, those were still huge footsteps to follow. My parents are my rocks. My dad retired from Ford Motor Company and my mom is a retired high school teacher. My dad convinced my mom to retire early since he did. Well, we all convinced her to do it so they could enjoy their time together. Financially, they're fine, so they may as well enjoy it. Brandon and I are grown and doing our own thing, so they don't have us as dependents anymore. It took a minute, but she finally agreed on retiring and they have been everywhere. They've been to Africa, Hawaii, and Europe, and even on a Tom Joyner cruise, which was my Christmas present a few years ago. They had a ball and go every year now. They are two peas in a pod. When I meet a man like my daddy, then I'll know it's time to settle down. He is a great father, husband, and a real man, like they used to make them."

"Yeah, I know what you mean. These punks now days thinking they're a man just because they happen to be a male, that was definitely not the way I was raised."

They lay there discussing how the kids of today were definitely different from when they were growing up.

"So, what are your plans for today?" he asked as they were getting dressed.

"I don't know, probably hook up with Debra, do some shopping or something."

"Wanna go to the Aquarium?"

"Sure, I would love to." She had wanted to go since she'd seen it on Tyler Perry's movie *Daddy's Little Girls*. "But, I still have to go home and change clothes. I am not wearing the same clothes two days in a row, clean or not!"

"Okay, I'll tell you what we can do. I'll follow you to your house. You change your clothes and leave your car there, then ride with me and we can go eat and then head to the Aquarium."

"Now that sounds like a plan," she dimpled.

CHAPTER 19

Brook loved the Aquarium, and even though Gio had on a hat and shades, they still got stopped for a few autographs and pictures. Brook was amazed at how Gio always had so much patience with his fans. He always smiled and said thank you like they were doing him a favor, but she knew that was part of his charm. She would look at him and visions of their night together would come to her and she would blush. He really did turn her out. They left the Aquarium and Gio said he wanted to take her somewhere. They ended up at the studio where he recorded.

"I want you to hear the new single I'm working on and tell me, honestly, what you think. Of course, I do more ballads, but this is an upbeat cut," he said.

"You have upbeat cuts on your other albums," Brook said.

"Yeah, but I'm more comfortable with ballads. I'm always nervous about the dance floor cuts." They headed into the studio and there were a few people in there. Jermaine Dupri was one of them. "Hey, JD, glad you're here. I want to listen to that cut real quick," Gio said. "Oh, Jermaine Dupri, this is Brooklyn Bridges. Brook, JD," he introduced.

Wow, he is short.

Jermaine played Gio's song and Brook found herself bobbing her head. The beat was bumping and made you want to dance. Heck, she felt like dancing right then. Gio's beautiful voice singing the chorus was catchy. *Pull yo girl on the dance flloooooorrrr, and grind it on dowwwwwnnnn, just pull your girl on the dance flooooorrrr, and grind it on dowwwwnnnn.*

"So, what did you think?" Gio asked.

"Pssssh, I'm ready to grind it on down. In fact, I'm ready to go to the club right now," laughed Brook. "That was definitely hot!"

JD nodded his head. "Just the reaction we're looking for. I think it's a hot single, too. Good dancing music and you know how people love to dirty dance," JD said.

"Thanks, man. I appreciate your time. We're getting ready to head out, I'll holla at you later," Gio said to JD.

"Nice meeting you." Brook finger waved.

"So, you ready to go grab something to eat?" he asked.

"Sure. Where do you wanna eat?"

"Well you know I'm a meat and potatoes type of guy, so maybe some soul food. You ever been to Gladys Knight's restaurant, Gladys' and Ron's?"

"No, but it sure sounds like a good idea," she answered.

Getting a table was almost impossible. But, Gio spoke with someone who spoke with someone and they had a table. The food was delicious. Brook had gotten the barbecue turkey wings, macaroni and cheese, and some green beans. Gio had gotten the smothered pork chops with rice and collard greens.

"This is delicious," Brook said, stuffing her mouth with mac and cheese.

"Told ya," Gio said with mouth full of greens.

Brook saw the flash, but didn't realize what it was until she looked up, still chewing, and almost choked. There was a guy with a camera taking pictures of them eating.

"Gio!" Brook grunted, trying to swallow at the same time.

"Hmm," he grunted back, still grubbing on his food.

"Gio! There's a man taking pictures of us eating!"

"What?!" Gio said, looking around. When Gio spotted the guy, he hurried away.

"Was that the paparazzi?" Brook asked, shocked.

"Yep, live and in person," he said, shaking his head.

"He probably got a picture of you with a mouth full of greens," Brook laughed.

"Oh, you got jokes. I hope he got you in the picture with that mac and cheese on the side of your face."

"Oh snap," Brook said and grabbed a napkin. "Does it bother you when they do that?"

"Not normally, but if they'd just ask, I really wouldn't mind. When they sneak like that, now that irritates me."

"Yeah, I hear you. There are some times that are just personal, like when you have a mouth full of greens," Brook joked.

"Or mac and cheese on your face," Gio joked back.

CHAPTER 20

Gio had to admit, Brook might be 'special friend' material. She took her time getting to know him, Gio, not Giovanni Lay, the superstar. They hung out together and joked around. He stopped thinking only of getting her in the bed and started to enjoy hanging out with her. He still wanted her, badly, but, it wasn't the most important thing anymore. She went from a conquest to someone he actually enjoyed hanging out with.

And when they finally did the do, it was well worth the wait. He could feel her hesitation in the beginning, so he took his time with her. But, she warmed up quickly. Gio smiled to himself. But, that smile quickly turned to a small frown. She shook him a little because when he woke up, it looked like she was getting dressed and sneaking out. That was definitely a first. And, he thought the sex was off the chain. Maybe the sex was only great to him. For the first time in his life, she had him doubting himself and his lovemaking skills. A thousand thoughts went through his head when he saw her half dressed. He wanted her to climb back in bed for another round. He couldn't seem to get enough of her.

Women! They were supposedly so prepared for anything, but she hadn't even bought a change of clothes with her. Maybe he wanted her more than she wanted him. That sure wasn't the case anymore because she could go round for round with him anytime as well as hold an intelligent conversation with him, play a game of Wheel with him, and joke around. Hmm, she just *may* be girlfriend material.

CHAPTER 21

Brook and Gio fell into a friendship with benefits. They would play *Wheel of Fortune* or go out to eat. They went to a play and the museum, and he even went to Bible Study with her. Brook really liked Gio. He wasn't pretentious or full of himself at all, confident, yes, but a jerk, no. He was well grounded. And the sex, she thought the sex was amazing! They seemed to like the same things sexually, which was a great fit. The crazy part was, although she had his home and cell number, she never called him. She didn't feel comfortable calling him. If he wanted to see her, he'd call her. And he definitely called. She spoke with him at least once or twice a week.

Unfortunately, Gio was leaving to go on a short tour. It was called the Lovers Tour, with Mario, J. Holiday, and Trey Songz. Gio was joining the tour because Lloyd broke his leg playing basketball. Brook could imagine all the punani that was going to be thrown at them on that tour. It really didn't bother her because she wasn't his woman, they were just having fun. She was enjoying him and he was enjoying her, and besides, she was still seeing other guys, too. No one seriously, but she did go out on dates. One thing Atlanta had was a lot of brothas, she was always meeting somebody, but the problem was, she started to compare them to Gio. He had a great sense of humor and Brook loved to joke around. She wasn't sleeping with anyone besides Gio because she had a one man rule… sex with one man at a time. So, before Gio left, she made sure she sexed him down really good to make him remember her punani, and to hopefully give her enough to last until he got back.

Brook was meeting Debra and Carmen at happy hour at some new club that had a New Orleans theme and sold Cajun food. They also had a live band. Brook got to the club, looking around to see if anyone was there yet. Carmen was, bobbing her head to the music.

"Hey, sweetie," Brook greeted.

"Hey, girl," Carmen said as they gave the girlfriend hug.

"What you drinking?" Brook asked.

"It's a Hurricane. They have a little bit of everything in them. It's a New Orleans specialty and it's off the chain. Remember that song back in the day, Hurricane, you can call it slurricane," Carmen sang.

"Oh yeah, I remember that song. It looks good. I think I'll have one, too."

"Hey, heiffas," Debra greeted. "What ch'all drinking?"

"Hurricane," Brook and Carmen said at the same time.

"Jinx!" Brook yelled and pinched Carmen.

"Ow!" Carmen said. Brook and Debra started softly punching Carmen on the arm. "What in the world are y'all doing?" Carmen asked, laughing.

"Girl, you got jinxed. That means you can't talk until someone says your name," Debra explained.

"Now, you know y'all two been around each other too damn long. And, how old were you when you first started playing that game?" Carmen laughed.

"Hey, it's not a game, it's a reality," Brook said seriously while Debra nodded her head in agreement. She and Debra then cracked up.

"Sometimes, you two are in a world of your own," Carmen laughed.

"I know, girl, it's a Louisville thang," Brook said.

"But, you're welcome into our world anytime. You know you're our play cousin," laughed Debra.

Gio had been gone about a week when he called. Brook was surprised because she didn't think she'd hear from him that soon.

"So, how's the tour going? I know the concerts have been straight sold out," Brook said.

Gio laughed. "It's going well, but it's really tiring. We spend most of the time traveling on the road. Then, when we get to a city, it's radio, sound check, and the concert. Then, off to the next city to do it all over again. We're performing Thursday through Sunday night. It's really a lot of work."

"You mean there's no fun at all?" she teased.

"I'm not going to say there's no fun at all, but it really is a lot of work. But, I knew the deal, that's just how it is on tour. Heck, I've been on enough of them. I think with me joining in at the last minute, I wasn't able to prepare myself like I normally do."

"I had my events that I did as a Promotion Director, but that was one night every few months, not two and three nights in a row for weeks on end. So, I'm sure it's tiring."

"Yeah, it's all good though. The guys are really cool and that's always a plus. There's nothing worse than being on tour with egos, or attitudes, or even worse, somebody that's on the down-low."

"What?! Downlow brothas on tour? That sounds like a Jerry Springer show." She laughed.

He laughed, too. "It does sound like a Jerry Springer special. Unfortunately, it's true."

"See, that's why I look for the signs, plus, I have a gaydar. But, the scary part is when there aren't signs."

"I hear you on that. That's the hard part for women, they have to be careful and make sure a guy is not on the down-low. With us guys, we're kinda hoping the woman is on the down-low," he joked.

"See, you wrong for that!"

"Well, I just wanted to touch base with you to see how you were doing and to let you know I was thinking about you," Gio said softly.

"Awww, that's so sweet. And here I thought you were catching all of that downlowness that is being thrown at you."

"Well, that downlowness can give you something that penicillin can't cure or have you stuck for eighteen years! These chicks out here will puncture a condom and everything. After a while, it just gets old. I'm almost thirty years old! You start to see through the makeup and the weave and see the desperation and sneakiness. I've heard and witnessed so many horror stories, it makes you careful, and frankly, a little turned off. So, when I say I was thinking about you, I was thinking about chilling and playing some *Wheel of Fortune* instead having to be Giovanni Lay, you feel me?"

"I do. I really do. I never really thought about it like that. And, I do know there are females out there that plot to get pregnant by a celebrity or athlete. The sad part is that is their goal in life. So yes, I do feel you. It's been nice talking to you. When you get back, I'll whoop up on you in some Wheel to welcome you back properly." Brook chuckled softly.

"I hope that's not the only thing you'll be welcoming me back with," Gio said sexily.

"Oh, I got you. As long as you're not expecting any of that female downlowness." Brook laughed and hung up.

CHAPTER 22

Gio was back and Brook was excited. She tried to play it off, but she was really happy. He called her when he got back, actually while he was at the airport, and he got mad cool points for that one. He asked if she'd come over, but she played the waiting game. It was Thursday, and although she would have loved to drop everything and run over there, she still had work in the morning. One more day and it was the weekend. She could wait, and so could he.

"I understand. I know you're a career woman and I can't expect you to slack on your job because a brotha missed you."

"Now don't try to put the guilt trip on me." She laughed while really happy he said he missed her.

"I'm just teasing. I understand. I need to unpack and get together, too. And, tomorrow will be much better since we'll have the whole weekend." Brook felt a little flutter in her stomach, excited that he wanted to spend the entire weekend together.

"And, that means I can kick your butt in some Wheel, too," Brook said.

"Bring it on, baby girl, bring it on."

"Oh, it will be brought, trust!"

They laughed and said their goodbyes.

Brook was excited, and couldn't wait for the end of the day. She had gone and got prettified after she spoke with Gio. She took care of her female grooming the night before, so, all she had to do was go home, shower, and grab her overnight bag. Debra and Carmen were heading to Charlotte for the weekend, and Brook was set to go with them, but when Gio told her his return date the week prior, she told Debra she wasn't going. Debra told her she wasn't mad at her and to get some for her.

Gio greeted her with a big hug, picking her up and spinning her around. Brook squealed with laughter, happier to see him than she wanted to be. She liked to be in control of her feelings, but with Gio, she was always had butterflies in her stomach and was constantly on guard, making sure not to show too much. She tried to keep it in perspective that he was a celebrity who probably had other women stashed around. So, she kept it light. She was not trying to get her heart broken.

"Smells good in here," Brook said.

"Yeah, I thought I'd do a little sumthin' sumthin'. You've only had my grilling. I can also cook on a stove."

"What did you cook?"

"Smothered pork chops, rice, and green beans with homemade rolls."

"Homemade rolls! You made homemade rolls?"

"That's what the package said." He laughed.

"You are so crazy. Had me thinking you got a little Betty Crocker in you.

"Hey, I can cook, do a mean warm up, and even throw down in the microwave, but scratch is not even in my vocabulary. Dinner is ready if you're ready."

"See, you trying to spoil a sista. Mr. have the meal ready when I walk in the door. Now that's what's up."

"I told you I missed you. I want tonight to be special. See, first the meal, then I'll let you win in Wheel, then you can show me your appreciation later," he said with a wink.

"Oh, you'll let me win? I'll tell you what, if you don't let me win, then I'll doubly show you my appreciation later," Brook dimpled.

"How about we just forget about the meal and the Wheel, and get straight to appreciating." He laughed.

Brook blew him a kiss and headed to the bathroom to wash her hands.

"Wow, Gio, this really is good." She couldn't believe he could cook like that. It was almost as good as her mama's smothered pork chops, not quite, but pretty close. "These pork chops are so tender, the gravy is the bomb, and even the green beans are seasoned right. Be honest, did you run out and grab this meal?"

"No, I didn't, thank you very much. I slaved over a hot stove all day long preparing this meal for you, woman. And, in case you're wondering, the kitchen is clean because I clean as I cook." Brook reached over and pinched him. "Ow. What the…!"

"I'm just making sure you're real." She laughed.

Gio got up and left out of the room. He came back in with his apron that read *Real Men Cook... Well!*

She cracked up. "Ain't that it! They need to make that a law. Do you have a collection of aprons? Every time you cook, you have on a different one."

"Yeah, if I'm out and see one that catches my eye, I'll grab it. Some people collect coins, I collect aprons."

"That's pretty cool, especially since you have good ones with great slogans. It's not like they're frilly. Or, do you have some frilly ones, too?" she joked.

"Oh no! I don't own nothing frilly. In fact, I don't think I even like that word. Frilly. You know that's a girl word!"

"A girl word? I have never in my entire life heard of something called a girl word."

"Yeah, frilly, scrumptious, sweetness, fluffy, all girl words!"

"Man, you are trippin'. You're such a guy. You're not homophobic are you?"

"No, not at all. I don't care what someone does in their bedroom. That has absolutely nothing to do with me, as long as they don't bring it to me. I'll understand that you are, if you understand that I'm not."

Brook nodded in agreement, liking the way he broke it down.

They were battling. He must have been practicing because he was giving her a run for her money. He'd won three games, she'd won two, and they were playing the best out of seven. If he won this game, it was all over. The clue was a song title. Brook hated song titles because they were never songs she'd heard of. Brook though, *Yes! Gio just landed on Lose A Turn.* It was her turn and she landed on $500. She guessed an M and got two of them. It looked so familiar.

Give It To Me One More Time, Brook typed with seconds left. Correct! She jumped up and started doing her cabbage patch winning dance. "Now! It's not over 'til I say it's over," she laughed.

"Yeah, yeah, yeah. Don't get too excited. That's just gonna make my win all the more better," he boasted.

"Well, let's put a little wager on it then," Brook said.

"Okay. The loser has to do whatever the winner wants for the night."

"Cool. Now let's do this!"

"Rub a little harder boo. And don't forget each individual toe."

"Babe, how long does this foot massage have last?" Gio whined.

"Until right now. You're done."

"Good. That was too long. I'm trying to rub other things."

"Now, for my back," Brook said and turned over onto her stomach so he could massage her back.

"Huh!" Gio said, almost in a screech.

Brook laughed at the look on his face. "Come here, you big baby. I'll find some other things you can do with those hands."

"Now, this is more like it," Gio said, falling on top of her and then rolling so she'd be on top of him. He let his hands go to work as they tongue danced with each other.

CHAPTER 23

Gio and Brook went bowling with Debra and her friend, Ezra, and they were having a ball. Gio and Brook were kicking their butts, too. They had won the first two games and it looked like they were going to win the third. Debra was giving them a run for their money, but her friend Ezra was metrosexual and acted like the heaviest thing he picked up was a mirror. Brook could tell he was getting on Debra's last nerves acting like the bowling ball would mess up his manicure. He was pretty, not handsome, but plain pretty, the singer Genuine pretty. The big difference with him was he was soft, you could tell he was a white collar worker for sure. They ended up playing four games and Brook and Gio won them all. No one had even bothered them about autographs or pictures. They got plenty of stares, but that was it. In fact, Brook was getting used to the stares. Brook suggested they head out and stop somewhere to eat and Debra was just rude. She said that sounded great, told Ezra goodbye, and left with Brook and Gio. Gio thought she was hilarious.

"Girl, you are off the chain. I ain't even mad at you 'cause ole boy was getting on my nerves, too. I felt like going over to him and giving him nuggies, and messing up his hair," Gio laughed and the girls joined in. Brook could just see Gio putting him in a headlock and rubbing his head with his knuckles, like her dad used to do her brother, giving him nuggies.

"Okay, temporary lapse of judgment on my part, but he shole was pretty." Debra laughed.

"Yeah, and I bet his lingerie is, too," Gio joked.

"Ewwwww!" Debra and Brook screeched.

They ended up at Q-Time on Abernathy. You couldn't go wrong there, they had some great food. Gio got asked for a few autographs, but everyone was really cool. Brook, Debra, and Gio grubbed down, barely talking.

"Okay, now that was the bomb," Debra said, sitting back rubbing her non-belly.

"Okay! And I'm going to need a to-go box," Brook agreed.

"This was almost as good as my cooking," Gio said, and they all laughed.

"Okay, good peoples, y'all can drop me off at the crib 'cause I'm ready for a nap," Debra said.

They all agreed on that. Gio paid the tab and they all walked out lazily to go take naps.

They dropped Debra off and headed over to Brook's house. Brook had to go bad, but she was not comfortable doing a number two while Gio was in the house. She'd wait until he fell asleep and sneak to the guest bathroom. Her belly made a little gurgling sound.

"Babe, I know you're not still hungry," Gio said.

"No, just too full," Brook said, trying to play it off. She hoped she didn't accidentally fart.

They headed to her bedroom and fell across the bed. She turned on the television and turned to CNN. She laid her head on Gio's chest and started to doze off. She heard his light snoring and knew she could safely make it to the bathroom, but she was just so comfortable and sleepy, she didn't feel like moving. She started to doze.

Beerrrrmmmmmppppppp!

Brook's eyes shot open. It came out! Her fart had slipped out! She lay still to see if Gio heard it, but he was still snoring lightly. She slid out of the bed and hurried to her guest bathroom, then lit her candle and handled her business. As Brook walked back to the room, she hoped he didn't wake up while she was gone. He was still asleep and she breathed a sigh of relief. As she slid back in bed with him, Gio turned over.

"Babe, do you need me to take out your garbage? I think I smell it," he said groggily.

Brook's eyes got wide as saucers. She couldn't believe the fumes hadn't gone away. "Nah, I got it. I forgot I had left my salad out on the counter. I threw it out," she answered.

He fell back to sleep and soon Brook was snoring lightly with him.

CHAPTER 24

Gio was leaving to go on his movie shoot. He would be gone six weeks, and Brook knew six weeks was a relationship buster. She was going to miss him. They were staying in and Brook had stopped at Big Daddy's on Riverdale Road and picked up their meal. She was trying to keep it light, but she knew she was a little sad about him going. She hadn't seen him in over a week because he was tying up some recording stuff that he needed to handle before he left, so she couldn't wait to see him. They talked earlier in the day and he told her the door would be open and to come on in. She didn't see Tha Dogg's truck when she pulled up and figured he was already gone.

She let herself in and followed Jill Scott singing, *Come See Me*. She walked in and Gio was sitting on the sofa in the room off the kitchen, eyes closed, just bobbing his head, grooving to the music.

"Hey," she greeted softly.

He smiled and came over to her. He took the things out of her hands, sat them down on the table, and started kissing her softly, urgently.

"Gio, what are you doing?" Brook started, kissing him back.

His hands were everywhere as he kissed her mouth, her face, her neck. He pulled her blouse over her head and started to kiss her breasts while unhooking her bra.

"Babe," Brook moaned softly.

But, Gio was on a mission. He unzipped her jeans and slid them down, and picked her up and sat her on the kitchen counter. He finished pulling off her jeans started eating her out like she was the meal.

"Ohhhh," Brook moaned as Jill Scott's *Crown Royal* started playing in the background. Jill sang, "*your hands and your lips and your tongue tricks, and you're so thick, and you're so thick, Crown Royal on iiiicccceeee*."

Gio snatched off her panties and stopped teasing her. Brook's legs shook with her orgasm and she couldn't help but moan loudly. He dropped his pants, stuck his tongue in her mouth, and slid into her wetness.

"Wait, wait," Brook tried to protest, but it was so good.

As Jill continued singing about being in so deep, Gio pushed harder, deeper into her. With Jill still serenading them, Gio picked her up off the counter and held her while he thrust deep inside her. Brook wrapped her legs around his waist and tried to take all of him. Gio started trembling.

"Give it to me, baby," Brook said, coming for about the fourth time.

Gio growled and came so hard Brook thought it would shoot her off of him. He lay back against the countertop, still holding her in his arms, both of them breathing hard. He slowly let her down.

"I didn't hurt you, did I?" he asked softly.

They were the first words he had spoken since she had gotten there. She shook her head no, kissed him softly on the lips, and headed to the bathroom. She sat on the toilet and thought about what they had just done. It was the best sex they had ever had. Heck, it was the best sex she had ever had period. It was so intense. But, what was bothering her was they didn't use protection. She always used protection, always! She turned on the shower and got in. And then Gio came and joined her.

"Are you okay?" he asked, noticing something was going on with her.

"We didn't use protection."

Gio thought for a moment. "I'm clean, boo. I take an AIDS test annually, and I don't normally have sex without a condom."

"Since my girlfriend died of AIDS, I get tested annually as well. It's not just that, there also is the issue of birth control."

"Aren't you on birth control?"

"Condoms *are* my birth control. I haven't NOT used a condom since college when I was in a relationship. Using them as my only form of birth control keeps me straight. But, I should be okay, Mr. I gotta have it right now," Brook teased. "What was that about?"

"I was just sitting there thinking about how I'm going to miss you while I'm gone. Jill was singing to me and in you walk, looking all good. I just needed you at that moment," he confessed softly.

Brook smiled. They soaped each other down, almost getting started again, and finally got out of the shower, toweled off, and headed in to eat.

They were sitting there eating, each in their own thoughts when Brook said, "I'm gonna miss you, too." He reached over and softly rubbed the side of her face.

They played a few games of *Wheel of Fortune,* but they weren't as enthusiastic about it as normal, so they decided to go watch a movie. They went through the pay per view channels and tried to decide what to watch.

"Hmmm, how about porn?" Brook suggested.

Gio was like a kid in a candy store. "Forreal?!" He almost jumped up and down. Brook laughed.

"Yes, I do like porn, too. Well, just regular porn, nothing weird like animals or anything like that." Gio hit a few buttons and there came the porn music. Brook laughed, "Pretty familiar with that, I see."

He laughed, too. "Well, I've been known to watch a movie or two. I'm just happy you want to watch it with me."

"You'd be surprised at how many women really like porn. Of course, it has to be good porn. Don't be walking down the street and slip and fall, and a stranger jumps on you and you two start going at it."

"Aw, man, you want a plot and all that, too?" Gio joked.

They laughed and got quiet as the movie started. They watched all of fifteen minutes of the porn before they were going at it. Brook started it by sliding down in the seat and giving him head. Brook stopped him before they got too heavy and told him they still needed to use a condom. They ran up to his bedroom where the condoms were located and proceeded to get busy.

It was time for Gio to go. They stood at the door, smiling at each other.

"Good luck, Gio. I know you're going to do great on your first movie."

"Thank you, dimples. I'll give you a call as soon as I can. I don't know what to expect since this is my first time."

"I feel ya. You just go show them that you can do this, and do it well."

They stood there and held each other for a minute. Brook pulled back and gave him a quick kiss on the lips. She rubbed the side of his face with a smile and walked out the door with a little finger wave. She got in her car and drove off with a beep of the horn.

Alicia Keys was singing on the radio about holding her like it was the last time and tears ran down Brook's face. She got mad at herself. Why in the world was she crying! It wasn't like she was in love with him, they were just kicking it. That was exactly why she didn't want to get involved with him in the first place. She wiped her face and breathed deeply to calm herself. Last night had really been amazing. They ended up going three rounds and once more in the morning, and the morning sex had been slow and leisurely. It was that 'I'm going to miss you' sex. Brook smiled. Yep, that Giovanni Lay had definitely gotten under her skin.

She put in her old Beyonce CD, flipped to her jam, *Get Me Bodied remix*, pumped that song up, and got her head into something else besides Gio. She picked up her phone and called her girl.

"What'chu doing?" Brook asked when Debra answered the phone, bopping to the music.

"Finally got rid of Rantae's buggin' ass," she said. "Girl, he can work a sista out, but he always wants to stay longer than I want him to. Actually, he can leave right after the do, but damn, he always wants to hang around. I'm not letting his ass come back here. Next time, we're going to his place. I just hate traveling in the hood. Damn blue collar workers."

Brook just drove and listened to her friend rant and rave about her latest conquest and his being too clingy. It got her mind off of Gio and the fact that things were probably going to change with him being gone so long.

"You wanna go get something to eat?" Brook asked.

"Aw, boo, Gio's gone, huh? And, here I am going on about Rantae's needy ass. You okay?"

"Girl, boo, of course I'm fine. It's all good. He just worked me out and now I'm starving."

Debra was her girl and saw right through her bravado. "Okay, come scoop me and we can go eat up some stuff. Then we can head downtown and go to the Underground and laugh at people."

"Now that sounds like a plan," Brook agreed, already feeling better.

Brook had really gotten under Gio's skin. But, he felt himself actually liking it. It was something new for him. He hadn't been in a relationship in a long time. In fact, the last relationship didn't end well. It was actually pretty ugly. That's why he didn't put too much into females. Either they were trying to trap a brotha or they wanted to be seen out and about with him. That's exactly what he liked about Brook. She was just chill. She definitely wasn't the type to try and get pregnant by him. That much was proven when they slipped. She was a little freaked out about it, but then again, he thought she was on some type of pill or shot or something. Heck, who's only birth control method would be condoms just so they wouldn't have sex without a condom? Brook was really special. He was feelin' her, and she was feelin' him. They were just going to see where it took them. She didn't even want to go to any events with him. He jokingly asked her if she was secretly married. She just said that wasn't her thing, which for him was another plus.

But now, he had to get his head on straight. He was going to do a movie… a real movie, not a BET Special. As much bravado as he showed about everything, he was really nervous. He didn't want to mess up the opportunity. The night with Brook helped relax him. So he was feeling good, just a little on edge. He knew once they started, he'd feel more comfortable. He wasn't used to being out of his comfort zone, which was why he was jumping in head first into the movie thing. He was Gio Lay, he wasn't scared of anything.

CHAPTER 25

"What's up, sexy," Brook heard when she answered the phone.

"Hey, Gio," Brook answered with one of the biggest smiles, dimples almost reaching each other on the inside of her mouth.

"I'm missing you," Gio said seductively.

"The feeling is definitely mutual, and it's gonna be forever before you get back!"

"Yeah, I know. Probably another month or so."

"How's everything going? You remembering your lines, everything going okay?"

"Yeah, I'm accomplishing some things I didn't ever think I could do, bringing all kinds of emotions out. I just wish you were here to help me relax," he said with a chuckle. "So, I was wondering, how about you fly down here for the weekend?"

Brook's heart jumped. Wow, she really was on his mind, but she knew why, thinking back to the last night they had before he left.

"Hmmm, that could definitely work, which weekend are you thinking about? Aren't you shooting on weekends?"

"We have next weekend off. Now, I won't get finished 'til probably late on Friday night, but then I'm yours until Monday morning. Give me the word and I'll have your plane ticket waiting for you."

Aw man, Brook thought, *that's when Aunt Flo would be visiting. Dangit!* She wanted a repeat of those last sessions as well, without the slip up, of course.

"Well, I'd really love to come and spend time with you, but that is when I'm expecting Aunt Flo."

"Oh that's understandable. Is she visiting from Louisville?" Gio asked.

Laughing out loud, Brook explained, "Not a real aunt, just that monthly visitor, if you catch my drift."

"Ohhhhhh! Girl, if you don't get your behind down here and see me! As much as I would love to devour your hot little body, that doesn't mean that's the only time I want to see you. I just want to spend some time with you, whoop up on you in some Wheel, and have a nice, relaxing weekend to clear my head."

"Then, let's make it a plan," Brook said.

CHAPTER 26

Brook wheeled her luggage through Miami International Airport thinking, *Whoa, I understand that whole 'the border thing isn't working!'* She hardly saw any Americans, looked like it was about 90% Hispanic, and everyone was speaking in Spanish. Was this still America? As she was hurrying along, she noticed a driver holding a sign that said Brooklyn Bridges. Now, surely someone didn't have the same exact name as she did. She knew Gio was arranging transportation, but she didn't expect a driver of her own. She assumed the hotel shuttle would take her to the hotel.

Getting her strut on, acting like she did it every day, Brooklyn sashayed over to the man holding her name and said in her best Greta Garbo impression, "Yes, I'm Brooklyn Bridges."

"I'm Kenneth, your driver. Follow me," he stated, obviously not getting the joke and taking her luggage.

As they stepped outside and the warm weather washed over her, Brook looked around and was not impressed. Opening the back door of the sedan for her, and as if reading her mind, Kenneth smiled. "You're staying at The Ritz Carlton on the beach. You're going to love the view."

"Thanks," Brook dimpled.

Okay, this hotel is off the chain, Brook thought. She felt like acting like a Japanese tourist and start taking pictures everywhere. As she got out of the car and took in her surroundings, Brook thought Miami was a place she could get used to. It was October, pretty chilly in Atlanta, and down there it felt like mid summer. As she went to the front desk and gave her name, Brook got excited. *Okay, I have about five hours before Gio should get here.* That would give her time to check out some of the gift shops in the hotel, take a nice long bath, and be smelling good by the time he got there. Aunt Flo wasn't actually due until the next day, so she thought they could get busy all night long. She was so glad her cycle was predictable because she knew exactly how to plan it out. By tomorrow, she'd be on the Midol tip.

"Daaaaaaaaaang!" Brook said excitedly. "This room is crazy!" After she tipped the bellman and closed the door, Brook went around exploring each room. It was a suite, two bedrooms, a separate living and dining room, and a kitchen. Brook squealed, it had a huge Jacuzzi tub in the master bedroom. Walking out onto the balcony and looking where the ocean met the sky, Brook thought about it. She kept forgetting that Gio was technically a celebrity. Now she knew he definitely had bank. Whenever they went anywhere it was always first class, but daaaaaaang, she still didn't realize he had it like that!

Brook decided to cook him a home cooked meal. *I just have to find a grocery store since the hotel has all the pots and pans. Wow, real china... and silverware. Yep, this hotel is definitely off the chain*, Brook decided.

Brook wandered down to the front desk and asked about any grocery stores that may be in the area.

"There is a Publix grocery store not too far from here. Would you like me to arrange for transportation to take you there, ma'am?" the accommodating Concierge asked.

"Yes. That would be lovely," Brook answered graciously.

When they got to Publix, Brook had to hold in her amazement because it was two stories. She'd never seen anything like that anywhere, and it wasn't like she wasn't well traveled. *Go 'head Miami, y'all doing the damn thang. Oops, I mean dern thing.*

Arriving back at the room, Brook went straight to the kitchen to put on the steak. She figured she'd keep it simple and cook his favorites, steak, baked potatoes, a salad, warm bread, and dessert would be her. She laughed naughtily.

"Honey, I'm home," Gio's voice rang out, doing a Ricky Ricardo impression. "Man, it smells good in here," he noted.

Brook had candles burning, food ready, and the new Maxwell CD playing softly in the background.

"Hey, boo," Brook said as she sauntered into the room taking a page out of his book and wearing an apron that read, *Cooks do it better in Miami.* Underneath, she had on sexy matching red bra and panties.

"Damn!" Gio whistled and went to grab her in a hug. "Now, this is what a brotha needs when he comes home from a hard day's work," he groaned, kissing her deeply.

When they finally came up for air, he asked, "Is this a tease? Is the red signifying anything in particular?" He laughed.

Brook laughed. "No, silly. My aunt isn't due to arrive until tomorrow, so I figured I'd be your dessert tonight," Brook answered seductively.

"Well, forget dinner, I'll just take the dessert!"

"We have plenty of time." Brook laughed. "Go get your shower and get comfortable. When you get back, dinner will be ready."

Brook cracked up as Gio ran to the back to get his shower.

"I did not know you could throw down like that," Gio said while rubbing his flat abs.

"I do a little something, something. I just don't cook that often because it's easier to just stop and pick up something." Brook smiled, knowing she was showing off her dimples.

Gio stood up, went over and picked Brook up in his arms, and carried her to the bedroom. "Time for dessert," he said.

CHAPTER 27

Brook lay on Gio's chest, both lightly dozing when Gio said, "You know, they're talking an Oscar for me on this role."

Brook sat up suddenly. "Really! That is wonderful, Gio. Especially for your first movie role." She smiled and reached over to give him a light kiss.

"Yeah, but it sure takes a lot out of you because you have to use your true emotions, and working with these guys is no joke. They are totally serious! There are no screw ups. I've gotten so much advice, lessons, direction... I just really appreciate them so much. It's crazy because my role is getting bigger than what it originally was. They say I'm a natural," he said bashfully.

"Well you go 'head now! I ain't mad atcha. Get your acting on, boo," Brook teased.

"I don't know about that, but I am gonna continue to use their direction and learn as much as I can. You never know, if I do a good job in this movie, I'm sure there will be more. Singing will always be my first love, but I know singing. Acting is a new challenge for me and I love a challenge."

"I'm glad it's working for you. You seem to be taking the bull by the horn. I can't wait to see the movie."

They snuggled closer together and fell asleep.

Beach sounds awoke Brook the next morning, seagulls and ocean crashes. She stretched lazily and could hear the shower running.

As he walked into the room with a towel around his waist, he smiled. "Good morning, sleeping beauty."

Brooked grinned, admiring him in his towel and greeted, "Good morning. This has to be the most comfortable bed I've ever been in," Brook exclaimed.

"You hungry?"

"I'd say we worked up an appetite," Brook flirted.

Gio laughed. "I'll order room service. What would you like?" Gio asked, eyes following a naked Brook to the bathroom.

"Everything," Brook answered as she ran bathwater in the humongous tub and went to relieve herself.

"Wow, Gio, I didn't mean everything literally." Brook laughed, eying enough bacon, sausage, pancakes, French toast, eggs, grits, home fries, and fruit to feed a small family.

"Woman, I'm hungry," laughed Gio. "We worked up an appetite last night."

As they filled their plates, silence filled the air and soon, all you heard was forks scraping plates and slurps of orange juice.

"So, what's the plan for today?" Brook asked, munching on a piece of bacon.

"I figured we'd head downtown and do some shopping and sightseeing. They have glass bottom boat tours, jet ski rentals, all kinds of fun stuff we can do. Then tomorrow, we're going to Dwayne Wade's crib on Star Island for a little fun and relaxation. I want a totally regular and normal day because I really do have to get my head right. I have a love scene when we resume filming on Monday." He grinned.

"A love scene?" Brook teased. "With who, Nautica Diaz?"

"Yep, the one and only. And, I am nervous. Will she get offended if I don't get a hard on?" he asked. "Or, if I do?" he joked.

"What kind of love scene is it?" Brook asked.

"The kind that is really making me nervous. You'll see when the movie comes out."

"If it's anything like last night, then I'm the one that's nervous," laughed Brook.

Although Nautica Diaz was hot, really hot, Brook wasn't concerned, and it wasn't her style. They had a good thing going, had never even talked about anything serious. In fact, she didn't know who else he was seeing just like he didn't know who else she was seeing. She enjoyed spending time with him, loved the fact that he totally sexed her down, and yet, could still hold an intelligent conversation with her. Being single, she understood the two didn't always go together. Either the loving was great and they were dumb as a box of rocks, or he was a great conversationalist but had no skills in the bedroom whatsoever. Brook still tried to keep her cool with Gio. Although they had great times together, she kept in mind women threw themselves at him wherever he went. Heck, she had been with him a few of those times. He was always respectful when she was with him, but she didn't know about when she wasn't, and because they had never talked about a relationship that was the way it was going to be. That was one of the reasons she totally freaked out when they slipped up last month. She never did that, and never would again.

"Miami sure is a beautiful town, but I see it has its ghetto parts, too," Brook noted.

"Yeah, but that's everywhere."

"What type of dress code will it be and what are you wearing?" Brook asked as they loaded down bags from the various stores they shopped in.

Brook started out with that whole independent woman thing, declining his offers of purchases. She did okay by a long shot. Yes, she had two mortgage payments and a car note. However, she had investments, thanks to her parents who started her out when she became a teenager. They had instilled those values in her, so now she had a nice little portfolio. But, those stores were a little expensive for her pocket, so what started out as, "I got it," while whipping out her Visa, turned into, "Thank you," after about the third store. All the while, they got stopped for autographs and pictures.

"I think I'm just doing slacks and shirt, but people will be in everything from jeans to dresses."

"Hmmmmm," Brook said, hanging up her purchases. "I think I'll wear this cute little silk pants suit that someone bought me at Nordstrom today."

Gio grinned back at her. "With those shoes that the sales lady swore you had to have with it?" he questioned.

"And that you insisted on including." Brook laughed. "Without a doubt."

CHAPTER 28

Wow, so this is how the athletes do it, thought Brook. The house was a small mansion, there were probably fifteen bedrooms. Although they didn't go through the whole house, she could tell by her trip to the ladies room that it was laid out. She heard someone mention that the pool was the 'outdoor pool' and it was huge, complete with a Jacuzzi. No one was in it, but there were some women in bathing suits. The food was unbelievable. They had everything from fried chicken to caviar. And, everyone was so tall. There were only about one hundred and fifteen guests, but most of the guys were basketball players for the Miami Heat. Brook hadn't realized how tall they actually were. The women were normal size, but most of them were so hoochified. *Aw heckie naw! Her butt cheeks are hanging out the bottom of her shorts!* Those were the type of women that just irritated Brook. Their sole goal in life was to get pregnant by one of those men.

"Hi, Giovanni." Two of them sauntered past, asses just a shaking.

"Hello," Gio answered.

"Hi," Brook said, in a small voice.

Gio laughed. "You are so crazy."

"Just thought I'd throw that out there just in case they didn't see me standing here." Brook laughed.

"You 'bout ready to go?"

"Whenever you are."

They had been there a couple of hours, laughing, talking and having a good time. She was leaving the next morning and Gio had to be back on the set, so they didn't want to stay too late. They had a date with *Wheel of Fortune* when they got back to the room. And since it was apparent that Aunt Flo was a little delayed from all that sexing her and Gio had done, it looked like it was going to be on again.

"Leaving already?" asked Dwayne Wade.

Brook thought he was so tall, and fine.

"I have to be back on the set in the morning, so we're heading out. Thanks so much for the invite. We had a great time," Gio said.

"Nice meeting you." Brook smiled.

"Pleasure meeting you, too, Brook. And the invitation is always open. You don't need this knucklehead to come back," Dwayne teased.

"Slow your roll, bruh, or I'll have to hit you in the knees and take you out for the season," Gio joked.

"Whatever, man. I'm just glad to see you finally with a lady instead of a ahem, ahem," Dwayne faked as if he was clearing his throat.

"Ohhh, he got jokes," laughed Gio. "I'll holla at you later."

"Deuces," Dwayne threw back, laughing.

They arrived back at the room and got comfortable... Gio in boxers and a wifebeater, Brook in boy shorts and a cami. Brook put the *Wheel of Fortune* game in the DVD player and it was on.

"You really have gotten better at this game," Brook observed. "Almost as good as me."

"Dubrovnik, Croatia," Gio shouted, typing furiously.

"How the heck did you know that with only the d, t, r, o, n, and a? Why do you even know that place! I've never even heard of Dubrovnik!"

"Well, you know I'm pretty well traveled."

"You've been to Dubrovnik?" Brook screeched.

"Nah, I just remember it from my geography class back in school."

Brook threw the pillow at him. "You fraud," she yelled. Gio grabbed her and started tickling her. Laughing uncontrollably, Brook said, "I quit, I quit."

As their laughter subsided, they started kissing and it started getting hot and heavy.

"Did your Aunt Thelma come yet?" Gio asked.

"It's Aunt Flo, crazy. I think you delayed her," Brook whispered, giving him little nibbles on his neck and ear, making her way around to his mouth.

"Yes!" Gio shouted as he carried her back to the bed.

"Good luck with the rest of the movie, and your love scene. This weekend should give you all kinds of ideas," Brook joked.

Gio was getting ready to leave. He had to be on the set at 5am and her plane didn't leave until 9am.

"On the real, just do what you're doing because evidently, what you're doing is working," Brook said.

"Fo sho," Gio said. "Give me a call when you get in to let me know you made it safely. Just leave a message because I'll probably be on the set."

"Fo sho," Brook repeated with a grin. With a soft kiss on the lips, Gio was gone, mind already on the scenes he'd have to perform.

CHAPTER 29

Brook arrived back home, happy that she had the rest of the day to unpack and get ready for her work week. After unpacking her bags and hanging up her new clothes, Brook grabbed a shower, put on her comfortable PJs and called her mama.

"Hey, Mama," Brook greeted when her mother answered the phone.

"Hey, baby," Brook's mom said. "How was Miami?"

Brook's mom knew that Brook went to Miami, she just didn't know she was going to visit Gio. In fact, they still didn't even know about Gio. Brook didn't bring men home unless they were really important to her. It wasn't that Gio wasn't important, but that wasn't the nature of their relationship.

"It was absolutely beautiful! Mama, we went to a party in this mansion. Tell Daddy we went to Dwayne Wade's house," Brook said.

"He's in the garage fiddling with that car of his. I'll tell him what you said."

Brook's father had an old '63 Chevrolet Impala that he was restoring. Since they were both retired, that was his hobby. Mama took all sorts of classes at the Recreation Center, a place for retirees that was located downtown. She had even taken a self-defense class.

"I'll tell him when I talk to him. I just wanted to let you know I'm back."

"Alright, baby. I'm getting ready to head on over to The Center. We're doing flower arrangements today and you know I love flower arrangements."

"Okay. I'll talk to you later in the week. Love you," Brook said.

"I love you, too."

Next call was to Debra. Brook knew she'd never hear the end of it if she didn't call her girl.

"So did that bitch stay away long enough for you to get you some, Ms. I-only-sleep-with-one-guy-at-a-time?" Debra said, answering her phone.

"Well shoot, and how was your weekend?" Brook laughed.

"Girl, straight boring, except when me and Carmen went to the Obama rally."

"For real! How was it?"

"Off the chain! Girl, when I say every race was represented there... I mean from African to lily white. Even a Jewish guy was in line behind us.

And, girl, his speech was mesmerizing! I felt like I was in the most important place. I felt like I counted. But, then of course, there were some protesters there. You know I was hot. But, it was too funny 'cause the Obama supporters would follow them everywhere they went with Obama signs. It was hilarious," Debra hooted. "You know I was getting ready to step to them. Carmen made me slow my roll. How they gonna be at the Obama rally talking bad about him? I started to go over there and give them a piece of my mind."

"Pump your brakes, Sista Souljah. Dern, you wearing me out," laughed Brook. "You have to be the most militant almost-black person I know."

"You know how I get."

"Well, you need to run for somebody's office the way you're always breaking it down to people."

"Giiiiirl, you know I got too many damn skeletons in my closet. Hell, I got a whole science class in my closet."

"You ain't neva lying," laughed Brook, breaking into Ebonics with her girl.

"So how was your weekend, you never told me?"

"'Cause you got on your soapbox and didn't give me a chance. It was great. We had a really good time. Girl, you will not believe Dwayne Wade's house!"

"What?! You went to Dwayne Wade's house? Shutuuuuuppppp! Was it bad, girl?"

"What!" screamed Brook. "I'm talking at least 25,000 square feet. We didn't get to see the whole house or anything, but it was beautiful, not tacky, and very classy."

"So who was there?" asked Debra.

"A bunch of tall ass men."

"Yeah, them ball players are just too damn tall."

"Well, girl, I'm gonna get off here so I can finish unpacking and getting prepared for work tomorrow. I'll holla."

"Bye heiffa," said Debra, "I'll holla atcha on the weekend."

CHAPTER 30

The weekend with Brook was just what Gio needed. This acting thing was no joke. Gio didn't know what he expected, but it sure wasn't the hard work that went into acting. He didn't realize how much raw emotion he had to use and had a new respect for actors.

The great part was he was doing exceptionally well. They expanded his part some, and that was a major plus. He was feeling pretty good about what he was doing and enjoyed acting. It was something he could get used to. He officially had the acting bug. And the veterans guided him into pulling out Steve the character he was playing. He couldn't believe he was actually in a movie with Oscar winners. He was truly blessed.

With the expansion of his character, he had an upcoming love scene with Nautica Diaz, his love interest. He had never done a love scene, so was a little nervous about it. He would only be wearing a g-string, so everything would show if he got too excited. He knew off the set, he could do her. They had been lightly flirting with each other. She was a beautiful Hispanic woman with curves in all the right spots. And, she knew she was fine. He needed to clear his head, and Brook was definitely the way to do that. He needed her Zen to help him relax.

He was glad Brook was able to make it. He had one weekend off, and he knew he only wanted to spend it with her. It was just what he needed. They did the normal things that he liked about her to get his mind off the upcoming love scene, and her Aunt somebody stayed away long enough for them to have a weekend filled with great sex.

So now he was laid back, reading his script for the five hundredth time, and making sure he was ready. He had learned so much in such a little time. He practiced every night but there was no way to practice a love scene. He chuckled to himself and thought about all the things he did with Brook that would definitely give him some pointers.

CHAPTER 31

"So how did the rest of your work week go?" asked Gio.

"Tiring and too dern long. I'm so glad it's Friday. You know Debra had a fit when I told her I was staying in tonight," laughed Brook.

Gio chuckled. "It was all that Gio loving last week. By the way, isn't your aunt visiting you right now?"

Brook had such a week, she had totally forgotten about Aunt Flo.

"Well, not yet, but I'm sure it's the jet lag, coupled with our weekend and the stress of this week. No worries. Now, if Aunt Flo doesn't show up next week, then I'll worry."

They said their goodbyes and hung up the phone. But, Brook was worried. She was never late. Aunt Flo came monthly, on time, every month. "Oh shit, I mean shoot," said Brook aloud. She threw on her sweats, ran and jumped in her car, and sped over to Target. She found the aisle with the home pregnancy tests and was amazed. *Wow, how many different types are there?* she wondered. Just in case, Brook grabbed three different tests, went through the self check out just in case she saw someone she knew, and hurried back home.

Brook had tinkled on three different sticks and was ready to throw up. Two had come back positive and one was pointing in that direction. "No, no, no, no," Brook cried. "Mama and Daddy are gonna kill me!" Although Brook was a twenty-seven year old grown woman, she was still concerned with pleasing her parents. "I can't have a baby right now! Gio and I aren't even like that for real. I don't even know who else he is seeing!" She knew that before he went away to make his movie, they saw each other probably two, sometimes three times a month. She never questioned him, which was the reason she was worried when they had slipped up. Her fear had been a disease, not a baby. "OOHHH MMYYY GODDDD," Brook cried. But, she knew it was no sense in calling on God now. She wasn't thinking that when she was freakin' with Gio all over his kitchen counter. "I can't have a baby right now, especially without a husband," Brook cried. What was Gio gonna think? What was Mama and Daddy gonna say? And her job, she was a respected Account Executive. She couldn't be walking around being a baby mama! Noooooo! Tears streamed down Brook's face. *Wait, these things aren't fool proof. Heck they may even be wrong. I've had a stressful week, maybe that's why I'm late*, Brook hoped, making a note to make an appointment with her gynecologist, Dr. Baker. Brook curled up in her bed to go to sleep, tossing and turning the whole night.

CHAPTER 32

"You're pregnant," Dr. Michelle Baker said matter-of-factly, two days later.

Brook stared at her, the words not truly registering. She had half convinced herself that there was another reason her period was late. To hear Dr. Baker say it, after taking a blood test, Brook nodded her head. She really knew it. She had hoped, really hoped, that it wasn't so.

"Thank you, Dr. Baker," Brook said, head down, looking dejected.

"Brook, this isn't a death sentence. You're not a fifteen year old teenager. There is no reason why you couldn't have and raise this baby. Is the father in the picture?"

"Well, kinda. It was a slip up, Dr. Baker, with a man I'm just seeing. I never, ever have sex without a condom. And the first time I do, I get pregnant. Only me," Brook expressed pitifully.

"Well, you're still very early so you have time to think it out and decide what it is you want to do. Just call me and I can either start prenatal care or refer you somewhere to terminate the pregnancy," Dr. Baker said.

Ugh, terminate. Such an ugly word, Brook thought.

"Will do, Dr. Baker, and thank you for seeing me so quickly."

Brook's day passed by in a blur. She couldn't concentrate at all. Now, she was home and still staring at the phone. She didn't know if to call Gio or not. She just didn't know, period. She picked up the phone and called Debra.

"What'up, heiffa," answered Debra.

"One of these days, it's not gonna be me on the other end of the phone. I need to talk to you."

"Ut oh. Tell mama what's wrong."

"I need a face to face with you."

"Tell me when and I'm there."

"Now," Brook sniffled.

"I'm there," Debra said, hanging up the phone.

Brook felt like she had just hung up the phone and Debra was ringing her doorbell. She answered the door and as soon as she saw Debra, she burst into tears. Debra hugged her and walked back into the house. They sat in her living room and Debra rubbed her back and told her it was going to be okay, even though she didn't have a clue what was wrong. That was the great thing about good girlfriends they knew when silence was needed.

As the tears started to subside, Brook looked and Debra and blurted out. "I'm pregnant!"

Debra looked at her, stunned. "Ohhhh. You sure?"

"Yep, went to see Dr. Baker today."

"Aw, boo. It's not the end of the world. I can be an Auntie. You know it's gonna be a girl and she's gonna be just as fly as her Auntie Debra.

"Pump your brakes, girl. I just don't know. I'm not ready to be a mother. And Gio! Psssh, we're not even together like that. Suppose he thinks I'm trying to trap him or something?" Brook said.

"Girl, boo. You know Gio knows you not like that. And, from what you told me, he initiated that hot little love session where you lost your damn mind and didn't use a condom. You are going to tell him, right?"

"I have to figure out what I want to do first. How could this be happening to me?" Brook cried.

"Sistagirl, it ain't the end of the world. You have two choices, either have it or don't. You know I've made a trip to that clinic myself. The really sad part is it was entirely too easy. You go in, you go to sleep, you wake up, and it's over. This is a decision *you* have to make, but you have to tell Gio. It wouldn't be fair to him if you didn't."

"I know. You're right. I'll call him tonight when I think he's finished shooting."

"Hey, Gio, this is Brook. Give me a call when you get a free moment. Hope all is going well on your movie. Talk to you soon," Brook said into Gio's voice mail.

She was nervous, really nervous. She didn't know how he was going to react. She didn't have a moment more to wonder because her phone rang and she saw on the caller ID it was Gio.

"Hey, boo," greeted Gio. "I must have just missed your call."

"Hey," Brook said softly. "Are you busy?"

"Naw, I'm done, on my way back to the hotel. What's going on, you okay? You sound a little down.

"Well, Gio, I really don't know how to say this, so I'm just going to be straight up with you." Brook gulped and shouted it out. "I'm pregnant." Total silence. For the first time, Brook felt a bout of nausea. "You still there, Gio?"

"I'm here. I'm just in shock. Wow, I take it that means your aunt never came."

"Nope."

"Wow, I'm gonna be a daddy," he said.

"Wait. Don't you think we need to discuss this first? I'm not really sure I'm ready to be a mama."

"What are you saying, Brook, that you're gonna have an abortion?"

asked Gio, becoming agitated.

"No. What I'm saying is that I'm totally confused right now and I don't know what to do. I'm scared and I'm pregnant, and my mama's gonna kick my ass!"

"Baby, it's going to be okay. I don't have any kids. You don't have any kids. I have plenty of money and investments, so finance is no problem. We can do this!" Gio reasoned.

"I understand all of that. I'm just still in shock right now. I just... I don't know. I really just need to think."

"Okay, I understand. Just promise me you won't do anything without talking to me first."

"I wouldn't do that or I wouldn't have even told you in the first place."

"I really appreciate that, Brook. We're going to be okay. You'll see."

"Just give me a few days. I'm not going to make any rash decisions, either way. Let's talk again on the weekend and figure out for sure what we're going to do, okay," Brook said.

A couple of days later, Brook was in her cubicle at work getting prepared for her day. She'd had a restless night and was still a little tired. The receptionist called her.

"Hey, Dionna," Brook greeted as she answered her phone.

"Hey, girl, you have a delivery!"

"Okay, I'm on my way up."

As Brook rounded the corner at the front desk, she noticed about five dozen roses, red, pink, and yellow.

"Damn, girl. What did you do, or not do, to get all of these beautiful roses?" Dionna asked with a grin.

"Wow," was all Brook could say. "Where the heck am I going to put all these roses? I'll tell you what, leave them up here and give me the cards. I'll take them home with me at the end of the day."

As she read the cards, each one had the same message... *We can do this.*

Brook smiled for the first time since she found out she was pregnant and thought, *Maybe we can do this.* She dreamed that night of little girls with brown eyes and dimples.

Brook waited until the weekend to call Gio. She left him a message thanking him for all of the roses. When Gio called her back on his break, she asked him if he was trying to bribe her.

"I don't know. Is it working?" laughed Gio. "We have about three more weeks of shooting and then I'll be home. You feeling okay?"

"I'm actually feeling fine. I thought I was supposed to be feeling bad and throwing up all the time. I don't even feel different. But it is still really early, only about four weeks. I'm going to hold off on telling anyone until three months. That's when it's safe and minimal complications can happen."

"So, does this mean what I think it means?" asked Gio excitedly. You could hear the smile in his voice.

"I guess so." Brook laughed. "I didn't even realize it until I just thought about telling people. I guess that means we're going to be parents. But, promise we'll leave it between us until three months, okay."

"Fo sho," Gio said.

He couldn't believe it! She was PREGNANT! He was excited, but still a little leery. He felt like he knew Brook and didn't think she was 'that' type of woman. Unfortunately, he had been down that road before. He thought he was going to be a dad a few years back, but the baby was born entirely too soon, like three months too soon. He immediately got a blood test and as Maury would say, "You are NOT the father." He couldn't believe he had gotten played. The signs had been there, but he was too excited about the prospect of becoming a father, even if it meant with a baby mama, to even notice things were a little off. Yep, hindsight was definitely twenty-twenty! But this time, he was prepared. He believed in Brook and trusted her more than he had trusted any woman. But, his eyes were open, and he knew if the slightest thing didn't add up, she'd know about it!

Right now, he had to get his head back into his movie. The love scene had gone well, a little too well. At that point, Nautica Diaz was practically throwing the panties at him. There was only so much a red-blooded man could take. And, kissing throughout their scenes didn't help either, but it was all good because they were still adding on parts for him. He was starting to feel like a true, skilled actor.

CHAPTER 33

"How you feeling?" asked Debra.

"Girl, don't you ask me that any more. I told you, I'm feeling totally fine. No nausea or anything, just my breasts are a little sore and I have cravings for soul food, which isn't very good. I'll have to keep my behind in the gym for real," Brook exclaimed.

"Gio will finally be home next week, won't he, or has it been delayed again?" asked Debra.

"Yeah, but I'm really getting a weird vibe from him. I talked to him every other day at first. Then, it went to every couple of days. Now, it's time for him to come home and I hardly hear from him at all. I understand he's busy with the movie and all. It's just a vibe I'm feeling. Something is off."

"Girl, you know you are trippin'. There has been buzz about him in that movie and they're talking he's going to win awards, maybe even an Oscar! They're saying he put in a performance of a lifetime, kinda like Jamie Foxx did in *Ray*," Debra exclaimed excitedly. "It's just them pregnancy hormones messing your head up, crazy."

"Hmm, maybe you're right. Now, let's go on over to Deedy's Soul Food so I can get me some greens.

"Your ass gon' be big as a house," hooted Debra.

Brook gave her the middle finger.

"Girl, your ass really *is* gonna be big as a house," laughed Debra as she watched Brook eat barbecue ribs, potato salad, macaroni and cheese, greens plus cornbread, and now she was looking at the dessert.

"I do work out, you know! Now, leave me alone, woman, and let me enjoy my dessert," she growled. "When we leave here and my food digests, I'm going to head over to Ladies Workout Express and get my work out on," Brook said as she ordered a slice of chocolate cake with chocolate icing and vanilla ice cream.

As they were driving back to Brook's house, Debra asked, "So when are you going to tell your parents?"

"Probably on my way to the hospital to deliver." She laughed. "I don't know. Besides Gio, you're the only other person that knows. They say you're not supposed to announce until after three months because that's the danger period when you can have a miscarriage. But, for real, for real, I just don't want to disappoint them. Look at Brandon, he's the perfect son," Brook whined.

"One thing you know for sure, your parents love you and are proud of you. You're not some high school kid getting knocked up. You're a grown woman with a career. They'll understand. Heck, you know your mama been wanting some grandbabies."

"Well, I'm going home this weekend for Brandon's birthday. I won't say a word. I sure hope Mama can't tell. You remember how she knew everything when we were younger."

"She sure did! Remember that time I spent the night at your house and we snuck out your window to go see Darren and Quentin?" said Debra, cracking up at that memory.

"Girl, I thought she was gonna kill us. And she locked the window! When I saw those curtains wide open and that window was locked, I about peed on myself," Brook screamed, laughing hard at how scared they had been, out trying to be fast. They had to ring the doorbell to get in the house. Her brother's room was on the second floor so it wasn't like they could knock on his window. Her mother had ranted and raved for an hour about the dangers of young ladies sneaking out in the middle of the night. They were so tired because they had been drinking beer, which Brook truly hated, but they were trying to be grown. They were both still virgins and that was the highlight of their life at that point. They were only freshmen in high school and wanted to fit in. Then, Brook's mom made them write a five-page report on the dangers of teenagers in the streets after dark. And, they had to write it before they could go to sleep. Needless to say, they had never done that again. On top of that, Brook's mom had still called Debra's mom and told her what they had done. They were both on punishment for a month.

CHAPTER 34

"Hey, Daddy," Brook greeted as she walked up the driveway.

"Hey, babygirl," Brook's dad, Brian, greeted, giving Brook a nice, warm daddy hug, as she called them.

Brook loved her daddy. He hadn't changed a bit since forever. Her dad had worked at Ford Motor Company on the assembly line since Brook was a baby. They always had a new or nearly new Ford. Her friends often teased and called them rich people. When Ford downsized for the third time a few years ago, they offered him a really nice severance package to retire early. Daddy took the deal, so he was officially retired. Standing six feet even with a slender build, he was a very handsome and proud man who loved and took care of his family. He was proudly the head of his household. With a head full of curly, black hair, he loved to brag that he didn't have a strand of gray hair, while Brook's mom had silver and gray hair and would tease that he was the one who gave it to her. Brook remembered family vacations with her parents and her brother. They didn't do stuff normal families did like go to an amusement park like Disneyworld or anything like that, they would drive to educational places, like the Grand Canyon, went to DC to see the Smithsonian, even went to visit Mt. Rushmore. She remembered as a kid thinking, *Wow, they must have had to sit still for a long time for somebody to draw their face in there.* She could smell the fried chicken her Mama would fry for the trip.

Her parents still lived in the house she grew up in, a nice family neighborhood in Shively. The area had changed a lot with the homeowners dying and their children and grandchildren taking over their property, but not their block. Brook knew every family on it, from Mr. Gibson next door to the Booths and the Moores down the street.

Debra had grown up around the corner and her mom still lived there, and so did her grown behind brother, Greg. It just did not make sense that he still lived at home, and he had to be close to forty, still always changing menial jobs. He and Debra totally did not get along. She called him trifling. He called her a gold digger. She told him if he got a real job instead of flipping burgers or washing dishes, maybe he'd be lucky enough to get a woman like her. He really was jealous because Debra had finished college and he only went one semester. Look up loser in the dictionary and there his picture would be.

"The car is looking good, daddy!" It really was a beautiful car, in tip top shape. Her dad had gotten it painted black cherry and it glistened.

"I've been getting so many offers for this car, it's not even funny! I didn't put all this work into it to sell it," he exclaimed, totally bewildered that people thought he'd sell his prize possession.

"Daddy, that's what people do, buy cars, fix them up, and sell them."

"Well, not me. And, what is this your mama told me about you meeting Dwayne Wayne? Isn't that the guy that was on the Cosby Show spinoff about black college life?" asked Daddy. "That was a really good television show, showed young black folks that college life is for them as well. That Bill Cosby sure did a lot for our people. You remember the show *Good Times*? Had black folks struggling and living in the projects like that was the only life we could have. Cosby showed us that black people did live in other places besides the ghetto," Daddy ranted.

"Daddy wait, I didn't meet Dwayne Wayne, I met Dwayne Wade from the Miami Heat! I went to a party at his house."

"Is that right? That boy's got game, I tell you. Did you see his gym? I know he had a gym at his house? All those ball players have gyms in their homes. Full sized ones, too.

Let me get in this house before he starts talking about Dwayne Wade's game, his strengths versus his weaknesses, Brook thought. Her daddy loved some basketball. Louisville was definitely a basketball city and since they didn't have a pro team, college basketball was the sport the whole town loved and that eased over to pro basketball.

"Daddy, wasn't nobody in no gym" Brook laughed.

"Hmmm, I see you been around that Debra with that kind of language. You know you'll give your mother a heart attack with that sentence you just used."

"Shhh, don't tell her," laughed Brook. "I'll see you inside, Daddy. Have fun with your toy car."

"My car is going to be worth more than your house one day," Daddy laughed.

"Hey, Mama."

"Hey, daughter," her mother answered, giving Brook a hug and peck on the cheek.

Brook's mother, Frances, was a beautiful woman. Standing only about 5'2, she had a slender build, brown skinned with beautiful, long salt and pepper hair, always pulled back in a bun in the back. Regal was what came to mind when seeing her. Sometimes she'd wear her hair out, but not often, she said it was too much trouble. Brook had treated her to a salon visit once and her hair was beautiful, but Mama said the only time she'd wait that long again was for Jesus Christ himself, so it was back to the bun, or chignon, as her mother called it. Brook and Brandon always laughed that it was a fancy name for a bun. Mama was where Brook and Brandon got their dimples. She was the disciplinarian of the family and packed a mean whack! She did not play, probably because she was a high school teacher. She went to college as soon as Brook had started school. She remembered her and her Mom doing their 'homework' at the kitchen table together. Brook was glad that she didn't have to attend the same high school where her mom taught. Oh boy, that would have been the worst high school years. She could see her mom marching into her classroom and giving her a good one upside her head for acting like she had no home training. Brook groaned at the thought.

"Mama, didn't I tell you I'd tell Daddy about Dwayne Wade."

"Well, I told him you called and one thing led to another and I ended up telling him. What's the big deal?"

"Only that you told him the wrong person," laughed Brook.

"Oh." Mama laughed, too. "Have you talked to your brother?"

Brandon was a great example of a good man. He was an attorney for a very respectable law firm in downtown Louisville and his wife, Phyllis, was also an attorney. They'd been married almost five years and still didn't have kids. Mama always bugged them about bringing her some grandbabies, but they always laughed it off. 'Now isn't the time,' they'd say, 'we're still enjoying each other.' Her Mama really was ready to spoil some grandbabies.

"I talked to him yesterday. He said they'd be over later. Whatcha cooking?" Brook asked, lifting lids to pots and examining what her mom was throwing down on.

"I'm cooking all of the birthday boy's favorites. I have fried chicken, macaroni and cheese, greens, and hot water cornbread."

Soul food! Brook knew she'd have to eat slowly. She definitely didn't want to arouse suspicion.

"Happy Birthday, bighead," Brook said as her brother and his wife came into the kitchen.

Brandon came over and gave her a squeeze and kiss on the cheek. She really was proud of him.

"What's up bighead," he greeted.

"Hey, Phyllis," Brook greeted.

"Hey, sweetie," Phyllis greeted back as they hugged.

"How's ATL treating you? You ready to come back home yet?" Phyllis asked.

Phyllis couldn't imagine life outside of Louisville. She was one of those people that had loved her school, was in all the clubs, was now on the reunion committee for both high school and college, was active in her church as well as on the Democratic board, and worked the polls at voting time. While Brandon had gone to Loyola Law School in New Orleans, Phyllis had stayed right there in Louisville and gotten her law degree at the University of Louisville. Brook didn't blame her though. Phyllis and her brother owned a beautiful home in Hurstbourne, in an upscale subdivision. They had a huge four bedroom three bath home. And it was just the two of them. *This really should be Phyllis that is pregnant right now,* Brook thought.

They all sat down to dinner, Brook's father said the prayer, and they dug in.

"Pass me the greens, please," Brook requested.

"Goodness, girl, you already finished the ones you had on your plate?" exclaimed her nosy brother.

"Nobody makes greens like Mama." Brook grinned, hoping no one could see her heart beating through her chest. She just knew at any moment her mom was going to stand up and shout, "Ah ha, you're pregnant!"

Brook took it easy for the rest of the meal, making sure not to draw attention to the fact that she wanted to put the whole pot of greens in front of her and just chow down on them. She kept glancing longingly at the bowl that was on the table. She'd have to sneak some more later.

Brandon outlined a big case he had won while Phyllis looked at him lovingly. *One of these days, I'll find Mr. Right and have that loving look on my face*, thought Brook. Phyllis then went into one of her boring cases. While Brandon was an attorney at the D.A.'s office, Phyllis practiced corporate law and it was boring as heck. Brook glanced at her mother, who was trying her best to act interested, and her dad who just kept nodding his head like he totally agreed with all the gibberish she was speaking. She was glad Debra wasn't there because she knew by now, she'd be holding in her laugh. Phyllis really irritated Debra. Debra said no one could be that perfect and called her a black Stepford Wife. And actually, as much as Brook loved her sister in law, she had to agree, that girl was the most boring person in the world.

CHAPTER 35

Brook checked her answering machine when she got home. Debra was on there, talking about how she met Mr. Right at Starbucks and to call her when she got back. That was it. No word at all from Gio. He hadn't called her cell the whole weekend when she was at her parents'. Brook didn't know what was going on, but she was really feeling uneasy. Hormones didn't have anything to do with him not calling her all weekend. In fact, she hadn't talked to him since last weekend, and that was really short and to the point. *This Negro bet not be trippin!* He'd finally be home on Saturday, and she'd see what the deal was then. She knew one thing, she definitely wasn't going to call him first.

She couldn't believe that he was just now calling her, Saturday evening. She knew he was due to arrive that morning, but that was a seven hours ago. She had finally talked with him on Tuesday, briefly. He was in a rush, yet again. Brook knew for sure they definitely needed to talk because something was evidently on his mind.

"Hello," Brook answered.

"Hey, what's up," Gio greeted.

"So, are you home?"

"Yeah, I'm here."

"Okay, I'll be over there in a little bit."

There was a slight pause and then he answered, "Oh, okay."

They hung up the phone and Brook said, "What the heck!"

Gio answered the door looking super sexy. He was rockin' a nice, chocolate colored linen slacks and shirt outfit, some Kenneth Cole shoes, bling in his ear, and smelling absolutely fabulous. Brook's kitty kat did a little meow. He was on the phone and just gave her a head nod. She followed him into the house and as they walked through the various rooms to get to his bedroom, Brook saw Tha Dogg in one of the rooms playing Playstation.

"Hey, Dogg," Brook greeted.

"Hey, Ms. Brook," Tha Dogg said with a smile and a wink.

As they got to his bedroom, Brook headed over to the sitting area and put down her bags. She had stopped at Sticky Fingers and got some barbecue ribs, greens, and potato salad. She'd bought the same for Gio, except instead of potato salad, she got him baked beans. Lastly, she got a dozen of their wings, which where the bomb. She went over to his mini fridge he had in the sitting area and grabbed a can of Hawaiian Punch that he always had stocked in there, and sat down to commence to grubbing.

Gio finally started wrapping up his call. Brook heard him say he'd probably be through there later. Brook rolled her eyes starting to get irritated.

"Well, hello," Brook said as Gio finally hung up his cell.

"What's up," Gio gave her a head nod while fiddling with his phone.

"So, is this the M.O.?"

"Huh?" he said, still fiddling with his phone.

"Is this the M.O.? You know, get a girl pregnant and then turn into an ass?" Brook clarified calmly, getting a straight up attitude.

Gio's head snapped up. "Well, I wouldn't know, I've never gotten a girl pregnant before," he answered, throwing attitude right back at her.

"Speaking of which, I'm gonna need a DNA test," he said, not even looking at her, still fiddling with his phone.

Brook was in mid bite of her rib and stopped, rib dangling from her hand. She slowly turned her head toward him and nodded. "Yeah, we can do that," she said calmly. "So, you asked me to come all the way over here so you could ask me for a DNA test?" Brook asked incredulously.

"First off, I didn't ask you to come over here, you volunteered. And secondly, you can't blame a brotha. It's awfully suspect how you conveniently got pregnant," he said rudely.

Aw hell to the naw! He went THERE! She really could not believe this was the same guy who begged her to go through with the pregnancy barely a month ago.

"I got pregnant, Gio? It takes two to tango, sweetie. And if my memory serves me correctly, you're the one who couldn't stop to put on a damn condom," Brook shouted.

"And, how do I know that's even when you got pregnant?" Gio shouted back.

Brook's eyebrows raised so high, you'd think her eyeballs were about to pop out. She was totally in shock that he was saying those things. She stared at him for a few seconds. Of course, he went back to fiddling with his damn phone.

She politely put her rib that she had been waving around back into her container and calmly said, "Fuck you," as she wiped barbecue sauce off her hands.

"What?" Gio said, like he didn't hear her.

"I didn't stutter, muthafucka. I said fuck you!" she repeated loudly. "You know what, you're just like every other nigga out here," she said.

"Naw, baby, I got bank and about to get more! You know, y'all chics are the ones out here trying to trap a brotha." He laughed snidely.

"I wasn't talking about what you got, monkey ass nigga, I'm talking about who you are," Brook said, stabbing her finger to her heart. "Niggas like you are a dime a dozen. Me, I'm needle in a haystack, baby. And, mark my words, you'll realize that," Brook threatened as she put her plate back in the bag with his plate. Gio watched her grabbed the bag, her purse, and walk toward the door. "You just made a very hard decision really easy. Now, allow me prove you wrong," she said as she slammed his bedroom door with all her might.

Tha Dogg watched Brook fly past him, tears rolling down her face. He walked out of the room and saw Gio come rushing down the hallway. He looked at him and shook his head sadly.

Gio yelled, "Stay outta my fuckin' business, Dogg," and stormed back down the hallway. Tha Dogg heard him slam his door even harder than Brook had.

Brook knew she needed to slow down, but she was pissed. She couldn't believe what had just happened. As Brook sped to Debra's house, she tried to call her but her cell went straight to voice mail and she didn't answer the house phone. After weaving through traffic, Brook finally made it to Debra's and she was almost hysterical at that point. Her eyes were swollen, tears still streaming down her face. Brook jumped out the car and started ringing Debra's doorbell like there was no tomorrow.

Debra finally came to the door, peeked out and opened the door.

"Girl, why are you ringing my doorbell and beating on my door like you crazy? And why aren't you at Gio's?" she asked.

Brook pushed past Debra and went storming in the house. "You will not believe what that muthafucka said," Brook screamed. "Fuck that stupid, bama ass mutha..." Brook stopped mid sentence. There was a guy sitting on Debra's sofa, a really fine one at that. That's when she noticed the lights were down low, soft music was playing in the background, and a bottle was sitting in an ice bucket on the table with two champagne flutes half full.

"Uh, hi, I'm umm Glenn," Mr. Fine stuttered, half waving, totally embarrassed.

"Oh," Brook said. "I'm so sorry. I didn't know you had company. I'll talk to you tomorrow." Brook backpedaled and headed to the front door.

"Girl, if you don't get your ass in here," Debra said. "Glenn, let me holla at you for a minute."

Head down, Brook said again, "I'm so sorry. I really didn't mean to bust in here like this."

Brook headed to the kitchen and grabbed a glass. Not a champagne flute like they had, but a real Kool-aid drinking glass and filled it up with their champagne. As she gulped it down, Debra hurried back into the room, eyes going wide at Brook gulping champagne out of a regular drinking glass.

Debra screeched, "What are you doing! What the hell happened? You come storming in here, cursing like me and guzzling champagne when you're supposed to be at Gio's. And, what are you doing drinking champagne?" Debra yelled, knowing something was very wrong.

Debra turned on the big light and screamed. "What happened to your face? Is that blood? Did y'all get into a fight? Oh hell naw, we getting ready to do an old fashioned beat down on his ass! Bump that!" Debra screamed.

"What?" Brook said, feeling what was on her face. "Oh, that's barbecue sauce," she explained.

"Girl, shit! What happened?" Debra asked.

"This muthafucka wants a DNA test," Brook screamed, getting pissed even more now that she had her girl with her. "I told you his ass was trippin'. Nigga talking about how I conveniently got pregnant, like I'm trying to trap him and he didn't know if that night was even when I got pregnant. I don't even know who the hell he is! That's what my ass gets. Hell, we've only been kicking it what, about six or seven months, and that wasn't even consistent," Brook said, mad for falling for the okie doke.

"What?!" screamed Debra. "You have got to be kidding me! What's that nigga's number, let me call him," Debra hollered.

"No!" Brook said, "He can go straight to hell, do not pass go, do not collect $200! He ain't *never* got to worry about me ever again. And, you already know that I am making an appointment as soon as possible to end this fuckin' pregnancy, too!"

"Now calm down, Brook. You don't want to make any rash decisions. Just think about it first," Debra reasoned.

"Think about it! The father of my child just accused me of trying to trap him. How did it all turn around in just one fuckin' month!"

"Okay, cursing Brook is really starting to scare me. What happened to not cursing anymore, huh?" she asked, rubbing Brook's back.

"You're right," Brook said, taking a deep breath to calm down. "I am not going to let him change who I am!"

"Now, you know somebody has been in his ear. Who do you think he told?" questioned Debra.

"I don't know, and I don't care. All I know is I'm in a situation that I don't want to be in and, I'm gonna do what's necessary to fix my life. The drama is over and so is this pregnancy," Brook said with finality.

Gio couldn't believe Brook. She had the nerve to be upset with him for asking. He didn't know what she was doing when he was away. They weren't exclusive. That baby could be anyone's. Once the baby was born, then they would get a DNA test and go from there. As the saying went, fool me once, shame on you, fool me twice, then I'm a damn fool!

She was really pissed when she stormed out of his house, but Gio wasn't worried. She'd get over it. If she wanted him to even think of being with her, she'd get over it. He'd give her a call in a few days, or weeks if he felt like it, and let her make it up to him.

He had bigger things on his mind, like Nautica Diaz. That girl was a hot mess! He finally gave in and sexed her, and she was off the chain. She scratched up his back and bit his lip. They had to put extra make up on his lips to cover it. After that, he spent most nights in her trailer. She fed his ego. Between her telling him how great he was, the seasoned actors telling him what a great job he was doing, and the director telling him he was a natural coupled with his part being expanded six times, he had this acting thing down pat. Now they were talking an Oscar for his role. *Damn, his swag was just ridiculous.*

CHAPTER 36

"Hey, sleepy head," Debra greeted.

Brook woke up in Debra's guest bedroom. She'd been staying over there since 'the incident', as they now called it. Brook had gone to work Monday, Tuesday, and Wednesday, and had taken off Thursday and Friday. On Thursday she had the procedure done. It was Saturday and she knew she had to get back to the land of the living. It wasn't as easy as she thought it would be. The procedure itself was scarily easy, but the sadness that came with it surprised her. Now, that was the hard part, getting past what she had done.

"Hey, girl," Brook answered, sitting up in bed. "I've come to a conclusion, I'm going home today. I need to take today and get prepared for my work week."

"You sure? You know you are more than welcome to stay here until forever." She laughed.

"Girl, boo. I need to get on with my life. It's all good."

Well, I have a great idea," Debra said. "Let's have us a Diva Day. We'll go get manis and pedis, facials, let's do it up. Then, we can stop by the Mac store and get our faces done and go do dinner somewhere."

Brook smiled for the first time in a week, dimples deepening, and said, "Now that sounds like a great idea! That's just what I need to get out of this funk." Brook jumped out of the bed, raring to go.

Brook felt great and knew she looked great. It was just what she needed. She felt so refreshed and had on a new dress to make her feel even better. She and Debra sashayed into Justin's for dinner.

"Reservations for Debra Williams," Debra told the beautiful sista at the podium. Her name tag said Antonia.

"One moment, please," she said with a beautiful accent.

Then, not two minutes later, Antonia said, "Follow me, please."

A few heads turned to watch them as they strode to their table, admiring their different styles of beauty.

"How the heck did you get us a table at this late notice?" questioned Brook. Debra just smiled and winked.

As Brook and Debra were giving their order to the waitress, they heard a voice say, "Y'all divas know y'all fly as hell!" They both turned around to see Carmen standing there laughing. After hugs and squeals, Carmen teased, "Y'all know y'all see the looks these ladies in here are throwing as well as their dates."

"Don't blame me for their insecurities," said Debra. "And, I don't want nobody's man and definitely don't want nobody's husband."

"I hear ya, girl. That's what's wrong with us women today, too ready to share somebody else's man. Remember when we used to respect each other?" preached Brook.

"And ourselves!" Carmen chimed in. "Remember when being called a Ho was fighting words?"

"Pssh, still is for me," said Debra, complete with a neck roll. They all laughed.

"Who you here with?" asked Debra nosily.

"This guy I showed a house to," answered Carmen. "This is a first date and I'm not too sure about him yet. A girl has got to be careful! He was buying a house for himself, no wife, no kids. While normally that's a good thing, in Atlanta it screams down-low!"

"OH-kayyyyyy," Debra said as they high fived each other.

"So, we're just feeling each other out. In fact, let me head back over there."

"Alright, girl, enjoy your night, I'll holla at ya through the work week," said Debra.

"Fo sho," answered Carmen.

"Isn't it funny how we both have picked up the language of Atlanta?" laughed Brook. "And, I haven't even been here a year yet! I find myself saying 'fo sho' and 'y'all' and all kinds of southern words. It's so normal here."

"I know," Debra agreed, "I don't even realize I do it."

"Well, it can't be worse than saying har for hair and thar for there like we do in Louisville."

"Fo sho," Debra agreed, and they both burst out laughing.

CHAPTER 37

Brook had thrown herself back in to work with a vengeance. The great thing about her promotions background was that she constantly thought of ideas for her clients instead of just selling them advertising. And, the ideas were popping out. She hadn't been out in the last six weeks. Gio had called a few of times in the beginning but she had ignored his calls. He had even sent roses to her job which she left at the front desk and tore up the card without reading. She instructed Dionna that if any more came to not accept them and have them take them back. She was getting her grind on and that was what was working for her right now. She had seen pictures of Gio in some of the magazines with Nautica Diaz and she guessed they were an item now. Whateva! He could do him because she was definitely doing her! She worked hard during the day, went to the gym, and went home.

Mia came over and asked Brook, "So you gonna share some of those promotions or what? You have been cranking them out and closing deals like you're trying to bank money. Are you trying to give me a run for top salesperson?" She laughed with her mouth but not her eyes.

"Hey, Mia, the ideas just started flowing, and you already know you are welcome to any of them. It's not like I can't sell them if you do. We have totally different clients. Go for it," Brook offered.

Brook liked Mia well enough. She was a shorty, standing all of 4'9", Hispanic, loved the brothas and had more attitude than a sista. Brook had seen her jump bad on more than one occasion. Get that Grey Goose vodka in her and she was always ready to fight, swearing somebody was looking at her wrong. In fact, that's why Brook didn't hang out with her and had told her that she needed to change her drink of choice. Brook felt like she didn't get all dressed up to go out and mess up her clothes because her coworker was drunk. They had hung out three times and it had happened all three times, enough for Brook to know to be busy whenever Mia wanted to hang out. The really messed up part was they were either at client locations or some work function. Once she started drinking, she really didn't care. She was great in business, in fact, that's the part that Brook admired because she was a real go-getter. It was after hours that messed her up. Everybody knew about it but didn't mention it, that was just a part of who she was. Everyone knew to disappear when she started on her third or fourth drink.

"Girl, you already know I never have a problem with anybody sharing my promotional ideas. I just don't want to put them out there like that for people to criticize. You know you are always welcome! I appreciate all the help you've given me," Brook said.

"See, chica, that's why you're my girl. Wanna hit happy hour after work?" she asked.

"Nahhh, I have a six o'clock and then I know I'll be ready to go home," Brook said, happy that she really did have an evening appointment.

"All right, I'll drink a couple of them for you then."

"Don't hurt nobody now," Brook teased. "I'll email the promotion one-sheets. I can't send you the ones for clubs because you know we can't have the same promotion going on at different clubs, but I'll send you the rest."

"Cool beans," Mia said. "Ciao, chica.

Brook's cell rang and she answered, "Aren't you supposed to be approving somebody a loan or something?"

Debra laughed. "I can do more than two things at once. Just ask Glenn," she said with a giggle.

Glenn was Debra's new boo and the same man at Debra's when Brook barged in on the night of the incident with Gio. Thankfully, they met again under much better circumstances and he was a really cool guy. She couldn't believe there was someone who could make Debra blush, yet, he could. He was an investment banker, which was why Brook thought they had so much in common. He was divorced for about four years with a son that was seven years old, who he got every other weekend. Debra said he seemed to be a great dad, but she hadn't met his son yet and was not rushing it. The great part was Glenn told her he didn't bring women around his son because he didn't want to give him the wrong impression. He told Debra that he and his ex had a really good relationship. Debra said right now, they were just having fun, no commitments, no strings, and they were both enjoying it just like it was. She had spent the night at his house a couple of times and there was no drama, no late night phone calls, no blank spots on his furniture where it looked like a picture used to sit. It was really just all good.

"Okay, now don't get mad, but Glenn and I went to see Gio's movie, *Overproctective*, last night," Debra confessed.

"And, why do you think I would want to know that, you trader?"

"Girl, it was the bomb! Gio did a really great job in the movie! He played a teller in a bank. Nautica Diaz played the bank president's daughter who falls for him. He was so funny. You know they're talking an Oscar for his role and he really deserves it! As much as I wanted to hate the movie, I couldn't," Debra said excitedly.

"Ohhhkkkaaayyy, and what? You president of the Gio fan club now?"

Brook snapped sarcastically.

"No, girl, I'm just saying he was really unbelievable in the movie and he'll probably get the Oscar out of it. He is really about to blow up."

"Okay, whateva. I have to go. I have work to do."

"Now, Brook, all I'm saying is you may wanna call a brotha."

"For what, so he can impregnate me again and turn into every other jerk that isn't ready for responsibility?" Brook whispered harshly, losing her patience. "I can't even believe you went to see the movie, Debra, you're supposed to be on my side! We broke up with him," Brook said, sounding like a kid.

"I am on your side, boo. I'm just saying, I'm sure he was really under pressure with the performance that he gave in this movie and maybe you should just hear him out."

"The only thing I want to hear from Gio is silence, okay? And, if you keep bringing him up, that's the only thing I'll want to hear from you, too," Brook threatened and hung up on her best friend.

"Okay," Debra conceded when Brook answered her phone. "I won't bring him up again. And I'm sorry for going to see the movie, but Glenn wanted to see it and I hoped to hate it so I could call you and dog it out. Hey, Glenn and I are heading to happy hour after work, wanna come?" she asked.

"What? Two nights in one week? What's really going on?" Brook teased, never able to stay mad at her friend for long. "I'll tell you like I told Mia, I have a six o'clock and then I'm heading home."

"Ewwww, drunk ass Mia," Debra said. "I will never hang out with her again. Now that is Dr. Jekyll and Mrs. Lush," Debra joked.

"Ain't that it," Brook agreed.

"Brook, you said you wouldn't let someone change who you are, yet, you haven't been out in almost two months and you're working too hard. Loosen up and have some fun, girl. I miss my friend," Debra whined.

"I'm not letting anybody change who I am and it hasn't been two months," Brook said, knowing she was straight lying. "Okay, maybe it has been a while. I'll tell you what, next weekend, it's on and poppin', okay?"

"That will work, and I'll call Carmen, too. Next weekend is the annual All White Party, and you know it's gonna be off the chain."

"Aw man, that's gonna be a bunch of wannabes and think they ares," whined Brook.

"All the better to get your mind off of anything but having a good time because you know the deal up front."

CHAPTER 38

Brook couldn't decide what to wear. Her choice was white slacks and a white halter, but she knew everyone would be much dressier. Debra had called for the third time and asked where she was. She finally decided on a clingy, white KLS Collection halter dress with her white stiletto sandals that laced up her shin. The dress hugged her body in all the right places and wrapped around and gathered at the side on her waist. At the bottom, it curved outward with a flounce and fell a few inches above her knees. Since she had been working out more, her body was tight. She felt great and looked great. She was actually excited to go out. Hanging out with Debra and Carmen was sure to be a fun time. With one last look in the mirror, Brook grabbed her purse and keys and headed out. She called Debra when she got in her car. Brook was going to be the designated driver.

"I'm on my way," Brook said when Debra answered.

"Finally," she huffed.

Brook pulled up and honked the horn for Debra to come out. Her girl was rockin' a sharp, sleeveless white jumpsuit with some bad white stilettos. You could tell she knew she was the stuff just by her walk to the car.

Brook laughed when Debra got in. "You just know you are 'that girl', don't you?"

"Don't hate, appreciate." Debra laughed.

"Carmen has saved us a parking space."

"How do you save a parking space?"

"She takes up two spaces, then when we get there, she'll move in one and give us the other."

"Sneaky. Both of y'all are so sneaky, and brilliant," Brook squealed, happy not to have to worry about finding a parking space.

Debra called Carmen when they got at the club and Carmen hurried out to move her car.

"My cousin, Roz, is holding our table," Carmen said as they hurried to the party.

The party was definitely off the chain. There was a line of white all the way down the street. Brook, Debra, and Carmen strutted to the front of the line, Debra gave her name, and they entered the party. The party was just as packed on the inside as on the outside.

"Follow me," Carmen yelled and weaved her way through the crowd.

Two guys were talking to Roz. She was what people would call voluptuous. She looked like about a size twelve, which was small enough, but her booty had to be a size sixteen and her boobs a size 40DDD with clothes tight enough to show it all. She had on white super tight slacks and a see-through white blouse with a white bra, but her boobs were falling out. The guys were almost slobbering all over themselves.

Debra whispered, "Now that's not a booty, that's a big ole ass!" Brook nudged her with her elbow and tried not to burst out laughing.

"Here they are," Roz said. The guys turned to check out the ladies and grinned, obviously happy with what they saw.

"Ladies," greeted the tall one in his sexiest voice.

"Hello sexys," said the one with all the jewelry, looking like he had gotten his Mr. T starter kit.

"We were going to order a bottle of Dom and join you."

"No thank you, bye-bye," said Debra, always one to cut to the chase.

"We're just hanging out with the ladies tonight," elaborated Brook, trying to smooth it over. "But, thanks for the offer."

The two men walked away mumbling.

"Debra, Brook, this is my cousin Roz. She's visiting from Knoxville. Roz, this is Debra and Brook," Carmen introduced.

'Hey, girl' and 'how ya doings' went around the table.

"How long have y'all been here?" Debra asked.

"A couple of hours," said Carmen. "Y'all slow behinds are late!"

"For real! Y'all missing all the fun. And I can't believe y'all let those guys get away! They was gonna get us some Dom," Roz said, trying to act like she really knew all about the champagne.

Brook glanced over at Debra who had glanced at Brook and knew they were thinking the same thing... Bama! They both let out a little chuckle. The waiter came over and took their drink orders and the party was on.

Brook didn't know how many men stopped at their table. She had heard every line that was ever invented, but she was having a great time. Her, Debra, and Carmen laughed and joked all night long. Roz, on the other hand, only threw in what celebrity she saw. Brook was coming back from an overcrowded ladies room and was stopped by a fine, dark chocolate, bald brotha.

"Hey, dimples, where are you rushing off to?" He smiled.

Ump, fine. A little too fine. Probably got a bunch of women on speed dial, too, Brook thought, but then stopped herself. She was there to have a good time, not judge.

"Just trying to get through this crowd to get back over to my table," Brook said with a smile, making sure to show off her dimples.

"Well, why don't you slow down for a minute and talk to me. There's no one to rush to at that table is there?"

"Nope, just hanging out with my girls."

As she stood there talking to him, lightly flirting and people watching, her eyes locked eyes with Gio's glare. He was standing across the room shooting daggers at her.

She visibly jumped. *Oh shit, I gotta get outta here,* Brook thought.

"Well, it was nice meeting you," Brook said and hurried away while Mr. Fine watched her hurry through the crowd.

"Did you know he was gonna be here?" Brook whispered harshly to Debra as soon as she returned to the table.

"Huh?" Debra said, looking confused, bobbing to the music. "Did I know who was going to be here?" Debra asked. But after looking at Brook's face, her mouth went into a big O. "He's here?" Debra squealed, looking shocked herself. "What kind of question is that, you know I wouldn't bring you here if I knew he'd be here!"

"Well, he's here and I'm ready to go," Brook huffed.

"What? Who's here and why is this person running you off," Carmen said, getting all into their conversation.

"Nobody," both Debra and Brook answered.

Debra whispered, "You okay?"

"Yep, I'm straight. And, I'm not letting anyone run me off. I'm good," Brook answered, bobbing her head to the music.

A guy walked up to their table, that time straight to Brook, and said, "Giovanni Lay would like to meet you," like he was presenting her with a grand prize.

Brook smiled uncomfortably at the guy, hoping no one heard him and said, "No thank you."

But of course, hanger-on-guy just knew that Brook would jump up and go running, started getting loud, thinking he was important. "You think I'm lying? Giovanni Lay wants to meet you. He specifically asked for you," he said loudly with an air of importance.

"Look, sweetie, why don't you run along, find someone who's impressed, and leave me the hell alone," Brook said with a serious face.

Mr. Hanger-On got the message and beat it.

"Oh my God, he said Giovanni Lay?" said Roz excitedly.

Brook knew that girl would hear a celebrity's name from across the room.

"Oooo, girl, I just love him. Is he really here? Why don't you want to meet him? I wonder if he'll give me an autograph. He is too fine with them pretty ass eyes," Roz continued.

Carmen was looking at her like, What is going on?

Brook just shrugged her shoulders and shook her head. Giving them a fake smile, Brook said, "Now can we finish partying?"

"Sure can," said Debra and lifted her glass in a toast.

They were having a good time, flirting, laughing, just a good old fashioned girl's night out. Debra was telling a story about the time she was sleeping with this guy and his girlfriend came beating on her door. Brook had heard the story before but it was still just as funny that time.

"Not only did I tell this chic that I didn't know this asshole had a woman, I'm trying to explain to her how he did her wrong, not me! She was calling every name but the child of God and a home wrecker! And he was standing there with some *baby, baby please* bull while she's cursing me out. Finally, I had enough. I kicked him in the nuts so hard he fell to his knees. That shut both of them up. As he groaned on the floor, I told her to get her trifling, no good, cheating man away from my house and to never come back."

They were all hooting with laughter when everybody just stopped. Roz was sitting there with her mouth hanging open. Brook, still laughing turned around to see what everyone was looking at and there stood Gio.

Oh shoot, he looks good, she thought. He had on a white silk pants set that just made his skin glow with stunner shades covering his eyes.

"Good evening, ladies," Gio greeted. "Brook, can I holla at you for a minute?" he asked.

Roz leaned over closer to listen with no shame at all and Brook knew she didn't have a choice but to leave with him. Carmen's eyebrows were raised high, mouth in a big O. Debra was looking to see what Brook wanted to do. Roz was just trying to get in the mix.

"I'll be right back," Brook said and hurried away.

"You never returned my calls," Gio said.

"Gio, please! For what? What do you want?" Brook said angrily.

"I know you're mad at me. I'm sorry I flipped out on you. I miss you, Brook. And, you look beautiful. I can't even tell you're pregnant," he said, looking at her stomach, smiling.

"Probably because I'm not!" Brook said with a defiant look on her face.

"Huh? What do you mean you're not?" Gio asked, eyes widening, going from her belly to her face. That had thrown him for a loop and knocked that stupid smile from his face.

"Told you I'd prove you wrong," Brook said, rolling her eyes as she walked away.

"Brook! Brook! Brooklyn!" Gio called.

But, Brook kept walking and headed straight to the table where Debra was already standing with both of their purses in her hands.

"You ready?" Debra asked, and Brook simply nodded her head yes. "Let's roll," Debra said.

Brook finger waved bye to Carmen and Roz, who were still looking on in shock.

"I wish I had seen the look on his face when you said you weren't pregnant," hooted Debra.

"See, you think it's funny, I'm straight trippin'! I totally didn't expect to see him, so that in itself was a shock. The fact that he didn't know I wasn't pregnant anymore hadn't even entered into my mind."

Brook's phone rang again and asshole came up on her caller ID.

"He is blowing you up," Debra said.

"I just can't believe this," exclaimed Brook as she turned her phone off. "The first time I go out and I run into him. Dammit!"

"Well it was bound to happen soon or later," Debra reasoned.

"True. I just would've like to prepare myself to see him before it actually happened. I ignored him till he left me alone before, I can do it again," Brook said with resolution.

CHAPTER 39

Brook had an abortion. SHE HAD AN ABORTION! She had definitely messed him up. That was the last thing he thought she would do. He knew she was pissed at him because she didn't answer his calls and never returned his messages. The florist even told him they couldn't deliver at her job anymore because his flowers had been refused. So, he knew she was pissed, but he never thought she'd be that pissed.

Nautica Diaz was a wrap. He knew he should have never gotten involved with her. She was entirely too much work always wanting to go to this industry event and that party. And, she always made sure they took pictures. He figured Brook had probably seen pictures of them, but figured she was pregnant, what was she gonna do? Nautica was just fun for the moment.

Gio figured eventually Brook would have to cool off. He also knew he was the father of her child and did feel bad about being an ass. Yes, he probably did eventually want a DNA, but he didn't have to go about it the way he did. And, now that he thought back on it, he really didn't even want a DNA. He couldn't figure out why he was trippin' with her in the first place. Well, he knew, but was just too embarrassed to admit it. He was listening to the wrong people and it blew his head up.

He didn't want to even hit up the club, but Tha Dogg insisted he get his ass out the house. He was glad he did, otherwise, he wouldn't have run into Brook. When he saw her smiling into that nigga's face, he knew he had messed up, forreal. Later that night, he got wasted. Tha Dogg should have stopped him from drinking so much, but he seemed to be getting some kind of pleasure out of his pain.

Brook awoke to her doorbell ringing and beating on her door. "What the heck?" Brook said and stumbled down the stairs half asleep to answer it. It was Gio. "Dangit, why didn't I think of that?" Brook mumbled, instantly waking up. Had she not been half asleep, she would have considered it may have been him.

"Brook, I know you in there, I just saw you just peek out the peephole. Open the door, or do you want your neighbors to hear all of your business?" Gio threatened.

Brook called Debra. "Girl, Gio is over here beating on my door acting a plum fool," Brook said when Debra sleepily answered the phone.

"What? You want me to come over there. Glenn's here and we can be there in a hot second," Debra said.

"Girl, no. I just want you to know what's up just in case drama goes down."

"Okay, boo, call me if you need me."

Brook cracked open the door to Gio, who was roaring drunk. "So, you gonna let me in or what?" he slurred.

Brook opened her door wider to let him in because she definitely didn't want her neighbors hearing the ruckus he was out there making. Gio stumbled in the door.

"How you gonna come over here trippin' at this time of night, Gio?" Brook shouted. "You got your damn nerves and you're not welcome here."

Gio dropped to his knees and grabbed Brook around her waist, going from pissed off drunk to crying drunk. "Please, Brook. Tell me you didn't kill our baby. Oh, Brook, how could you do that? That was our child, our child we made in love and you killed it," he cried, tears streaming down his face.

Brook could not believe it. *This Negro is straight trippin'*, she thought.

"Gio, stop. Get up. You're drunk," Brook shouted. "You act a complete ass, accuse me of trying to trap you, question the fact if you're even the father, and then you come in here all shocked and surprised that I ended the pregnancy!" she screamed.

"I know, baby, I know. I was trippin'. You know I was trippin'. I didn't mean any of it, but you wouldn't take my calls and I was trying to explain. I just figured I'd have time to explain it better as you got further along in the pregnancy. I never thought you wouldn't still be pregnant. Why, Brook? Why didn't you just answer my calls? I would have made it up to you," Gio cried drunkenly, tears streaming down his face.

"I don't do make-ups, Gio, I told you, I'm a one of a kind type of woman."

"I know that now, that's why I want you to marry me, Brook." He clumsily pulled a box out of his pocket and it really was a ring in it. "See," he slurred, wobbling on one knee on the floor. "I love you, Brook."

"Are you kidding? I don't even know you," yelled Brook. "It's time for you to go, Gio. Not only do I not want to marry you, I don't even want to see you, so bounce!" Brook said, walking to the door.

"I don't have a ride," Gio confessed as he stumbled over to the sofa. "I had Tha Dogg drop me off since he said I couldn't drive."

"You did what?! What, did you actually think I would let you in my bed, in my life? Then, you really got me twisted!"

"No, that's not it at all. I just figured we'd be able to talk this all out."

"There is nothing to talk out, remember, I'm not pregnant anymore so there is nothing left between us. Now look, I'm over this whole conversation. You can sleep right there on the sofa and Tha Dogg can pick you up in the morning." Brook marched down the hallway to her linen closet and snatched down a sheet, blanket and pillow, then put a pillow case on the pillow. "Stand up, Gio," Brook said angrily. He was already dozing off.

As Brook made up the sofa for him to sleep on, Gio just kept mumbling, "I'm so sorry, Brook. I'm really sorry. It's my fault. I know I messed it up."

Brook went and got two aspirin and a glass of water, and gave them to him. "Take these," she barked.

Gio threw the aspirin in his mouth and drank the water. "Thank you, baby."

Brook didn't answer, just left him there on her sofa. She had hardly reached her stairs when she heard him snoring loudly.

Brook's phone started ringing as she made her way to her bedroom. *If this is Tha Dogg, he can come pick his ass up right now*, thought Brook angrily. She didn't want to call him to have him come all the way back to her side of town at that time of the night, well morning, but if he called first, then it was on.

"Girl, why didn't you call me back," Debra said. "Got me up all worried. I couldn't even go back to sleep."

"'Cause the negro is downstairs asleep on my sofa."

"What?! Why in the world is he sleeping on your sofa?" screeched Debra.

"He's drunk as hell. And I'm talking stumbling, fall down drunk. He had Tha Dogg drop him off, so his drunk ass is passed out on my sofa. I'll call Tha Dogg in the morning to come get him."

"You gonna be okay?" Debra asked.

"Girl, I'll be fine. It's all good. Don't worry. Now go on back to sleep or whatever it was y'all were doing over there," laughed Brook.

"Fo sho," laughed Debra.

Brook tossed and turned all night. She kept having nightmares about Gio and babies. In the latest one, there was a bassinet in her bedroom and a baby was crying. Brook got out of her bed and walked over to the bassinet. When she picked up the crying baby, the baby had Gio's head and was screaming, "Why mommy, why did you kill me?" in one of those scary Freddy Kruger voices.

Brook awoke with a start, heart racing. She glanced over to the clock to see what time it was. Eight am, time to get up and get him out. Brook walked downstairs to see if Gio was still asleep. Yep, he was, snoring hard. Brook went and got her cell and called Tha Dogg.

"Yeah," Tha Dogg answered sleepily.

"Dogg, it's me, Brook."

"Hey, Ms. Brook. Did everything go okay? You guys work everything out?" Tha Dogg asked hopefully.

"Dogg, there is nothing to work out. Now, when are you coming to get him?"

"His car is there. I had a couple of the boys drop it off. The keys are in your mailbox."

"Oh, okay then. Sorry for waking you. You take care, Dogg."

"Ms. Brook, wait. Look, I know you pissed at Gio, and I know how he showed his ass so can I understand why. But after about the fifth bottle of Dom, when Gio convinced me to bring him to your house, he kept saying how much he loves you and how he messed it all up and he wanted you to be his wife. Now, I know it's not my business and I probably don't know everything that happened, but just know this, he has never had anyone in his life like you, so just hear him out, okay? I have never, ever, heard Gio say he loved any woman, Ms. Brook, none of them! And for him to say he wants you to be his wife!"

"Dogg, he was drunk! It doesn't count."

"No, that's exactly when it does count. That's when the truth comes out, Ms. Brook, when you're drunk, and you know it."

"I hear ya Dogg. I hear what you're saying. Is there anywhere he has to be this morning? I don't want him to oversleep."

"No, he's good today. See, that's exactly what I'm talking about. Although you're pissed at him, you're still looking out. You are a special woman, Ms. Brook."

"Well, that and a skittle will buy me a river," joked Brook dryly.

Brook was cooking breakfast, she needed something to do. She had been cooking and thinking since she got off the phone with Tha Dogg. She knew she had to hear Gio out for closure, and she wanted to get the conversation over with and move on, but she was nervous and when she was nervous, she cooked. She heard Gio stumble to the bathroom about five minutes prior. As Brook was putting the plates on the table, Gio came in the kitchen looking a hot mess.

"So, I guess this means last night wasn't a dream." He nervously chuckled, looking embarrassed.

"Have a seat, eat," Brook answered.

Gio sat and they both bowed their head in prayer. Gio took a sip of his coffee, "Brook, I'm sorry. Just here me out, please," he said when Brook was getting ready to interrupt him. "I know I was an ass. I don't know what came over me, listening to the wrong people I guess, letting all that get in my head. I was stressed about the role I was playing and they were filling my head with all this talk of an Oscar, thinking you conveniently got pregnant, and I don't know. I had a bad lapse of judgment. I was straight trippin', and I apologize for insulting you and who you are. Please, accept my apology. You don't ever have to see me again, but please accept my apology. Real talk, I understand why you did what you did. That was all on me and I don't blame you at all."

Brook didn't say anything, just kept slowly chewing on her bacon, listening.

"You know, Gio," Brook finally said, "I do accept your apology. It's all good and it's water under the bridge. Let's just close that chapter of our lives and move on."

"And, what if I don't want to move on?" Gio asked softly. "Wait, before you say anything, just don't shut me out. Heck, play a game of *Wheel of Fortune* with me sometimes. I miss hanging out with you. Even if you never want to take our relationship further, I miss your friendship and would be happy if you would still be my friend."

"We can do that, Gio. We can be friends. Let ye who is without sin..." Brook quoted.

"Well alright then," Gio grinned. "So, after we eat, wanna play a game of Wheel?" he asked hopefully.

"Let's take it one day at a time. Maybe next week. I'll give you a call," Brook said.

"I know you're not going to call me," he said sadly.

"I will. This is just a little too sudden for me. You hurt me really bad, Gio. I can't just shake it off and go play a game with you. Just give me a minute," she said. "I'll tell you what, if I don't call you by next weekend, then call me," she said.

"Thank you, Brook," he said, reaching over and rubbing her hand.

Brook smiled softly, nodded her head, and moved her hand away.

Gio thought about the night before. He called some friends to find a jeweler that would be available whenever, and actually had him bring rings to his house and bought an engagement ring. He figured that would get her back. Wrong! Again! He took his drunk ass over to her house and proposed. She straight clowned him, and he really couldn't blame her. When he woke up the next morning on her sofa, he knew it hadn't been a dream. He had truly shown his ass. But Brook was cool about it. She had definitely calmed down since the night before and had even cooked. He didn't know if he should eat though. Was she poisoning him? But, then they said grace, and he didn't think she would poison him if they prayed before the food.

And, now, he was really trying to get back to where they were, to take it even further. He didn't care about his ego or what anyone thought, he wanted Ms. Brooklyn Bridges. He wasn't going to stop until she was his. She hadn't even slept with him. DAMN! That woman could hold a grudge. But, he didn't think it was a grudge, she was hurt, and it was his fault. So he didn't care how long it took her to trust him again, he was there. Forget girlfriend material, she was wifey material.

CHAPTER 40

Gio was trying to win her back. She knew it, hell, even Tha Dogg and Debra knew it. They had slowly gotten back into an easy friendship. He came over, they played *Wheel of Fortune*, and he left. He was also in the studio a lot working on collaborations. They hung out sometimes and went to the museum, a play, and even a poetry reading. Nothing heavy. Nothing serious. Every time, he went home and so did she. When they were out and he was spotted, Brook stepped back and let him do him. And, even though things were going well, Brook still hadn't been back over to his house and still hadn't had sex with him. They had been hanging out together for a little over a month and although it had been entirely too long since she had sex and she was starting to get withdrawal symptoms, Brook wanted to make sure she was really ready first. However, she did eventually go and see his movie and she loved it! She went by herself during a weekday when she was supposed to be out seeing clients. He really did a wonderful job and she finally saw what everyone else had been talking about. He became Steve, his character in the movie. Steve started off as a small character in the movie, just a bank teller. The president's daughter started flirting with him and they end up sleeping together. She started to fall hard for him and the President wasn't happy about his daughter dating a black guy, and one of his tellers to boot. Gio told her originally he was going to be just a fling of hers, but they ended up extending his part, which was why his return home kept being delayed. Gio and the daughter, played by Nautica Diaz, end up together, but the bank President tried everything to come between them, including framing Gio for stealing. The daughter found out the truth and confronted her dad. Either she'd go to the authorities or he had to leave her and "Steve" alone. And, that love scene that Gio had been worried about really was hot, really hot. In fact, Brook was not even feeling that at all and decided she hated Nautica Diaz.

Brook's doorbell rang and it was Gio, looking all fresh and outdoorsy. They were going to Debra's for a barbecue. Glenn supposedly made the best barbecue, he bragged. Carmen was also coming with a friend, but Carmen had to clown her once she found out Gio was coming, the man who ran Brook out of the club, she teased.

"You look like a barbecue." Brook laughed.

"How do I look like a barbecue?" Gio laughed.

"I mean, you have the whole Fourth of July look going on, with the red, white, and blue."

"Oh, she got jokes!"

He really looked good. He was dressed casual in a navy linen short set with red pinstripes and white sandals. White cap and shades completed the look. He loved his linen. He did look like a picture of a backyard barbecue.

"Let me go grab the potato salad and we can head out."

"Let me get that for you," Gio said as he grabbed the bowl of potato salad that Brook had prepared for the barbecue, acting like he was protecting it with his life. "We definitely don't want anything to happen to this potato salad," he joked.

"Now who's got jokes?" laughed Brook.

They were having a good time at Debra's, and Glenn's barbecue was all that he had promised. It was all about the sauce, he said dramatically. Brook really liked Glenn, and it looked like Debra did, too. He was cool, laid back, and just what Debra needed. She even called him boo. He got mad cool points for that one. Debra said they were just kicking it, but Brook knew better than that. They saw each other once, sometimes twice a week, which was a record for Debra. He didn't sweat her, which was definitely what Debra needed. *Yep, Debra had found herself a man*, Brook giggled to herself. But, Carmen's date, Maurice, was irritating everyone. Brook could tell Carmen was embarrassed. He thought working at an advertising agency meant he was in 'the business'. Brook worked with advertising agencies daily and knew they just bought advertising for clients. In fact, the one where Maurice worked was a smaller agency. He kept asking Gio stupid questions like had he ever thought about doing commercials and asked for Gio's card so he could hook him up. Finally, Brook couldn't resist jumping in because he was on her last nerve.

"What exactly would he do commercials about?" Brook asked.

"Well," Maurice said importantly, happy to have an audience, "just about anything like cars, anything you're interested in, I can make happen for ya," he said with a wink, looking around to make sure everyone was paying attention to him.

"Well, Maurice, you sound like you're talking about sponsorships and clients would have to pay him to sponsor their product," Brook said innocently.

"Yeah, Maurice, that's a sponsorship," Debra chimed in, not knowing what the heck she was talking about, but happy to put that smug Maurice in his place.

"And, he couldn't just say it in a commercial, he'd actually be required to use the product as well," Brook finished.

"Well, yeah, I know that," Maurice said stumbling over his words. "What I was saying was, umm, I could get with some clients and hook the two of them up," he smiled, thinking he'd recovered.

"In order to do that, Maurice, don't you have to get with the head of these car companies? In fact, what car company are you speaking of, because your agency doesn't handle any of the big ones, so you wouldn't be able to hook him up since that would be a conflict of interest, don't you think? Unless you're talking about Joe Schmoe on the corner in the hood," Brook said sarcastically.

"No, what I meant was...," Maurice started, but Carmen interrupted him.

"Aw hell, you don't even know what you meant, let's go," she demanded.

He looked like a kid who had to leave the birthday party right before they cut the cake. "Leave! You're ready to go already?" he whined.

Carmen just shook her head and got up. "Thanks for everything, y'all. I'll see ya on the flip side," Carmen said as she headed out to leave, clearly pissed.

Debra and Brook both knew that Maurice was toast.

They were playing spades, girls against the boys, and the girls were winning big time.

"Nnnow, dddon't tttake this aasswhhooopping ppppersonally," Debra stuttered like the guy on Harlem Nights, Richard Pryor and Eddie Murphy's big hit, as she slammed down the big joker, setting them once again. Debra and Brook squealed and gave each other high five, laughing and screaming.

"Okay, the score is now two hundred and seventy six to ten," screamed Brook as she and Debra fell out laughing again. They jumped up and did their dance routine they learned when they were cheerleaders for Pop Warner back in the day.

"W.I.N.N.E.R.S. That's the way you spell success," they cheered.

"I think you two are using telepathy on us," Gio said, trying to hold in his own laugh.

"Yeah!" agreed Glenn.

"What it's called, sweetie, is skills," joked Debra.

"Yeah, yeah, yeah, well I quit," said Glenn, scratching out the score so you couldn't tell what it was. They all cracked up.

"Sore losers," laughed Debra as she and Brooked hi-fived each other.

"Well, good peoples, it's getting late so we're gonna head on out. It's been fun," Brook said. "Oh snap, let me help you clean up."

"No, don't worry about it, I'll help her," Glenn said.

Brook raised her eyebrows and looked at Debra. "Well alrighty then," Brook said with a smirk.

Glenn and Debra stood in the front yard waving good bye as they drove away. Brook smiled, so happy her girl was happy.

"That was fun. Well, after that guy left. What was his name again?" Gio asked.

"Dumb-ass," Brook answered with a laugh.

"So, are you ready to turn in or do you want to watch a movie or play a game of Wheel?" Gio asked.

"You know what? I recorded the movie *Boycott* with Terrance Howard and Jeffrey Wright on my DVR. That looks like that'll be good," she suggested.

"I can get with that."

After a moment of comfortable silence, and the radio playing softly in the background, Brook asked, "Are we boring? I mean, it's Saturday night, well, it's still early, only a little after nine, and we're going in to watch a movie." She laughed.

"No, we're not boring," Gio answered, "we're just content."

Brook and Gio watched the movie and really enjoyed it. The discussed how powerful Martin Luther King, Jr. was back in the day and how that was what they were missing now days.

"We have a start with Obama. He is making us accountable for our own actions.

"But, did you see how long those people walked!" Brook said. "We could never get it together like that these days. And, I don't necessarily mean walking, I mean coming together as a people in general. Yes, Obama is a start, but we have to get some act right ourselves. Bill Cosby totally hit that on the head when he said we can't get all shocked and bothered that the cop shot little Tyrone in the back when bad-ass Tyrone was robbing someone. Don't do the crime! At first, I was undecided on whom to vote for, Hilary or Obama, but as Debra so eloquently told me, *ain't no middle aged white woman gonna know about my damn struggles. It's a black thing, she wouldn't understand.*" Brook laughed. "Debra may get a little radical on the whole politics thing, but she really does know what she's talking about. And, it's true, I feel like Obama does care more about me and my needs. And, that statement is the truest statement ever, unless you've lived in *my* skin, you'll never know *my* struggles," Brook said, getting a little heated.

"Whoa, pump your brakes, Cynthia McKinney, you're gonna make me wanna go march somewhere." Gio laughed and Brook joined him.

Gio's cell rang. He looked at the caller ID and then looked at Brook with a frown on his face. "I wonder what he wants?" he said and answered his phone. "What's up, bruh," Gio answered. Brook got up and picked up their glasses and bowl of popcorn to take in the kitchen and give him some privacy. "What!" Gio screamed. "You are shitting me! You are shitting me, man." Brook ran back in the room to see what was going on. Gio was pacing the room with a big Kool-aid grin on his face. "Alright, yeah, okay, I'll talk to you tomorrow," he said and hung up the phone. He looked at Brook with a look of wonder on his face.

"What? What!" Brook yelled, excited but not knowing why.

"Not only did they ask me to perform at the Academy Awards, but I also got nominated, baby! I've been nominated for an Oscar for Best Supporting Actooorrrrrrr," Gio screamed, grabbing her in a big hug and spinning her around.

"Shhuuttt uuppppp! Oh! My! God! I can't believe it! And for your first movie! I am so happy for you," she said, hugging him.

Gio said, "I doubt if I win, but that doesn't even matter. All I know is that I did good. Baby, I really did a good job because if I didn't, I never would have gotten nominated," he said.

"Do you want to call people, let them know you got nominated?" Brook asked excitedly. "I understand that you need to go."

Gio thought for a moment and said, "No, not really. I just want to share this with you, right here, right now."

Brook hugged him again and they stood there hugging and smiling. Brook didn't know when the kiss started, only that she didn't want it to end. It was a sensual kiss, soft and slow, a kiss that had been building up since they had started back seeing each other.

"Do you want me to stop?" Gio asked hoarsely, trailing kisses down her neck.

"No," Brook answered, feeling entirely too good.

"Look at me, Brook," he said, stopping the kiss. Brook looked him into those beautiful eyes. "Are you sure you don't want me to stop?" he asked again, making sure she knew where they were headed.

"I'm positive," Brook smiled, desire making her knees weak.

Gio whispered softly, "I need you, baby," and grabbed each side of her face kissing her softly. He grabbed her hand, and led her to her bedroom.

CHAPTER 41

Brook woke up the next morning and Gio was still asleep. She watched him sleeping with a soft smile on her face. The night had been amazing, and she was sore! They had foreplay for what felt like hours, and had made love forever, fallen asleep, made love again, and then they had a good old get down and dirty session. Brook got up to go relieve herself and run bath water, she definitely needed to soak. As she made her way to the bathroom, she picked up the empty condom wrappers, three of them. *Ump, we sure made up for lost time last night*, Brook thought with a smile, getting a tingle just thinking about it.

When Brook returned to the bedroom after her bath, Gio was still knocked out. She headed to the kitchen to make breakfast with a smile on her face. That was a sure sign of good loving when you got up to make him breakfast. While she was cooking, Brook grabbed the cordless and called Debra.

"Whatchu doin?" Brook asked when Debra answered the phone with, what up, heiffa.

"Cooking breakfast, whatchu doin?"

"Aw snap, you must've got some good loving last night to be making that man breakfast," teased Brook.

"How the heck would you know, you don't even remember what good loving is!"

"'Cause I'm standing here making breakfast myself."

"What!" Debra screamed. "I can't believe it! You done finally gave that man some!"

"Shut up, big mouth, before Glenn hears you."

"Girl, he is in there snoring. You know I put it on him." Debra gave a naughty little laugh. "And, it's about time you quit making that man suffer and got over it."

"What do you mean quit making him suffer? We were just taking it slow."

"No, *you* were taking it slow, he's been ready! I see the way he looks at you. You can be across the room talking to somebody and he'll be over there just gazing at yo crazy ass."

"Gazing! Whateva, heiffa!"

"You did remember to put a lid on that pot, didn't you?"

"Girl, boo, you know that will never happen again! I wish he coulda wore two condoms! Plus, you know I'm on the pill now, too. A sista is using all kinds of methods to make sure I don't mess up because I can't go through that again."

"Well I'm just glad to hear you got you some, 'cause you was really getting on my nerves," Debra teased again.

"Anyway, I was calling to see what you all were doing today. I have something special planned and I want you all to be a part of it."

"Count us in, and why do you have something special planned? You gonna have a 'I finally got me some' party or something?"

"Oh, that's just so funny. No, it's something else and I don't want to ruin it. So, just come by around six'ish. I'm cooking dinner, so don't eat."

"You want me to bring anything?"

"Nah, I'm cool. And it's a surprise for Gio, so don't say anything."

"Alrighty then. See ya later, alligator," Debra said.

"After while, crocodile," Brook answered, both of them laughing as they hung up the phone.

Brook brought Gio's breakfast in the bedroom on her bed tray and said, "Wake up, Mr. Nominee."

Gio grinned as he opened his eyes. "I'm up," he said. He scooted back in the bed to make room for the tray. "Wow, is this all for me? 'Cause I sure worked up an appetite last night!"

Brook blushed. Dimples deepening with her smile, Brook said, "Yes, it's all for you. Mine is in the kitchen. I'll be right back. Do you need anything?"

"Just you," he said with a wink. Brook hurried to the kitchen and got her tray. When she got back in the bedroom, Gio was just finishing his prayer. "Babygirl, are you trying to fatten me up? You know television adds ten to fifteen pounds to you." He laughed.

"Just trying to show off my skills," she bragged. They were both silent as they ate their bacon, eggs, and French toast. "So, do you have any plans for later?" Brook asked.

"Not really, just have to stop by to see my manager to go over the nomination thing. I don't have anything pressing in the studio, just some collaborations I'm working on with a few people, so I'm not even thinking of going to the studio today. And, I've been cutting tracks for the next CD, but that's a long way off."

"Cool! I wanted to cook you a celebration meal. What time do you think you'll be finished?"

"Umm, probably around six or seven."

Brook thought that was perfect. It would give her time to get it together and get everyone over to the house for his surprise dinner.

"That'll work. I'll have dinner ready around seven then."

"Thank you, baby," Gio said and reached over and kissed her. "I really appreciate that. I'll tell you what. Next weekend, I'm taking you out. We'll go out to dinner, a play, a club, whatever you want to do. We're going to go celebrate not only my nomination, but also to celebrate us."

Brook grinned. "That's a plan."

Brook knew the nominations would be announced soon, she just didn't know when. Hopefully, their friends wouldn't find out before he had a chance to tell them. Brook had a lot to do. She knew he liked soul food, and always said he was from the country and that he was a meat and potatoes man. Brook went to the grocery store, planning to make a good ole Sunday after church, soul food meal. She could fry the heck out of some chicken. She wasn't as good as her mother, but that was who taught her how to fry it, so she was really close to it. As she was going down the aisles getting her groceries, she called Tha Dogg.

"Dogg, don't say my name if Gio is with you, this is Brook," Brook whispered, not knowing why she was whispering.

"Hey, Ms. Brook. No, he's not with me, he's in his office," Tha Dogg answered. "That's what's up, my boy got nominated," Tha Dogg said proudly. "He really deserved it. You know he played that part to a tee in the movie!"

"Hey, Dogg," Brook interrupted before went on more, "I'm planning a small dinner party for him tonight to celebrate. It's a surprise, so I don't want him to know. So, when he's on his way to my house later, call me and let me know. Then, wait about ten minutes and come on over. I want you to be a part of this, too. It's nothing fancy or anything, I'm just going to cook him a home cooked meal of his favorite... soul food. I've invited a few friends."

"You know what, Ms. Brook, you are on point. One of these days, I'm gonna find me a woman just like you. So, are any of your single girlfriends coming?"

"Dogg, this is not a hook up Tha Dogg party. You just worry about making sure I know he's coming before he gets here." Brook laughed.

"I got you, Ms. Brook. He is going to be so surprised."

The next call was to Carmen. "Hey, girl," Brook greeted when Carmen answered the phone.

"Girl, I am so sorry for that asshole yesterday. I swear he was totally not like that! We'd been on at least four dates and I never saw that side of him. I even let that fool inside my garden. Man, I am still pissed. You know I cussed his out good, too!"

"No worries, it's all good, just please don't invite him again." Brook laughed.

"Pssh, invite him again! Girl, his ass got kicked to the curb last night. There's nothing worse than a damn wanna-be," Carmen fumed.

"Well, bump him then." Brook laughed. "You know the old saying, there are plenty more fish in the sea! Anywho, girl, I was calling because I'm having a small dinner party tonight around six'ish. Can you come?" Brook asked.

"Oh yeah, that'll work. What type of dress is it?" Carmen asked, always the one concerned about what to wear. She was worse than Debra.

"Totally casual. It will just be a few friends over, play some music, food, fun, you know the drill."

"Well, I'm coming solo 'cause I just don't even feel like being bothered with none of these trifling men!"

"Just remember, girl, one monkey don't stop no show," Brook said reassuring her friend.

"Pssh, that negro ain't stopping nothing! Do you need me to bring anything?"

"No, I'm straight. Just get here before six-thirty because it's a surprise for Gio."

"A surprise for Gio? Why is it a surprise for Gio?" Carmen asked.

"I'll tell you tonight. See ya then," Brook said, and hung up before Carmen could ask any more questions.

Next she called Pam. "Divvvaaaaa," Pam said, answering the phone.

What in the world did they do before the caller ID, thought Brook. "What's up, Diva! You got plans for later?" Brook asked.

"Not really. Danielle and I were thinking about heading over to Churchill Grounds for happy hour. Danielle has a friend in the jazz band that's playing over there. Why, what's going on?" Pam asked.

"I'm throwing a little dinner party for Gio tonight and wanted to see if you could come. Heck, bring Danielle with you."

"Oh yeah, count me in. You know, I *am* the reason you two are together," Pam reminded her for the fiftieth time.

"Girl, whateva, witchyocrazyself. I'm looking at around six'ish, but before seven because it's a surprise for Gio."

"Awwww, y'all are really a couple now. I'll be there. Do you need me to bring anything?"

"Nope, just be here on time, no CP time. Can you think of anybody else I need to invite that's a really good friend of Gio's?"

"Hmmm, what about Randy? Although he's Gio's attorney, they're still really good friends."

"Great idea! Can you get in touch with him and let him know?"

"I gotchu," Pam said in her best Wanda impersonation, the ugly lady character Jamie Foxx used to play on the TV show *In Living Color*.

"Make sure Randy knows it's a surprise for Gio and to be here by six-thirty," Brook said.

Next, Brook called her Promotions Director, Tonya, from the radio station. "Hey, Ta-Ta, it's Brook."

"Hey, Brook, what's up?"

"I desperately need a favor. Do you think you can get in touch with your contact over at the AMC Theater? I'd like to get a poster from the movie, *Overprotective*, and I need it as soon as possible."

"Hmm, I'm trying to think if I still have any in my prize closet. Let me call over there and see who's there. If I can't get it from them, I'll look in the prize closet at work. I'll call you back within five minutes." Three minutes later, Brook's cell rang and it was Tonya. "Ask for April. She'll have your poster for you."

"Thank you. Thank you. Thank you! You are a life saver!"

"No problem. I appreciate all the giveaways you're always getting for me," Tonya replied.

That was another benefit of coming from promotions, Brook understood how important it was to help promotions with giveaways, and her clients loved her for it.

"Well, it looks like I definitely have to hook you up for getting this. Thanks again. See you at work."

Brook swung by the movie theater, picked up the poster, and drove over to Kinko's to have them mount it onto a foam poster board. Next, she headed over to Target and picked up plates, plastic forks, and cups. She didn't plan on having to do a bunch of dishes after the little shindig. She had a beautiful painting set up on an easel in her living room and was going to take the painting down and put Gio's movie poster on the easel. She then swung by the Dollar Discount and bought balloons and a congratulations banner. Brook was set.

The house smelled fabulous! Macaroni and cheese was in the oven baking. Green beans were simmering on top of the stove. The sweet potatoes were already done and covered in foil, and she had a toss salad in the fridge. Brook was frying chicken in her fryer on her back patio when she heard the doorbell.

"Hey, girl," Brook greeted, kissing Debra, then Glenn, on the cheek.

"We brought some ice since you can never have enough. And, I bought a cheesecake just in case you needed dessert," Debra said as Glenn brought the bags of ice into the kitchen.

"Hey, Glenn, can you ice up the beer? There are a couple of cases in the refrigerator and more ice in the freezer in the garage. There's an ice chest in the kitchen to put the beer in," Brook said.

"Sure can," he said and hurried off to get the beer ready.

Debra went into the kitchen, stirred the green beans and checked on the macaroni and cheese. She snuck a wing off the platter of chicken and joined Brook out back. "How many people did you invite?" Debra asked. "You have enough food to feed a small army."

"Probably about eight or nine people. I just didn't want to not have enough."

"What else you gotta do and what can I do to help?"

"I'm almost done. I just have to finish this last batch of chicken and get my shower. I know what you can do. Grab those Lunchables out of the refrigerator, the tray is on the table in the living room, and do your thing."

Debra was one of those people that could turn an apple into the most appealing thing you'd ever seen. She had skills like that. She had taken the regular kids snack Lunchables, placed them on a fancy tray, and simply added grapes. It looked like a picture it had turned out so well. Brook didn't know where her girl got her great ideas from. Her house looked like it belonged in someone's magazine.

"I'm gonna jump in the shower and get ready before anyone else gets here. And please look over the living room to see if anything else needs to be done?" Brook asked.

Brook finished her shower and went to her closet. She had no idea what she was wearing. She wanted to be casual, so she grabbed a black pair of Juicy Couture jeans and a black tank top that spelled Juicy across the front in faux diamonds. Her black belt with the big clear rhinestones and some Ferragamo ankle boots completed her casual look. It was six fifteen.

As Brook was finishing her makeup, she heard the doorbell ring. She sure hoped that wasn't Gio. If Tha Dogg forgot to call her, she was going to kill him. With one last look in the mirror, Brook headed downstairs to see who was there. It was Carmen.

"Hey, girl," Brook greeted giving her a quick hug.

"What is the occasion?" Carmen asked, looking at Brook and then Debra.

"Don't look at me, I don't know, either," Debra said. "I see the congratulations banner, I see balloons, so I know there is an occasion. But, what is it? And, why in the world do you have Gio's movie poster over there on your easel?" Debra questioned.

"The poster was a gift that Tonya, our promotions director gave me. It's been there for a couple of weeks," Brook lied, trying to throw them off. She just knew at any moment, someone was going to guess what they were celebrating, and she really wanted Gio to tell them.

The doorbell rang and Brook hurried away to the door with relief. It was Randy. As she gave him a hug, she whispered to him that if he'd heard any good news about Gio, not to say a word because it was a surprise. He looked at her and gave her a wink.

"Everybody, this is Randy. He's Gio's attorney. Randy, this is my best friend Debra, her boyfriend Glenn, and my girl Carmen. Carmen is actually the one who sold me this house."

Hellos echoed through the room and the doorbell rang again. That time, it was Pam and Danielle. Introductions were made again and everyone started trying to guess what the occasion was.

"All y'all need to worry about is when Gio comes in to yell surprise," Brook said.

"Ohhh, it's his birthday?" Debra said.

"Girl, you coulda told us that. We didn't even bring a gift. But, why does your banner say Congratulations instead of Happy Birthday?" Carmen asked.

Just then, her cell phone rang. Brook hurried to answer it, and it was Tha Dogg. "Ms. Brook, he just left, he just left!" Tha Dogg said excitedly, happy to be in on the surprise.

"Okay, Dogg, how long do you think it will take him to get here?" Brook asked.

"Hmmm, let's see, you're in Marietta, and he's leaving Jamar's office, so probably about forty minutes."

"Okay, Dogg, you know he drives fast, so give him about a ten minute head start and then you come on," Brook instructed.

"Will do, Ms. Brook. See you when I get there, and save me a plate."

"I got you, Dogg." Brook laughed. Her cell phone rang again and it was Gio. "Quiet, everybody, this is Gio. Turn the music down," Brook said. "Hello," Brook answered calmly.

"Hey, boo, I'm on my way, do you need me to stop and pick up anything?" he asked.

"No, I'm good. Don't forget, I cooked. You didn't eat, did you?" Brook asked.

"No, and I'm starving!"

"Alright, well let me finish cooking so it will be ready when you get here."

"Okay, I should be there in about a half hour."

"See ya then," Brook said and hung up.

Every car that went down the street, they just knew was Gio's. Brook hoped the house looked normal from the outside. They turned the music off and only the light in the kitchen was on.

"That's probably him," Danielle whispered as Gio's Benz turned into the driveway.

"Ya think!" laughed Pam.

"Everybody, quit peeking out the window," giggled Brook.

Gio rang the doorbell and Brook waited a couple of seconds, looking around to make sure everyone was hidden. Brook opened the door and as Gio walked in, then she flicked on the light.

Everyone yelled, “Surprise!”

“What the hell?” Gio said, looking around at everyone in surprise.

“Happy birthday!” Debra screamed.

“It’s not my birthday,” Gio said. Everyone looked confused, including Gio.

Brook burst out laughing. “Come in, boo. Quit standing there like you’re about to run. Now, I put together this little soirée at the last minute because we have something to celebrate. I didn’t want to tell you all what it was because I wanted Gio to be the one to tell you. So, ladies and gentlemen, I present to you Mr. Giovanni Lay,” Brook said dramatically.

All eyes turned to Gio. “Aw, man,” Gio said, blushing. “I can’t believe you did this,” he said, looking at Brook with a big grin on his face. He gave her a big hug and kiss while everyone was still standing around looking and wondering what the heck was going on.

“Uh, excuse us, but we’re still here. If y’all keep that going, ya gonna have to take it upstairs,” Debra said sarcastically.

Gio grabbed Brook’s hand and said to everyone, “Well, everyone, I got nominated for an Academy Award for Best Supporting Actor for my role in *Overprotective*.”

Congratulations were heard around the room, and everyone went over to give him handshakes and hugs.

“And, Randy, how in the heck did you get here?” Gio asked, still amazed that everyone was there for him.

“That would be my doing. You know, I’m the reason you two are even together,” Pam said with a laugh.

“Girl, don’t you even start that again,” Brook laughed.

Everyone was fixing their plates when the doorbell rang again. “Now who?” asked Gio excitedly with a big grin on his face.

“Well, it wouldn’t be complete without this person,” Brook said mysteriously and went to open the door for Tha Dogg.

“Dogg!” Gio shouted. “You mean to tell me you knew and you didn’t even tell me?”

“And have Ms. Brook on me, not even,” Tha Dogg answered with a laugh. Brook introduced Tha Dogg to Glenn, Carmen and Danielle. He already knew Debra, Pam, and Randy.

“Babe, when did you put all of this together?” Gio asked, still not believing the surprise.

“After you left, I thought about cooking you a big celebration meal, and then figured I’d invite our friends so you could tell them in person.”

"You are amazing," Gio said, smiling at Brook. She blushed.

"The nominations were announced today. I'm just glad none of you watch much television," she laughed. "With the exception of Randy, no one here knew what the celebration was even for," Brook told Gio.

"Ohh, that's why Debra said happy birthday?" Gio laughed.

Everyone laughed, remembering Debra yelling happy birthday. Brook turned back on her mix CD and turned on the television and put it on mute. She changed the channel to CNN just in case they showed something about the nominations.

Brook was so happy she had decided on paper plates because the clean up was really easy. When everyone finished eating, she pulled out a game of *Taboo*.

"Okay, boys against the girls," Brook yelled.

"Hey, there are more girls than boys," Gio said.

"Don't be skurrred, boo. We'll take it easy on you," laughed Brook, blowing him a kiss.

"Whateva, just bring it on," Gio said.

Brook noticed that Randy and Carmen were into a deep conversation… again! Danielle thought that everything Tha Dogg said was just hilarious, and Tha Dogg was eating it up. Brook smiled at them. It is turning out to be Matchmakers. She couldn't wait to find out what Randy and Carmen had been talking about, they both were cool people. Although she had only met Randy a few times, he seemed like a really down to earth guy. A little nerdy, but sweet.

After the girls beat the guys every game, they changed from *Taboo* to *Guesstures*, which surprisingly, the guys ended up winning seven to two.

Pam said she was heading out and Danielle looked like she was ready to cry. So, Tha Dogg offered to take her home when she was ready.

"No, I told Pam I'd go with her," she said longingly.

"Girl, keep your butt here, I'm grown. I'll be okay. I'll holla at you later. Dogg, take good care of her," Pam said.

"And you know I will." Tha Dogg almost blushed, if that was possible.

They had a great time and ended up sitting around talking about everything from the funniest movies to Obama to the sudden death of Michael Jackson.

"Well, my friends, it's getting late," Brook said. "And, as the saying goes, y'all don't have to go home, but you got to get the heck out of here." She laughed.

"Come on, diva, we'll help you with the clean up," Carmen said, getting up and going to clear off the table.

"Hey, we can help, too," Gio offered.

"No thanks, we got it," Brook said.

The ladies started grabbing platters while the guys got into the own conversation about, what else, sports.

The house was back in order. Leftover food was put away and they were waving goodbye to their friends.

As they walked back in the house, Gio said, "I can't believe you. I can't believe you put all this together in a few hours. And for me! This was so nice," he said, giving her a hug.

"You deserve it. This is a huge accomplishment and I'm so proud of you," she answered, hugging him back.

"Now where in the heck did you get the poster?" he laughed.

"From the movie theater."

"You really are special," Gio said, giving her a kiss on the lips. "Now, come on in the bedroom and let me show you my appreciation," he said, wiggling his eyebrows.

Brook ran off to the bedroom with a squeal with Gio chasing behind her.

"Hey babe, sing for me," Brook said as she was getting undressed.

"Sing for you?" Gio chuckled. "What do you want me to sing?"

"I dunno, sing anything," she responded, sitting on the bed in her panties and bra.

"Ummm, okay."

He thought for a second and then started singing Robin Thicke's jam, *Lost Without U*, sounding even better than Robin Thicke.

"*I'm Lost Without You…,*" Gio sang.

Brook leaned back on her elbows and watched him as he sang the song to her, a half smile on her face. She thought he'd sing one of his songs, but he had surprised her. His singing really could melt the panties off of you. He got through the end of the second verse and stopped. He asked bashfully, "Okay, was that enough?"

Brook reached down into her panties and rubbed herself. "Yep, it's true. Your singing really does make you wet," she said seductively.

"Well, let me taste it and see," Gio said, removing her panties and tasting just how wet he got her.

CHAPTER 42

They were definitely now a couple. They had been doing couple stuff with Debra and Glenn, and even Carmen and Randy, who had really hit it off and were starting to hang out together. They had been to see *The Lion King*, had done Six Flags, and all of them even had a cookout at Piedmont Park. They swam, halfway played softball, and her and Gio had played badminton. Glenn barbecued and the ladies bought the sides. It was a really fun time.

Gio had even invited Debra and Glenn over to his house for a cookout because Gio had to show off his barbecuing skills. They swam and hung out, and Debra tripped out on Gio's house. She pulled Brook to the side, "Girl, damn! I cannot believe he's ballin' like this," she said excitedly.

"I know. I was a little put off at first, but now, I've gotten used to it," Brook confessed.

"Pssh, I half expected Jeffrey from *The Fresh Prince* to answer the door," Debra laughed.

Gio found out a week prior he had another movie project to do. It was a part added in especially for him and a great opportunity. He was only going to be gone for three weeks, but Brook was feeling nervous. The last time he went away to do a movie, a different person came back. They had made love that night, really made love, and not just had sex. Gio told her he loved her, and she told him she loved him back. He promised to never hurt her again, and Brook admitted that she couldn't take it if he did. They established their love for each other and knew it was the turning point for their relationship.

Brook was leaving church and called Debra to see if she wanted to do brunch. She got her answering machine. Next, she tried Carmen. *That heiffa must be still sleep.* She tried Pam and got her machine as well. *Where the heck is everyone? Oh well, I'll just go do brunch by myself.* She was totally fine with going somewhere by herself. She went back to Gladys' and Ron's, and who was in there but Debra and Carmen.

"Well, well, well, what do we have here? How y'all gonna go to brunch and not call me?" Brook joked as she walked up to their table.

"Girl, where the heck have you been? I called you and you didn't answer. I left a message on your machine at home and your cell," Debra said.

"Oh, I didn't check my messages. I went to church, something you two heathens evidently know nothing about," Brook joked. "Now, scoot over.

I take it y'all already ordered."

"Yes, and you are not gonna hold up our food, either, waiting for yours," laughed Debra as the waitress came to their table to take Brook's order. Of course, Brook asked her to bring all the meals together.

Brook got home and saw she had a couple of messages on her machine. One was from Gio and one from her brother. She got her cell out of her purse and saw she had two missed calls there as well, one from Gio and another from Mama. She had put her phone on vibrate in the movies and had forgotten all about it.

She called Gio back and got his voice mail. "Hey, boo, looks like we're playing phone tag. If you get a chance, give me a call. Talk to you soon. I miss you."

Next, Brook called her Mama, and they were on the phone a good hour. The great news was Phyllis was finally pregnant. Her mama was ecstatic. Brook was so happy, too, she was going to be an auntie.

"Now, don't tell him I told you," Mama said.

"I won't. I'll act totally surprised," Brook agreed.

Next, she called her brother and acted all surprised when he told her. She talked with Phyllis as well and told her congratulations.

"How far along are you?" Brook asked.

"About nine weeks," Phyllis answered.

"Well, congratulations again. I finally will have someone to spoil. Hopefully it's a girl, then you can name her Brooklyn," Brook teased.

"Well, I'd have to make sure that was okay with Brandon," Phyllis said.

That girl clearly had no sense of humor. She wished them a goodnight and hung up with a smile on her face. They really deserved it. She felt a little twinge, but would not let herself dwell on it. She was going to be the best auntie there was.

CHAPTER 43

Gio had been gone two weeks and they spoke a few times a week. They had even had phone sex, too. Gio told Brook one would never think by looking at her that she was really a little freak. "You give that whole lady in the streets and a freak in the bedroom a new meaning," he had joked. He said the movie was going well. His part wasn't big, but was important. He was the long lost brother whose return actually turned the whole movie in a different direction. He said he was really enjoying the experience.

"You know, the Oscars will be coming up soon," he said.

"Wow, that was really fast. Seems like you just found out about it," Brook said.

"You are going with me, right?" Brook hadn't really thought about it. "Whoa, total silence. That isn't a good sign. I'd like you to be there with me. This is an important moment in my life and I'd like to share it with the woman that I love," he said.

"Awww, boo, of course I'll go. Wow! That means I have to find a really bad dress to wear. You know, you absolutely have to have an Oscars dress," Brook said, getting excited.

"I'll tell you what, when I get back, we'll go shopping together. I have to find something to wear as well. I don't want to wear the normal tuxedo. A brotha gotta be clean!"

"I know that's right. And we are gonna fresh to def! I'm too excited. I've never been to the Oscars before. And on top of that, you're performing and nominated. This is going to be a great night."

"Even better with you sharing it with me. I know this isn't really your type of thing."

"It's not that it's not my type of thing. It's just that it's your thing and I want it to be about you. You deserve this. I don't want you to feel that I need to be included in your fame. People want to see you, not me. Heck, I sell radio advertising. I like being me. And I like you being you," Brook explained.

"I hear you, babe. And I appreciate the way you see it, too."

"I'll be glad when you get back," she said.

"I'll be glad when I get back, too," he said.

"You have some making up to do," she said seductively.

"Oh yeah, well I can't wait to give you some making up," he said laughing softly.

"Well, babe, I'm going to get off this phone before you have me taking a cold shower." She laughed.

"Alright. You have a good night's sleep. I love you," he said.

"Good night, babe, I love you too."

Brook's phone rang and it was Gio. "Where's my woman," he said gruffly when she answered the phone.

Brook laughed, "Waiting on your call. I'm on my way, boo."

Brook was driving to Gio's when Debra called. "So, did you find a dress yet?" she asked.

"No. Gio said we were going shopping this weekend, so hopefully I'll have better luck. You didn't find anything?"

"No. I've seen some cute dresses, but nothing Oscar worthy. And, you know you're gonna need a bad-ass designer gown. You know they're gonna ask who you're wearing."

"They're not going to be asking me anything," Brook exclaimed.

"Girl, please. Of course they're going to ask you. You're going to be with Gio. It's time for you to stop being afraid of being seen out with him. What is up with that, anyway?" Debra asked.

"I don't like being in pictures with him because Mama and Daddy might see them and start asking questions. What am I gonna say then, Oh yeah, he's this celebrity that I'm bangin'!" Brook answered.

"You just tell them the truth, that this is the man you're in love with."

"No way, heckie naw, unt uh," Brook said. "Then, Daddy is gonna want him to come home to meet him and I don't know if I'm ready for all of that, or even if Gio is ready for all of that. Sure I love him and he loves me, so I guess I'm his girlfriend. I don't want my parents to think anything crazy. I've never gotten involved with a celebrity before and I don't want them involved just in case it doesn't work out."

"Girl, boo. You're the one that is over thinking this. Have you all ever even talked about meeting each other's family?"

"No. I know he has two older sisters and a younger brother. We talk about our family, just not about meeting them. We're just getting us together. I don't want to complicate it by bringing family into it yet. I love Gio. I love being with Gio. And, that's enough for right now."

"I hear you. You're still taking it slow. You have to be the taking-it-slowest person I have ever known," laughed Debra.

"Whateva, heiffa. I've made it to Gio's. I'll talk to you tomorrow."

"Alright, don't hurt him now," Debra said.

"Hurting is definitely not what I have in mind." Brook laughed and hung up the phone.

Brook and Gio had played a short game of *Wheel of Fortune* and couldn't hold off any longer. It had been almost a month since they had last seen each other and they were ready to make up for lost time.

"I have a surprise for you, boo," Brook said seductively.

Gio smiled that sexy smile of his and said, "Oh yeah, what is it?"

"I can show you better than I can tell you. Get comfortable," she said and went and lit the candles that were all around the room. "I'll be right back."

Brook came back in the room dressed in very sexy and revealing lingerie.

"Oh, *hell* yeah," Gio said when he saw her. She went over to the CD player and put in a song.

"Don't know if you've ever heard this cut before," she said as Jamie Foxx's voice filled the room, a cut off his very first CD called *Experiment* played. Jamie sang, "*I feel like I want to love you, in a different waaayyyy.*"

Brook came over to Gio and pulled out a pair of handcuffs with pink fur on them. Gio's eyebrows raised and a big grin spread across his face. She straddled him and grabbed his wrists, handcuffing him to the headboard. She slid down his body, all the way to his feet, and slid open his legs. She began kissing and sucking on the insides of his calves and worked her way up. Gio's boxers slid open, showing what she couldn't wait to get to, standing at attention. Brook took her time kissing the inside of his thighs and kissed around his the magic pole, making him throb harder. Jamie sang in the background about doing things you'd never done before while Brook stuck her tongue in his mouth and began grinding on him. Gio was grinding back and moaning softly. She worked her way down his body from his neck to his chest, taking time to lick each nipple, and slid him between her breasts while softly licking the head.

"Damn, baby," Gio groaned.

Brook took him into her mouth, sucking hard while rubbing it up and down, trying to swallow him whole. Gio's hands were pulling against the handcuffs. He wanted to grab her but couldn't. The handcuffs looked frilly and had pink padding and fur around them, but they were still handcuffs.

"Oooh, baby, you need to stop. You really need to stop," he begged. Brook stopped because she felt him on the brink of explosion and reached on the night stand for a condom. She slid the condom on him and slowly slid onto him. She started working him slowly at first, going in circles, working her body.

"I need to touch you, baby," Gio groaned.

"No, you don't." She smiled and started going faster. She'd raised up half way and then slam back down onto him, getting ready to explode herself.

"Oh, baby, oh, baby," Gio sang as he thrust back up to her. Brook grabbed his shoulders to brace herself and rode the wave.

"Ohhhssshhhitttttt," she moaned loudly as Gio thrust deeper and deeper into her. The tables had turned. While she had control at first, Gio was now working her deep. She was coming so hard and could feel Gio swelling.

"Ahhhhh," Gio screamed, bucking her and almost knocking her off of him.

Brook fell onto his chest, breathing hard, listening to his heart beating fast. They laid there, both catching their breath.

Gio's heartbeat slowed and he said, "Aw, damn, baby. Will you please let me out of these handcuffs?"

Brook giggled and got up off of him, making sure to hold onto the condom so it didn't come off. She grabbed the key off the nightstand and let him loose.

"Damn, we're lucky this didn't break," he said as they looked at all of the sperm in his condom. Gio went into the bathroom to dispose of his condom, then came back in and grabbed her in a hug. "You really are full of surprises, aren't you?" he said with a grin.

"Only good ones, boo, only good ones," she answered as they snuggled up and fell asleep.

"Now I have a surprise for you," Gio said. He had wakened her in the middle of the night, grinding into her and they made love again, slowly, lazily and were laying there, half falling back to sleep.

"Really! What surprise?" Brook asked, head on his chest.

"Well, you know how we have to find something to wear to the Oscars, right? So, how about we fly out to LA next weekend and go shopping on Rodeo Drive? There is bound to be something you can find out there. And, I can go to Armani and find a nice suit. I have two first class, round trip tickets. We can leave Saturday morning and come back Sunday evening. How does that sound?"

Brook jumped up and squealed, jumping all over him. "That's a great surprise! Aw, babe, I hadn't even thought of something like that. I'm just thinking that I've been in almost every shop in Atlanta and still haven't found the perfect dress." Brook gave him a kiss. "So, what time is our flight?" she asked, lying back down on his chest.

"I don't remember, but I'll look when I can move my legs again," he joked.

Brook laughed, too, and they dozed back off to sleep.

The next morning, Brook asked Gio if she was dreaming about going to LA to find a dress. Gio walked over to his dresser and grabbed the airplane tickets.

"Here you go," he said, smiling. Gio loved to surprise her. Her face lit up and those dimples, they would deepen so much he'd just watch them, mesmerized.

"Who in your family has dimples?" Gio asked, sticking his finger in her dimple.

"My mom does. My brother Brandon also has them," she answered, still studying the tickets. Brook had never flown first class before, but she didn't want to let on that she was excited about that, too. "My mom's dimples are deeper than mine," Brook said.

"Is that even possible?" He laughed and Brook smiled.

"So, we're staying the night in LA, too?"

"No, babe, we're staying in Beverly Hills at the Beverly Hilton Hotel," he answered, smiling.

"You're just full of surprises," Brook said, grinning. Gio grinned, too.

"Let me go run our bathwater so we can go eat something. I'm starving and in a minute, I'm gonna start eating on you," he said

"Again?" Brook asked with a laugh.

"Hey, babe, do you know how to skate?" Gio asked.

"Of course, I can skate. But, I'm talking real skates with four wheels, not rollerblades."

"That's what's up. Let's go skating. I haven't been in forever."

"I'm game. Hey, let's see if Debra and Glenn want to come."

"Sounds cool with me."

Brook called Debra and asked if they wanted to join them skating. Debra asked Glenn and, of course, he said he was the skating champion.

"They have Adult Skate over at Robin's Roost Skating Rink. Let's go over there," Glenn suggested.

They agreed to meet at the rink in an hour. They stopped at Brook's so she could change into skating clothes, jeans and a tee shirt, and to grab her Strawberry Crème Pastries. She just loved those shoes.

They were having a ball, until Brook fell. She felt like she was going down in slow motion. She knew she was going to fall, but she couldn't stop it. The look on Gio's face was what made her laugh. He looked so surprised. He skated back to help her up, but she was laughing so hard and could hardly get up.

"What the heck are you laughing for?" Gio asked, laughing, too.

"At the expression on your face. You looked like you were about to have a heart attack," Brook replied, laughing even harder.

"Well, you fell hard as hell," Gio said, cracking up too.

Debra and Glenn whizzed by, pointing and laughing. Brook and Gio skated toward the exit of the rink, still laughing, and then Gio fell. He tried to show off and turn around to skate backwards, but his skates got twisted so he fell.

Brook screamed, laughing hard. She got out of the rink and stood to the side, bent over cracking up. Gio was still on the floor, cracking up himself. Debra and Glenn were on their way over to where Brook stood laughing, and they were cracking up, too.

Then, the DJ announced to the whole rink, “Giovanni Lay has just busted his ass on the floor y’all,” and everybody cracked up.

People were being really cool about him being there. No one had bothered them, and aside from the looks, everything was going smoothly until he fell. Then, the camera phones started clicking pictures of him on the floor, laughing hysterically. They knew then it was time to go.

CHAPTER 44

Beverly Hills was amazing, and the streets were so clean you could actually eat off them. And, the cars were ridiculous! She figured out who lived in those beautiful mansions up in the hills... it was the car salesmen! The Beverly Hills Hotel was absolutely beautiful, even the elevators were laid out. They entered their suite and Brook was again amazed. It was absolutely stunning. One whole wall was glass and overlooked the city. Brook couldn't hold it in any longer.

"Woooow," Brook said.

"You like it, baby?" Gio asked with a smile.

"This view is amazing," Brook answered.

"Wait until you see it at night."

"This isn't the room you take all the ladies to, is it?"

"Of course not! I've never even stayed in this suite. But, I have stayed at this hotel before and I've seen this view, only from a few floors below."

"Okay, I just wanted to make sure I wasn't one in a long line of women that Gio has bought to the Beverly Hilton hotel! I told you, I'm a one of a kind type of chic," she said with a smile.

"You are special and I know you're one of a kind," Gio said seriously, giving her a hug. "Now, let's go, woman, and get our shopping on. Hopefully, we can find something today and then we'll have the rest of the time to play," he said.

"Now, that sounds like a plan," Brook said and she grabbed her purse and followed him to the door.

Gio rented a two-seater Miata convertible. Brook loved it when they picked it up from the airport, but looking at the other cars on the road, they may as well have gotten a Gio Metro. They parked the car and walked down Rodeo Drive. Brook was totally impressed with Beverly Hills, even the stores were impeccable. And, some of them were so exclusive you had to have an appointment to come in, unless you were famous enough.

They went inside a beautiful boutique that looked like you had to be rich to just step in the door. The saleslady greeted Gio.

"Hello, Mr. Lay. And you must be Ms. Bridges," she greeted.

Brook looked at Gio, eyebrows raised, and turned to shake the lady's hand. "Uh, hello," Brook said.

"I'm Jannie, and I'm here to help you find the most fabulous dress for the Academy Awards," she said grandly. Brook looked at Gio, who had a big grin on his face.

"Definitely full of surprises," Brook grinned.

"Now, if you'll just follow me, I have a few selections for your perusal," Jannie said importantly.

Brook followed Jannie to a rack of gowns, turning to blow Gio a kiss as they walked away. His nasty behind acted like he caught it and then rubbed it on his crotch, making Brook burst out laughing.

"I know, shopping is always so much fun," Jannie sing-songed, thinking Brook was laughing at shopping, causing Brook to roll her eyes at Jannie's back.

Jannie looked her up and down and told her to turn slowly in a circle. The first gown Jannie pulled out was just plain ugly. Brook said no without even trying it on. It was too drab, a nondescript gray. The second gown was black and clingy, very pretty. Brook went to try it on. It fit her well, but a little too tight. Instead of looking sexy, it looked a little slutty and it made her butt look even bigger.

She walked out to let Gio see it with a little frown on her face. Gio burst out laughing. "You look like you hate the dress," he laughed.

"I don't know. I feel a little hooker'ish in this," Brook said.

"Well, go get my money then," Gio teased.

"Next!" Brook said, heading to the back. That gown was doing too much.

The next one was a beautiful dress. It was pale blue with ruffles from the neck to the ground, but she thought it had too many ruffles. Brook walked out to show Gio. He burst out laughing. "Looks like a prom dress," he joked.

"I know, it's really pretty, just too rufflely," Brook agreed.

Brook tried on two more dresses that just didn't quite do it for her. She was surprised that Jannie could just look at her and know her size. Gio liked one of the dresses, but it still wasn't what Brook wanted for her first Awards show. She wanted something that would take her breath away. And then, she saw it! Jannie was rambling on and said something about Dior as she pulled out the dress and Brook caught her breath.

"Oh my," Brook said, staring at the dress. She took it out of Jannie's hands right in the middle of her conversation, and walked into the fitting room. The gown was a caramel color and had a strapless, fitted bodice with little popcorn-type puckers all the way down mid-hip, and then fell into little soft feathers to the ground.

Brook glided out and Jannie finally stopped talking. "You look amazing," she said.

Brook smiled, nodding her head.

She walked out to Gio who simply smiled. "You floated out here, babe. You look beautiful."

"You like?" Brook asked as she did a slow model spin.

"The important question is, do you like it?" Gio said.

"I love it," she smiled.

"Then, I love it, too," Gio smiled back. "And, you really do look beautiful, but you still looked beautiful in the little hooker dress too. Hey, maybe we can take that one for later," he laughed, wiggling his eyebrows.

"We'll take this one," Brook said to Jannie with a giggle.

"Wait, how much is it?" Brook asked. She hadn't even thought of the price.

"Don't you worry about how much it cost. This is the perfect dress. You love it. I love it. That's all that matters. Now, go take off the dress while I go settle the bill. You didn't think you were wearing it out of here, did you? I know you love it, but sheesh," he cracked.

Brook giggled and headed back to put her clothes back on. She gave the dress to the assistant to bag up and headed back up to the register with Gio. The dress cost six grand. Six thousands dollars for a dress! Brook wanted to protest, then thought about the dress and how it already fit her perfectly with no alterations needed. Now, *she* wasn't about to pay six grand for a dress. It was pretty and all, but she wasn't the six grand for one dress type of shopper. She sure couldn't wait to show Debra.

"So, you knew all along that we were going to that store?" Brook asked.

"Of course. I asked around and heard she had all of the designer gowns and figured it would be easier to make one stop in her store instead of having to go to all the different stores.

That was a great idea. And, thank you for my beautiful dress."

"Anytime, boo. You know we gotta be funky fresh on the red carpet," he said and crossed his arms in an old school homeboy pose.

"Now we have to find you something to wear."

"We're gonna head over to Armani. It's Armani, so you know I'll find something quickly. Mine will be a lot easier than yours."

They had been in the Armani shop for two and a half hours and Gio was finally done. They had such a huge collection and Gio didn't want the standard tuxedo. He ended up with a hella fly three piece suit. The suit was chocolate with an old school double-breasted vest that was almost the same caramel color as her dress. It looked great on his skin tone and the vest pulled out his eyes. They seemed to sparkle. Caramel was definitely his color. Their purchases would be shipped to them and his still had to be altered. Jannie had given her a swatch of material from her dress so she could match her shoes and handbag, which had come in handy when selecting Gio's vest. Debra would help her find the perfect shoes, and she needed to get accessories. Those movie stars weren't gonna have jack on her, Brooklyn Denise Bridges.

She was gonna represent! They headed out of the store and were ready to eat. They hadn't had anything to eat since they left that morning and it was close to five pm.

CHAPTER 45

It was finally the big night. Brook was excited, yet nervous. She had to admit, she and Gio were looking awfully fly. Their outfits blended well. Brook had gotten a nice massage and facial, and had her face made up while Gio had gone for sound check, so she was feeling relaxed and refreshed. Their limo pulled up in front of the venue and it was packed out there. It was finally their turn to get out and Brook was suddenly really nervous. She hoped she didn't fall. Those were four inch heels she was rockin'.

"You ready, babe?" Gio asked, smiling.

"As ready as I'm going to be." Brook smiled back nervously.

The limo door opened and she heard, "Mr. Giovanni Lay and guest."

The crowd went wild. Gio got out first, and then put his hand out to help her out of the limo. She was blinded by the flashlights. She heard Gio's voice somewhere in the light saying, "Just hold onto my hand and smile." So, Brook kept smiling, hoping she wasn't looking crazy.

Gio pulled her to his side as he did an interview with Joan Rivers. She heard him ask who he was wearing. Gio answered, "Armani."

"Ah, yes, simple, yet classy," Joan River said.

Wow, her face looked like wax, Brook thought. Brook wanted to rub it with her thumb to see what it felt like. That woman really didn't need any more face lifts. She kept trying to slide out of the way, but Gio wouldn't let her go. So, she just stood there and continued to smile.

"And, you are?" Joan Rivers asked her.

"Hi, I'm Brooklyn." Brook smiled.

"And, who are you wearing?"

"Christian Dior," Brook answered.

"That is absolutely stunning. You two look gorgeous, dahling. Now, are you married, dating, co-parenting, or what?" Joan asked, as nosy as ever.

"No, we're just dating right now," Gio answered with a smile. "Thank you, Ms. Rivers, as always, it's been a pleasure," Gio said graciously and they walked away, only to be stopped by another crew.

Brook just hung onto Gio and said as little as possible. She had gotten very good at saying, "Christian Dior." Gio answered questions about his role in the movie and what he thought of being nominated.

Finally, it was time to take their seats, and they had really good seats, too. She saw a little bit of everyone. It took everything in her to not stare at the array of stars. There was Denzel, and he looked just as good in person, with his wife, Pauletta, who Brook thought was classy and stunning. There was Will and Jada, looking the absolute perfect picture of the handsome husband and beautiful wife. Brook loved them. And, there was Jamie Foxx, just seeing him made Brook blush, thinking about her night with Gio while they listened to his song. Tyler Perry was in the next row and Brook almost stopped and waved. She loved Tyler! Gio did a lot of handshaking and received a lot of congratulations on his nomination. They were sitting a few seats down from Nautica Diaz and her date. Gio uncomfortably introduced them and they sized each other up as she gave Brook a fake smile. Brook threw a fake one right back at her said it was nice to meet 'them' and included her date. She then turned away, not even giving her any more of her attention, letting her know that she did not consider her threat. *The games we women play*, Brook thought. The lights blinked and it was time to start.

"They'll come get me when it's time for me to perform, but meanwhile, I'll be right here." Brook just shook her head okay, too overwhelmed by everything to do anything else.

The Awards show was actually pretty boring. She only wanted to hear about the good movies, and that was only about ten percent of them. It was time for Gio to go perform, so he headed backstage. The seat filler came and took his seat. Brook smiled politely, then she snuck out her phone and sent a text message to Debra.

Girl, this has to be the most boring thing. I feel like I'm back in Mr. Sutton's history class.

Brook felt her phone vibrate. *Did you see Denzel? Where are you sitting? And Idris Elba knows he is foinne!*

Brook giggled and typed back, *you little groupie hoochie, get it together. I'm sitting near Denzel and Tyler Perry, not too far from Jamie Foxx and Columbus Short's fine self.*

Debra typed back to her, *Go sit on Columbus' lap and give him a slow grind for me.*

Brook almost laughed out loud. Her girl was a certified nut! She just typed back, *nasty Heiffa!*

When Gio performed, Brook was so proud. At first, all you heard was his amazing voice singing the beginning of his song. Then, he came up on a round stage through the floor and the crowd went wild. He looked so good. He had changed into a simple black suit with a salmon colored shirt and tie, stunner shades on his eyes. He sang *Heartstopper*, the hit that everyone was familiar with. It was a song about a woman that was so beautiful she could cause a man's heart to stop. Brook hadn't seen Gio perform live in over a year, when they first met at her station event back in Louisville. His performance was very sexy. He moved smoothly and exuded romance. He didn't jump around on stage with the latest dance moves, or grind all over the stage showing everyone his business. He did a few of the dance moves with the background dancers. The lady dancers hung all over him as he sang to each one of them, but it was tasteful. Mainly, he sang beautifully and did his own groove, which was dripping with sex appeal. At the bridge of the song, he took off his glasses and showed off his beautiful eyes. Brook was smiling so hard, she couldn't wait to get him back to their hotel room.

Finally, it was time. Gio had changed back into his Armani suit and was sitting next to her. They held hands and they waited anxiously.

"... And, the Oscar for Best Supporting Actor goes to... Giovanni Lay in *Overprotective*!"

Brook's mouth fell open. Gio's mouth fell open. They looked at each other, eyes wide, mouths hanging open, yet, still smiling. Gio grabbed her, kissed her, and jumped up. He quickly made his way to the stage, shaking his head and grinning. Brook clapped so hard, her hands hurt. She couldn't believe he actually won. He was up against some stiff competition.

"Oh! My! Goodness!" Gio said, grinning and looking down at the award in his hand. "I'm so surprised. I feel so honored even being in this category. I first have to thank my God, my Savior." Everyone clapped politely. "I'd also like to thank my director, Jordan Woods, for pulling this performance out of me. He is who made me into the character, Steve McAlister. I want to thank my parents for teaching me to be all that I can be. I want to thank all the other actors on this movie that had a lot of patience with me," he chuckled. The audience laughed at that one. "If I'm forgetting someone, I'm so sorry. I know I don't have a lot of time." Brook was trying to telepathically send him thoughts to get the card they made earlier with whom to thank, just in case he won. Finally, he started patting on his pockets. He finally remembered. Gio said, "Y'all, I want to do something a little different. I want to ask my woman to marry me. She turned me down cold the first time, maybe she'll show me mercy with the whole world watching. Brooklyn Denise Bridges, will you marry me?" Gio pulled out a ring box and got on one knee, opening the box. Brook was in shock. She was sitting there with her hands covering her open mouth, looking at him but not really comprehending. He had caught her completely by surprise. "I had planned on doing this later tonight, but I think this is a better time. Brook?" Gio said, smiling nervously.

Brook just nodded her head yes. She couldn't speak. Gio ran down the steps and came over to her and slid the ring on her finger. The audience clapped and whistled loudly. Brook was still in shock. She looked up into his eyes with happy confusion and smiled.

"I love you," Gio whispered and kissed her. They hugged and everyone clapped.

"Oh my gosh," Brook said to Gio. She looked down at her hand and saw a beautiful, very large, engagement ring on her finger that had to be at least five carats. Brook's phone started vibrating in her purse, probably because the award show was live, but on a delay. "Gio, what... when..."

"For a long time, baby. I told you, I love you and I'm not going to lose you again."

At that point, the program had continued and Brook and Gio were whispering to each other. Brook was trying to blink back the tears that threatened to fall. Then, it dawned on her, "Baby!" Brook squealed softly and rubbed his Oscar. She looked at him, grinning and hugged him. "You did it, babe, you really did it," Brook said excitedly. They looked at each other, both smiling hard. It was a night they'd remember forever. He won his first Oscar for his very first movie role and they got engaged.

"So, you really wanna marry me or did you just not want to embarrass me in front of the whole world?" Gio asked with a grin.

"Yes, I really wanna marry you," Brook grinned back at him, grabbing his hand and looking him in those beautiful brown eyes, her eyes getting watery again. She wanted to hug and kiss him, but she knew everyone was looking. Everyone around them had been congratulating them since it happened.

"And, my phone has been ringing off the hook. I know it's Debra." Brook giggled.

"Let's go out for a minute and you can call her back," he said.

She felt the stare and turned to see Nautica Diaz staring at her. Brook just smiled and winked, showing off her dimples. *Check Mate, Bitch!*

Gio and Brook got up as soon as it was possible and headed out to the lobby. Seat fillers came and sat in their seat. Everyone was shaking Gio's hand as they made their way back up the isle. Brook kept walking, smiling the whole time. They got to the lobby and more congratulations came. Brook wanted to find a quiet corner somewhere and digest everything. They were engaged! He really loved her! She was smiling so hard, her cheeks hurt. Her heart was bursting with joy. She never even knew she could feel that way. Although she loved him and they had wonderful times together, Brook always still held back a little, making sure he wasn't going to hurt her again. But, her guard was down and she was happier than she had ever been.

They found a little corner off in the cut and Gio grabbed her in a big hug. They stood there, holding each other, not saying anything. Gio looked in her eyes and told her he loved her and wanted to spend the rest of his life with her, his eyes tearing up. Brook started crying and babbling, about loving him too, and kissing him when her phone started vibrating again.

"I'd better grab this before Debra comes marching up in here," Brook said, laughing and crying at the same time. She answered the phone and there was screaming on the other end. She and Gio cracked up laughing. "Girl, quit screaming," Brook said to Debra.

"Oh, hell yeah!" Debra screamed. That was hella fly. Tell Gio he just won five thousand cool points."

"I'm sure he heard you." Brook laughed.

"Congratulations, girl. I am so happy for you both. We'll see y'all at the after party. I just wanted to be the first to tell you congratulations," Debra said with tears in her voice.

"Okay, girl, my phone is beeping again. I'll see you there," Brook said and clicked over on the phone.

"Hello," she happily singsonged into the phone.

"Brooklyn Denise Bridges, what is going on and who is this stranger you are about to marry?" Brook gulped and looked at Gio with big eyes.

"Daddy!" Brook squeaked.

Gio's eyes popped out and his mouth went into an O. Brook didn't even think about her parents watching the show. She knew Debra was watching because Gio was nominated, but her parents didn't even know that she and Gio were dating, so she knew the engagement was definitely a shock to them.

"Umm, Daddy, ummm. I didn't know either. This was a total surprise to me, too," Brook explained.

"But, daughter, you've never mentioned him. And, how serious can it be if you've never even brought him home?" Mama said. They had her on speaker phone.

"I love him, Mommy, and I want to be his wife," Brook said with tears in her voice.

A moment of silence passed. "Well, that's all you had to say, baby," her mother said, instantly understanding. "Oh my gosh! My baby is in love and getting married," Mama said excitedly. Her mother knew Brook wasn't a rash decision maker, and she could hear it in her daughter's voice that she was serious.

"Put him on the phone," Daddy said. Brook gulped and handed the phone to Gio, who was listening to every word.

"Hello, sir, ma'am," Gio said nervously. All she heard was Gio saying, "Yes, sir, why yes, yes, sir, with all my heart, yes, ma'am, it will be a pleasure, sir, okay, thank you, good bye." He looked at Brook and said, "I have to go meet your parents and soon." He laughed and Brook laughed, too. He picked her up and spun her around. "I love you, fiancée," he said, making Brook squeal, laughing and kissing him, neither of them noticing the cameras flashing, taking pictures of them.

On the drive over to the club, Brook changed out of her gown to a cute little halter mini dress. She knew she was not going to last a whole night in the long gown, so she brought the dress and left it in the limo. It was silver with shingles all over it, but every color would reflect off of it making it look multi colored. They sat in the back of the limo, finally alone, her head resting on his shoulder, holding hands and talking softly.

"So, had you planned to do that?" Brook asked.

"No! I didn't even know I was going to win. I had planned on doing it tonight though, when we got back to the hotel. I was up there feeling for the card that we had made, reminding me of who to thank when I felt the ring, so I threw caution to the wind and said, I'm gonna go for it," he said excitedly. "But, I was nervous, babe. I was scared you'd say no in front of the world."

"Is this the same ring from the first time?" Brook asked.

The first time was still a really sensitive subject for them and they never talked about it. They just left the past in the past and learned from it.

"Yes, it is. It's been in my safe since then. I knew then that I was going to do everything in my power to get this ring on your finger. And, it looks like I did it," Gio grinned.

"I don't do unfaithful, Gio," Brook said softly, yet seriously.

"Look at me, Brooklyn," Gio said, raising her head with his finger. "Don't you think I know that? I wouldn't ask you to be my wife if I wasn't 100% sure I was ready to dedicate my everything to you. I've never proposed to anyone in my life. You told me something a long time ago, and that is that you're a needle in a haystack. You are, boo. I love you, Brook. You're the only woman that I want. Forever, baby."

Brook smiled into his beautiful brown eyes and they kissed, and kissed. In fact, they didn't stop kissing until they felt the limo stop at the club.

"Well, fiancée, let's go celebrate," Gio grinned.

They were at the club and they were partying. Brook and Gio were both slightly drunk and having a ball. They had been dancing and drinking, and drinking and dancing. Gio insisted on giving everyone Dom to celebrate his woman agreeing to marry him and Brook would throw in, "and his Oscar!" It was the first time they had ever really danced together. Sure, they had slow danced at the house or joked around doing old school dances, but never on a dance floor, dancing to the music. She knew he could dance because she had seen his videos. It was nice to be the one dancing with him.

"Aw, shit, work it, baby," Gio taunted as Brook turned around and worked him out, slowly moving her body against him. Brook had the sexy dance down to a science. She didn't drop it like it was hot and shake her goods all over the dance floor. She just moved her body sensually to the music.

"Diiivvvaaaa," Pam squealed. "Girl, let me get a look at that rock!"

Brook flashed her engagement ring for the one-thousandth time. It really was a beautiful ring. She hadn't looked at it the first time he proposed because he was drunk and she thought he was full of crap.

"And, what is this about you turned him down the first time?" Pam asked.

"Long and boring story. Come sit with us," Brook said, heading back to their table.

"I'm over here with my girls, so I'll have to pass. Congratulations. And don't y'all forget, I'm the one who introduced you two," Pam laughed.

Their table was already a little crowded. They had Debra and Glenn, Randy and Carmen, plus Jamar and his wife, Stacey, and another couple, whose names Brook had forgotten. And, there was Tha Dogg, standing around making sure everything was everything.

Tha Dogg had given her the biggest hug. "I'm so happy for you two, Ms. Brook. I knew you were the one. I told Gio that, too! Ask him, I said 'Ms. Brook is the lady for you,'" Tha Dogg said.

"So, is this going to be a long or short engagement?" Carmen asked them.

Brook and Gio answered at the same time. Brook said, "Long," and Gio said, "Short." Everyone at the table started laughing.

"I guess this is something we'll have to discuss," Brook said, smiling at Gio. Just then, the DJ played Robin Thicke's cut *Lost Without You.*

"Sounds like they're calling us on the dance floor, babe," Gio said as he grabbed Brook's hand and led her to the floor. Brook wrapped her arms around Gio's neck and they slow danced, whispering softly about love and happiness, and reminiscing about what they had done when Gio had sung that very song to her. Brook had thrown her head back in laughter at Gio talking about the repeat performance he was going to give when they got back to the hotel, and another picture was taken with Brook laughing and Gio smiling at her, looking like a man in love. Again, they were oblivious, only seeing each other.

They half stumbled into their room, both laughing hysterically at Gio's rendition of Eddie Murphy in *Coming To America*, singing the song *I'm In Love*.

"Ssshhh, you're going to wake people," Brook whispered loudly.
They made it to the bedroom and fell on the bed. Gio grabbed her and started kissing her.

"Wait, babe. I gotta go potty. You just get ready for me. I have something for you."

Brook grabbed something out of her suitcase and went to the bathroom. She had just the thing. She'd bought a sexy little lingerie set, complete with garter belt, a while ago and bought it on the trip with them. It turned out to be the perfect occasion for it. She was getting ready to rock his world. She went over and put on her Beyonce CD and skipped to *Video Phone*. The music started playing and Brook started dancing, "*Shawty what yo name is?...*" Beyonce half sang, half rapped and Brook danced. Slow and sensual, Brook worked it. A big grin was on Gio's face as he watched her, sexy, working it better than any stripper he'd ever seen. Brook worked her body to the floor and twirled it back up. As she made her way closer to the bed, she turned around and stuck her butt out and shook it from side to side, and then smacked it. By the time she had danced over to him, his smile was gone. Instead, there was a look of desire on his face and a tent in his boxers. "*You can watch me on your video phone...*" Beyonce sang. Gio got up and started dirty dancing with her. His hands were all over her body. He turned her around and grinded into her booty while kissing the back of her neck. Brook's legs were getting weak with desire. Gio trailed kisses down Brook's back. He slid her panties down and he kissed all the way down her body. He turned her around and opened her legs, licking her wetness. Brook grabbed his head as her knees got weak. Gio pulled her over to the humongous window with the beautiful view of the city. They were on the fifteenth floor and the view was spectacular, especially since the window almost covered the whole wall. He turned her around, placed her hands above her head like she was under arrest and spread her legs. He stood behind her, slipping on his condom and slid into her. Brook groaned. She felt like he was going to reach her heart. It was amazing, making love to the night lights of the city.

"Slow down, baby," she moaned.

Gio slowed, moving in and out, in and out until Brook cried out her orgasm, her knees getting weak. Gio kept going. Brook tried to stop him but he wouldn't stop.

"Wait, baby, wait, I can't...," she cried out until another orgasm erupted from her.

Gio pulled her over to the bed and got on top. He placed her legs on his shoulders and slowly grinded into her. They tongued each other, getting faster and faster. He flipped Brook on top as she started riding him. She grabbed both of his arms and held them above his head and would rise up and back down onto him. Gio couldn't take much more and grabbed her hips, starting to buck wildly under her. Brook got off of him as he was ready to explode.

"Oh, shit," Gio said.

Brook smiled and lay back, motioning him to climb on top. She wrapped her legs around his waist and he gave her all of him. She looked into his eyes and told him she loved him.

"Forever, baby," was his answer as he kissed her deeply. He grabbed her waist as he exploded into her. He stuck his tongue in her mouth to silence his groans. Brook started exploding, as well, his intensity making her erupt again.

Gio fell onto of her with a big, "Ump!"

"Baby, you're too heavy," she grunted. Gio flopped over onto his back, breathing hard. They both fell asleep just like that, condom still on.

Gio was officially off the market, and he was totally cool with that. He didn't know one person could give him so much joy. But, that's exactly what Brook did. She was classy, sexy, crazy, and a little freaky, she was the perfect wife. Overall, he had to say he was the happiest he had ever been in his life. His dad told him when he went through the heartbreak of finding out he wasn't a father that he would know when love was right. And as always, his daddy was right.

When he talked with Brook's parents on the phone, they seem really nice, but her dad made him a little nervous. But, he wasn't worried about meeting him. He loved Brook and knew that her parents would see that.

Life was definitely in order. He was going to be married to the woman of his dreams. Who would have thought Giovanni Lay would be getting married? He surely didn't. Not to sound cocky, but he just couldn't imagine a woman that held all his interests. He'd dated and slept with a lot of women in his lifetime. He'd lost his virginity at twelve years old. Women loved singers and he loved women. But, there came a time in his life when it just became routine. He did it because there was nothing better to do. And then he met Brook. She sure turned his life around. And, he knew she was the one because she wasn't trying to turn his life around, she was just being Brook.

CHAPTER 46

"Wake up, sleepy head," Gio said, softly planting soft kisses on Brook's face.

"What time is it?" Brook croaked.

"It's almost noon."

"Man, I was knocked out," she said, stretching and yawning. "I can't believe it's that late. How long you been up?"

"Just long enough to brush my teeth and get a shower. You want room service or you wanna go out and eat?"

"Let's do room service. I'm starving, need some coffee, and don't feel like rushing." All of a sudden, Brook screamed. Gio jumped and spun around, dropping the phone. "We're engaged," she screeched, jumping up and hugging Gio.

"Are you trying to start something?" Gio asked, eying her naked body. Brook laughed, planting little kisses on his mouth and jaw.

"Fiancé, don't you start nothing," she said as Gio grabbed her waist and grinded into her, kissing her on her neck. "Boo, you just got dressed and I'm starving. Call room service while I go grab a quick shower, pllleaasseee," Brook said sweetly, blowing him a kiss as she walked to the bathroom, giggling while Gio stood there with a visible hard on. She was no longer shy about being nude in front of him.

"You're gonna make that up to me later, woman," Gio yelled.

"And, you know this, maaaaan," Brook yelled back, doing her best Chris Tucker impression.

They were hungry. All you heard were sips of orange juice and the fork scrapping the plates with an occasional grunt. Brook let out a huge burp.

"Oh my gosh! Excuse me. I am so sorry," she said, turning slightly red.

Gio cracked up. "Ask a girl to marry you and it all comes out," he teased.

"Oh yeah, my moms called while you were in the shower. She's all excited. Of course, she wants us to come there today." He laughed. "My phone rang so much last night, I just turned it off. Of course, she called and got my voicemail. And, she's offended that I never bought you home. I told her that we'd be there in a few weeks."

"Oh wow. I didn't even think of that. We were so caught up in the moment. We shoulda called her. I don't want to start off on the wrong foot,"

Brook said.

"You're not. She is so happy. And, of course my dad was like, son, are you sure this is the woman you want to spend the rest of your life with, because you know Lay men stay married! We're honest men. If you're going to be a husband, you have to be the best husband and you're a husband for the long haul. I got the whole lecture." He laughed happily. "But, it was all good. I know they love me and want what's best for me. And, they're going to love you, too," he said, reaching over and giving her a kiss. "Now, get dressed, woman, so we can go out and do some shopping. Remember, we're going to see *The Color Purple* tonight and that starts at eight. So, we have to get going."

"Won't take me long at all," Brook said, and she stood up and dropped her robe.

"Ouuuuu, you are really trying to start something." He laughed, eying her in her bra and thong. "Hey, babe, so how often do I get that dance?" Gio grinned.

"Hmmm, I guess we'll see now, won't we?" Brook dimpled.

CHAPTER 47

Brook could not believe all the pictures of them in the newspaper and magazines. Of course, there were the pictures of Gio proposing, but there was also a picture of them hugging. It looked like it was right after they got engaged when they went out into the foyer. There was one of them kissing with Gio holding the sides of her face, and a picture of Gio on the phone with her parents, serious expression on his face, with Brook watching anxiously. They even had a picture of them looking lovingly into each other's eyes on the dance floor at the nightclub they had gone to. Her mom said she was making an album of the pictures. They were back in Atlanta and Brook was talking to her mom on the telephone.

"When I say everyone has called, I mean everyone, even students I taught years ago."

"But, Ma, don't you think that's weird. I mean, I'm still me. Why in the world would everyone now want to call? Would they call me if I got engaged to Joe Blow down the street?"

"Probably not, baby. People love to be associated with celebrities."

"I just can't believe the coverage it has gotten. There must be nothing else going on for them to have us all over everything."

"Well, your Aunt Camille said she read in one of the rags that you all had been dating since high school. So, they're even making up stories. Said she was standing in line at the grocery store and there you and Gio were, on the front cover, talking about high school sweethearts get engaged at the awards show. Speaking of which, when are you two coming to visit. I'm so excited. My baby is finally getting married. Have you set a date?"

"We'll be there in a week or two. And, no, we haven't had time to set a date yet. I was thinking maybe next spring. Gio is thinking next week." She laughed.

"You are getting married here at the church, right?"

"Of course, I am! Reverend Coleman wouldn't have it any other way. Gio and I haven't confirmed anything yet. I'm still trying to get used to the fact that I'm engaged."

"You're not having second thoughts, are you? We never really talked about how you met. I know you said you all have been dating a little over a year. Don't let the whirlwind of it all get to you. If you're not sure, that's fine. You just say the word."

"Of course, I'm sure. We just got engaged two days ago. And, he's going to be super busy in the studio. He's doing a song for the soundtrack of some cartoon movie that's coming out. That's going to be huge for him because it's hitting the young mothers, and that is definitely the big movie market right now. I'll let you know more after Gio and I talk."

"Okay. I love you, baby. And congratulations again."

Brook hung up from her mother and went to get ready for her work week. *Time to get back to reality.* She was glad she had taken the day off from work to unwind from the weekend.

She had just gotten out of the bathtub when her phone rang.

"Hello, handsome," she answered.

"Hey, baby. You gettin' ready for work tomorrow?"

"Yes, just got out of the bathtub and getting ready to turn in. I'm still tired. You wore me out this weekend," she teased.

"I wish I was still wearing you out," he flirted back. "My moms called. Baby, she is straight buggin'. She wants to know when I'm bringing you home. Oh yeah, and the date for the wedding, what church, and on and on and on."

"Wow, I just got off the phone with my mom, and she had her fifty million questions going, too." They both laughed. "I tell you what. You focus on finishing your recording. That is going to be huge for you. Once you're done there, then we'll discuss the rest."

"But, the rest is more important than this song."

"No, sweetie, we have forever to plan, you have one week to finish the song!"

"Right, right. I love you, babe. Thank you for being you."

"You already know. You handle being famous, I'll handle the other stuff. I do have one question. Do you have a problem with us getting married in Louisville?"

"Of course not, boo. Heck, I'll marry you in the mall if that's what you wanted," he joked. "But, I have a question for you."

"What's up, babe."

"How long are we going to continue to use condoms? You said you were on the pill now and you know we're both clean."

Brook laughed. "I was thinking on our wedding night."

"Hmmm, okay, that's a bet. I had my argument ready on why we didn't need to use condoms anymore and you just shut that down." He laughed. "I love you, baby."

"I love you, too. Sweet dreams. I'll talk to you tomorrow, fiancé." Brook giggled.

As Brook snuggled into her bed, she smiled thinking about Gio, about being his wife and the exciting life she had ahead of her.

Brook pulled up to work the next morning and there were television station vans and photographers all around. She hoped nothing crazy had happened, but it must have been something major because people were all around. Brook hoped it had nothing to do with any of her coworkers and hurried to the building.

"Brook!" she heard her named shouted. She turned around in surprise, hoping to get a clue as to what had happened, yet a little nervous to find out. Cameras starting flashing. People started calling her name, yelling out questions about Gio and their engagement. Brook stood there, totally confused. How could those people out there covering a crime, or maybe even a death, have the nerve to ask her about Gio! How rude was that!

"Have you all set a date yet?" someone screamed. Brook just shook her head and hurried inside.

She got to her office and everyone was standing around. "Hey, what the heck happened? Is everybody okay?" Brook asked, looking around at everyone.

"What in the world are you talking about?" Mia asked.

"All the media outside, what happened? There were even television crews, too."

"Chica, they're for you. They questioned all of us coming in."

"For me!" Brook screeched. "Why in the heck are they here for me? What did I do?"

"You got engaged to a very famous, award-winning, sing-his-ass-off, superstar," Mia said snidely.

"You have *got* to be kidding me! They're here because Gio and I got engaged?" Brook shouted incredulously, her voice going higher with each word. She couldn't believe it. "Wow," she said, still tripping that a bunch of paparazzi were outside, for her. "I guess they'll leave. I just can't believe they're here. How the heck did they even know where I work? This is just too weird. I gotta go call Gio," Brook said, and hurried into her cubicle. But then, she looked at the time and realized Gio worked late the night before and would be in a deep sleep. She didn't want to disturb him, she'd call him after lunchtime. Besides, she had a busy day ahead and needed to get busy.

Brook finished up a few proposals, set up some appointments, and had a busy morning. She didn't have an appointment until later that afternoon so she headed to Gio's, calling him to let him know she was on her way. Even though they were engaged, she still wouldn't just drop by his house unannounced. She thought that was rude.

Gio answered the phone groggily. "Babe, you are not going to believe what is happening! The paparazzi were at my job!"

"Huh, they were at your job? What do you mean they were at your job? Where they there for you? What did they say?" Gio said, sounding more awake.

"There were television people and a bunch of photographers. They were taking pictures and shouting questions like have we set a date and stuff like that."

"Oh, babe, I'm so sorry. I had no idea this would happen."

"I know, babe, it's not your fault. I'm on my way over there. Do you have anywhere you have to be anytime soon?"

"No, I didn't get to bed until around five this morning. But we got most of the song done. I just have to go in later and clean up a few things. Bring that beautiful and perfectly plump ass on over here."

Brook giggled. "Okay, I'll be there in about forty five minutes. Do you want me to pick you up something to eat or anything?"

"No, I'm going back to sleep. I'll run down and unlock the door now, so just come on in. And, remind me to give you a key."

"Alright, boo. I'll see ya in a few." Brook's next call was to Debra. "Giirrrlll, you are not going to believe my morning! First off, I get to work and the damn paparazzi are out front waiting on me!"

"What! Shut up! Awww hell yeah, my girl is a star-rah!" Debra squealed.

"Girl, this junk isn't even funny. How did they even know where I work? There are real celebrities out there, why the heck are they following me for. I wasn't even with Gio!"

"'Cause you're the one the star loves. So, that makes you news."

"Girl, this is just too crazy to me! Well, on another note, Gio and I are officially going home next weekend."

"Oh, hell yeah! That will be the perfect time for me to bring Glenn home. I can't believe how cool his moms was when we went there. And, you know she emails me all the time. His sister is a little trifflin', but so is Don, so I feel his pain."

"Have I ever told you that sometimes you can really be a selfish little bitch? Don't try to change the subject talking about his mom. You know you are sitting there thinking about how it will be easier for you to bring Glenn. And, here I am scared one of my crazy cousins will try to sneak something half-eaten off his plate and sell it on Ebay!"

Debra cracked up. "Brooklyn Bridges, damn and bitch all in one morning! Yep, you are stressing entirely too much. This is your time, boo. You are engaged to a man you love very much, and more importantly, who loves you very much. To top it off, he's hella fine and a super star. Now, what exactly is it you're complaining about again?" Debra was right. Brook was really getting herself all worked up for nothing. "Sure, the Paparazzi are a headache. Yes, there will always be people wanting a piece of Gio, and maybe even you. But that is part of the package that comes with Gio."

"You get on my nerves, trying to get all deep." Brook laughed. "Thank you, girl! I really needed to hear that because I was really getting frustrated. And, that is just dumb. This too shall pass."

Brook undressed and slid into bed with Gio. She snuggled under him and he wrapped his arms around her.

"You okay?" he asked, kissing her on the forehead. "I'm sorry, baby. I know this can be a bit overwhelming. I think since I won the Oscar, it's just gotten crazier. I didn't mean for all of this to get in your way," he said.

"No, it's okay. I just have to get used to it. It took me completely by surprise, that's all. I expect it when I'm with you, just not when I'm not with you."

"Come here, woman, and let me help you relieve that stress."

"Now, that sounds like the best thing I've heard all morning," she laughed.

Brook and Gio were lounging in his huge bathtub, relaxing. Gio said, "Hey, babe, I have a question for you."

"Sure, what's up, boo?"

"I was thinking, since the paparazzi are hounding you, why don't you move in here with me?"

"Move in here with you? But, what about my house?"

"Well, you were going to move in here after we got married, right?"

"Well, yeah. I guess I just hadn't really thought about it. What am I going to do with my house when I do move in here? I guess I could sell it."

"You don't have to do anything with your house. Or, better yet, rent it out. Didn't you say you were renting out your other house in Louisville? So, rent this one out, too. You said one day you wanted to invest in rental property, well, here's your start."

"Hmmmm, you've really thought about this. But, don't you think we should wait until after we're married to live together?"

"Babe, how often are you at your house? You spend most nights here anyway."

"That is true. Okay, that's a bet. I'll move in here," she dimpled.

"So, do you want to bring over any of your furniture? This is your home, too."

"No, I'm good. I've pretty much gotten used to this. Maybe I'll bring a few of my paintings. You don't mind?"

"Of course I don't mind! This is our home." Brook reached back and kissed him.

"Okay, babe, we're officially living together." She giggled.

They had decided on a wedding date. Gio was working on three months and Brook was going for a year, so they compromised on seven months. They had already decided to have it in Brook's childhood church, and that's about all they had gotten done on the wedding planning. They headed out to eat and sure enough, there were paparazzi outside.

"There they are again. Do they know where you're going to be or something?"

"You know how I see it. This is their job. Yes, sometimes they can be harassing, but if you just give them the picture, they'll be a lot nicer to you. They love me. You wanna know why? Because I take the time out to talk to them, even answer a few questions. Can they be nerve-wracking, yes, but all it takes is about three minutes, and they'll leave you alone."

"Okay, I'll try it. They're just so aggressive and I really didn't know how to handle that. But I'm ready now!"

They parked and were headed to the restaurant when the paparazzi caught up with them. "Hey Gio, taking the fiancée out for dinner, huh?"

"Yeah, I gotta feed the woman. And, you all are scaring her, she's not used to this. You have to ease her into it," Gio half joked.

"We're sorry, Ms. Bridges, but you're hot news right now. Can we get a picture of you two?"

Brook and Gio posed. They gave a few pictures, Gio gave a few jokes, and they were left alone.

"Wow! That went smoothly. You da man, baby."

Gio smiled, slightly blushing. "You just have to give them what they want and then they won't drive you crazy trying to get what they want."

They ordered their food and were going over wedding plans. "Okay, let's decide on how many in the wedding party. How many guys are a must?" Brook said.

"Hmmm, at least five. What about you?"

"Hmmm, at least seven. This is gonna be hard because we're really not going to be able to leave anyone out."

"True dat. I get it so much with old friends. They're always looking for a reason to prove I've changed. I'll tell you what, you tell me how many and I'll match it."

"Okay, that's a bet. Lastly, the only other input I'll need is any colors you absolutely do not want in the wedding?"

"Yes, pink! I know that's the new black or whatever, but I'm not feeling it. I don't do pink, period."

"Oooo, I love it when you get all manly and masculine," Brook joked. Gio laughed and their food was served. "Okay, babe, if there's any other input you want, just let me know. I'll let you know how many bridesmaids for sure. Oh yeah, I'll eventually need a guest list of your side of the family with addresses. I can probably get that from your mom when we go there. Otherwise, just bring your fine self to the church and become my husband."

"Now that, I can do," Gio said and leaned over to give her a kiss.

Next, they headed over to Randy's office, he said he needed to go over some paperwork with them. Gio said Randy asked that she bring her attorney. Randy's office building was located in Buckhead and was very nice and modern, all steel and glass. She knew Randy was an attorney, she just didn't know he was big time like that. She'd have to tease him about that. First, the receptionist greeted them. She was the receptionist for all of the attorneys in the firm. Her name was D'Erica and she was a total Barbie... all blonde hair, blue eyes, tall, leggy, but spoke with a French accent. They walked down a hallway here and a hallway there and they were at Randy's office. His secretary, a beautiful chocolate sista named Phylicia, greeted them with congratulations and ushered them right in. Randy's office was beautiful with mahogany wood and lots of books. Brook was truly impressed. Randy greeted Gio with a brothaman shake and one-armed hug.

"How's my favorite soon to be married couple?" he asked.

"It's all good." Gio laughed and Brook grinned hard, both looking like the happiest couple.

"That I can see." He smiled "Brook, didn't you want an attorney present?" Randy asked.

"Nah, I'm straight. Gio said we'd go over the pre-nup and I'm fine with that. Gio was successful when I met him and even though I don't even want to think of ever getting a divorce from this man, if that unfortunate incident does happen to us, Gio was still successful when I met him. I'll sign whatever," Brook said.

"Damn, Gio, you really are a lucky man," Randy said with a smile.

Gio nodded and grinned. "But, wait a minute. I want to put a stipulation in this pre-nup. I want to make sure she's taken care of until she remarries. If the unfortunate does happen, I love this woman and don't want her hurt. Hey, wait, let's make that stipulation if she doesn't leave me for another man," Gio laughed.

"You two are just so special," Randy joked dryly.

Randy put the changes in the pre-nup and took it out to his assistant to retype. They sat around and shot the breeze for a minute until Phylicia brought the document back in.

"Let me go over this with you, Brook."

Randy went over the legalese with them, running through the document. It pretty much said what they had talked about, if they divorced, Brook would keep what she came in with. She would be allotted a huge allowance per month if they divorced, and would continue to receive it until she remarried, unless it was due to Brook being unfaithful. Brook signed the necessary paperwork and stuck her copies in her purse.

CHAPTER 48

Debra was helping Brook plan the wedding while her mom was doing her part back home. The wedding was going to be bigger than originally planned. They ended up with ten bridesmaids as well as a Maid and Matron of honor. And, true to his word, Gio came up with ten groomsmen and had two best men. Brook wanted The Dogg to be a groomsman, but he declined. He wanted stand guard to make sure everything was going according to plan. The colors were chocolate and powder blue. They were heading to Louisville the next morning so Gio could finally meet her parents. Debra was bringing Glenn as well, the sneaky heiffa. She knew everyone wouldn't pay much attention to Glenn since they'd be all over Gio. Brook's mom was having a ball getting the wedding together. She didn't like the colors at first, but once she saw them together, she loved them. They talked everyday about something for the wedding. Brook was excited herself. She had successfully moved into Gio's house, and she kept most of her stuff in her house. She was going to have to find a storage place eventually. She ended up taking more stuff than originally thought to Gio's, her family photos, her wet bar, a few strategically placed plants, and her paintings. Gio's house was definitely feeling like home for her.

As for Mr. Giovanni Lay, she was falling more in love with him each day. Although he was working in the studio most nights, it was nice to feel him slide into bed when he got home. And, he was right, the paparazzi did finally leave her alone, for the most part. The only problem was work. Everyone had changed. She was still the same Brook, but the people around her were either standoffish or overly friendly. She felt like screaming. Gio's solution was for her to quit her job, something she just was not feeling. She did not want to be dependent on him. Her mama didn't raise her like that. What in the world would she do all day if she didn't work? The other problem was she worked in the morning, he worked at night. He was asleep when she left and she was asleep when he got home. They were able to spend time together when she got off work and he wouldn't leave out until she was going to bed. So, they were able to still have dinner together each night and watch *Wheel of Fortune* or go to bible study, where no one even thought of bothering Gio for autographs. He went from going to the studio nightly, to only going Sunday through Thursday so they'd have the weekend together. That worked out better for them at the studio as it was always crowded on the weekends. Most Sundays, Brook went to church while Gio went and balled with the fellas. Some Sundays, he went to church with her, but people always stared. He couldn't even praise the Lord without someone watching him, so he mainly went to bible study where things were a lot calmer. Life was definitely falling into place.

The plane was landing and Brook was excitedly pointing out the landmarks to Gio that he hadn't paid attention to on his first visit. "See, babe, that's Kentucky Kingdom over there. Man, when we were younger, they had this Friday night teen thing going on called Day Five Alive. It would be shown on television the next night. Those were the days. Debra and I never missed a weekend. Of course, now they couldn't do that. The kids would be fighting and shooting. They just don't know how to have a good time," Brook said sadly.

"I bet you were the flyest girl at Day Five Alive, too." Gio grinned.

"And you know this." Brook laughed.

Gio went to get the luggage while Brook went to get the rental car. They were renting a convertible Benz and for once, Brook didn't mind. She just couldn't believe they were three hundred dollars a day.

The first stop they made was to White Castle. Brook loved White Castle and she missed not being able to get them. Every time she came home, that was her first stop. She told Gio about them and couldn't wait for him to try them.

"These ain't nothing but Krystal burgers," Gio said.

"What?! Krystal burgers! Yeah, right! Krystal burgers buns aren't steamed and soft! They don't even taste the same!"

Gio bit into his double cheeseburger and chewed thoughtfully. "Yeah, it is nice that the bun is this soft, but it's kinda soggy. Kinda makes you think there's gravy on it or something."

"But, it's good, huh? And it's better than Krystal's, too!" Brook said, munching on her onion rings.

"Yeah, okay, they may taste a little better than Krystal's, but they still remind me of them."

"And, I want you to taste Indi's wings. They are the bomb! But, wait until you taste my mom's chili. You know our chili has spaghetti in it."

"Then that's called spaghetti!" Gio laughed.

"No, it's Louisville chili that comes with spaghetti in it, and my mom's is the best. You'll see," Brook said proudly

They pulled up in front of her childhood home and Brook didn't see any extra cars out front. With the way people were acting lately, she was afraid there'd be a parade or something at her house. Brook opened the door and could smell the chili as they walked into the house.

"Maaaaaa, we're here," Brook yelled.

Brook's mom rushed into the room and gave her a hug, then gave Gio a hug. "Welcome Gio, I'm Brook's mom, Frances."

Brook's daddy came in and gave Brook her daddy hug. He shook Gio's hand with a smile on his face. "Hello, son, I'm Brian. Welcome to our home."

Gio thanked her daddy and told her mom that the house smelled wonderful.

"Why thank you, Gio. That's Louisville Chili."

"I was telling him about your chili. But we're not hungry yet, we just had White Castle."

"I figured that. The chili isn't ready yet, it's simmering. Well, come on in. Brook, show Gio to his room," her mom said.

"Do you need help with your luggage?" daddy asked.

"No, sir, I'll get it." Brook and Gio walked out to the car to get the luggage.

"I told you sleeping in the same room was *not* gonna happen," Brook teased. Gio laughed.

"I hear you. And, I thought you had the deepest dimples ever. You were right your mom's dimples are even deeper, kinda like that actress Debbie Morgan who's married to that actor that played Roc."

"Oh, you mean Charles S. Dutton? Everybody always trips on her dimples."

Brook was rolling her luggage and Gio took it from her. "I got it, babe. Don't have me out here looking like a punk in front of your dad."

Brook cracked up. "Okay, you big, strong man, you!"

They were sitting in the family room discussing the wedding plans. "When is Brandon coming?" Brook asked.

"Well, tomorrow I thought we'd do a little cookout in the back yard. They'll be here then," Brook's mom said without looking at her. Brook looked at her dad, who had that "ump, ump, ump" look on his face.

"Cookout?" Brook asked.

"Well, yes. I'm sure Gio wants to meet his future family," Brook's mom said.

"Who all did you invite?"

"Just your Aunt Bonnie and Uncle Kyle, your Aunt Sherry and Uncle Stefan, and of course, your Aunt Camille and probably a few of your cousins," Brook's mom said, smiling at Gio but still not looking at Brook.

Brook gave her dad 'the look.' Her dad gave her the 'I know, but you know your mama' look right back.

"Well, is London coming? That's my cousin that is going to be our Matron of Honor," Brook explained to Gio.

"You have a cousin named London Bridges? And you're Brooklyn Bridges!" Gio laughed.

"Yeah, real funny parents we have," Brooklyn said dryly. "She's London Bridges Britt now. She got married and lives in Jacksonville, Florida with her wonderful husband, Malik." Brook's dad gave a weird look. "Daddy, why'd you look like that?"

"I don't know. There was just something about him. Brandon and I were discussing it. Brandon said it's like he's playing at being a great husband, like he's doing what he thinks he's supposed to do."

"Well, isn't that the point?" Brook asked.

"Not when you're not sincere. Not when you're doing it because people are watching."

"But, he even cried when she walked down the isle."

"Exactly, playing at being a great groom. Brandon and I just felt something a little off about him, that's all. And his family, they were down right creepy!"

"Brian, that isn't nice. So anyway, London won't be able to make it," Brook's mom said, looking at her husband to let him know the subject was changed. "Gio, you're going to love Brian's barbecue."

"It's all about marinating," Brook's dad said.

They heard the front door open and close. Brandon and Phyllis walked in the room.

"Hey, I didn't expect you two until tomorrow," Brook's mom said as she got up to give hugs.

"Hey, bighead, hey, mommy," Brook greeted them and got up to give hugs. She rubbed Phyllis' little protruding belly.

"Hi, baby, here's your Auntie Brook," she baby talked to Phyllis' belly. She did the introductions and Gio gave Brandon the brothaman handshake and Phyllis a hug.

"It's a pleasure to meet you. I loved the proposal," Phyllis gushed. "And Brook, did you know you're like in all the magazines and all over television?" Phyllis asked excitedly.

Brook then told them about the paparazzi at her job. Phyllis looked excited. Her mom understood her plight.

"So, Phyllis, have you picked out any names yet?" Brook asked cleverly changing the subject.

Gio rubbed her back. She knew he was feeling uncomfortable talking about how the Paparazzi had hounded her.

"Well, of course if it's a boy, it's Brandon Dion, Jr. If it's a girl, we're thinking about Breanne Chantell." They decided not to know the sex of the baby.

"Oh, that's pretty," Gio said.

Phyllis blushed, and Brook couldn't believe it. She never would have thought of Phyllis as the groupie type and had definitely never seen her blush before. She couldn't wait to tell Debra.

"So, Gio, do you have any children?" Brook's dad asked slyly.

Brook almost choked on her Big Red soda she was drinking. "No, sir. I was waiting for that special woman to make my wife before I thought about starting a family," he answered.

Good answer, Gio, Brook thought and smiled at him.

"But, I have two wonderful twin nieces, Kennedy and Kendyl. They are my two princesses. Of course, I spoil them to death." Gio laughed. He went in his wallet to take out their pictures, just like a proud uncle.

"Oh, they're adorable," Brook's mom said. "And, they're identical. Wow, I always wanted identical twins."

"Yes, ma'am, but they're easy to tell apart. Well, they are to me, anyway." He laughed.

"Hey, do you all want to go downtown and show Gio Fourth Street Live?" Brandon asked.

"That'll work. Come on, Ma, Dad, come with," Brook said.

"Let me turn off the chili and freshen up," her mom said.

Brook's mom always freshened up. She never went in public without making sure she was 'presentable'.

Fourth Street Live was really nice, and they had a good time. Thank goodness no one asked Gio for his autograph. People weren't that bold in Louisville, they just stared. Brook and Gio were used to it and ignored them. Brook was telling Gio how this used to be *the* mall back in the day.

"Oh, Brook would just die if she couldn't go. She and Debra couldn't miss a weekend. I'd drop them off and Debra's mom would pick them up, or vice versa. She and Debra were two were peas in a pod. Still are. I'm sure you've met Debra," Brook's mom said.

"Oh yes, ma'am. We hang out with her and Glenn quite often," Gio said.

"Glenn! Who's Glenn? Debra has a boyfriend?" Brook's mom asked, looking at Brook.

"Yes, nosy, and you'll meet him tomorrow. They're coming in town. I'll let her know about the barbecue. I'm sure Ms. Ava would love to come as well," Brook said.

"That's a good idea. Should we also invite her brother, Greg?" Brook's mom asked.

"Heckie no! Debra wouldn't have him around anyway. Those two still don't get along." Brook laughed.

Brook called Debra and told her about the barbecue they were having and told her to tell her mom.

"I know Greg's fat ass ain't invited, right?" Debra said.

Brook laughed. "Somehow I knew you'd say that."

They were in the kitchen, digging into the chili.

"This really is good," Gio said, putting chili on his cracker like Brook had showed him.

"I told ya," Brook said, crunching on her crackers herself. "So, Phyllis, you have to let me know when the baby shower is so I can come back for that," Brook said.

"Probably in a few months. I'm only five months now. They say you're supposed to have it in your eighth month. We're going to have a co-ed baby shower.

"A what?!" Gio shouted, and then looked like he was ready to crawl under a rock. "I mean, umm, I'm so sorry. I had just never heard of that before," he sputtered, clearly embarrassed he blurted it out. Had his complexion been lighter, he would have turned red.

"In the words of Curtis Payne, what the hell!" Daddy said. "I have never heard of it, either. What kind of sissy stuff is that, a co-ed baby shower? What guy is going to want to come to a *baby shower*!?" Daddy asked incredulously.

"Now, honey, times are changing. Of course men want to be part of the whole experience," Mama tried to reason and hold in her smirk at the same time. At that point, Brook was doing everything in her power to hold in her laugh. It had Phyllis written all over it.

"Thank you!" Brandon shouted. "I told her men don't do baby showers. That just ain't natural."

"Man, all of this testosterone in here! Now, you know you all don't want to miss out on the baby's first event," Brook teased. Everybody got the joke except Phyllis.

"That's what I'm saying, Brook. This is our baby's first introduction into the world. I don't want Brandon to miss that," she reasoned.

"Babe, who in the heck am I going to invite, the guys I ball with, some of the partners at the firm? Hey, bruh, wanna come to my *baby shower*? Yeah, right! I wasn't really on board with this whole co-ed thing anyway. Almost had me looking a complete fool. It's settled. We're doing it the normal way," Brandon said with finality.

"Okay, fine," Phyllis said, always one to keep the peace.

"So, who's up for a game of *Wheel of Fortune*," Brook said, changing the subject. Brook had sent her parents a game as well because they all loved playing it.

"Sound great. We can play couples," Phyllis said, thinking just because she and Brandon were both attorneys they'd win. She seemed to have forgotten her mom was a retired school teacher. Brook had a surprise for all of them, they didn't know Gio was a huge fan, too, and gave her a run for her money every time they played.

"Sounds like a winner to me. Why don't you men folk go set up the game while I help Ma with the kitchen," Brook suggested.

"So, Mr. Bridges, Brook was telling me you have a beautiful '63 Chevrolet Impala. You definitely have to let me have a look," Gio said as they walked out of the kitchen. The guys headed into the garage to take a quick look while the ladies finished the kitchen.

Brook and Gio were kicking butt, and that wasn't an easy task. Her mom and dad were really hard competitors as was Brandon and Phyllis. They were battling like they were on the live show. Everyone was yelling and high fiving, they were having a great time. Brook and Gio won five games, her mom and dad won three games and Phyllis and Brandon had only won two games.

"Well, that's ten games, looks like Gio and I are the champions," Brook squealed. They high fived each other, grinning hard.

"Whatever. That's because this is your favorite game. Bring out the *Boggle* then," Brandon said, always the competitor.

"Aw heckie naw, then we'd have to pull out the dictionary for every word you put down." Brook laughed.

"Heckie naw," Gio repeated, laughing.

"That's a childhood word. That's the polite way of saying hell naw," Brandon said with a laugh.

"Or, in the words of Whitney Houston, hell to the naw." Brook laughed.

"We'll have to save *Boggle* for another day. We have to get some sleep. I'm a little tired from the trip and we have a full day tomorrow. Not to mention that I'm sure there's a lot of cooking that has to be done. Ma, what time is everyone coming?" Brook asked.

"I told them two o'clock. But you know how we can be, they'll probably get here around three," she said.

"Gio, did you bring your trunks so you can swim?" Brandon asked, acting like he had a new best friend. Brook's parents had a pool in the backyard.

"No, we didn't know we were having a barbecue," Brook answered.

"Ohhh," Brandon said and looked at their mother.

She ignored him and said, "Most of the food is already prepared. I already made the potato salad, macaroni salad, and deviled eggs. The macaroni and cheese and baked beans are already prepared. I just have to slide them in the oven. Your dad has the meat marinating and he's going to throw some ears of corn on the grill, too. Tomorrow is mainly for my desserts. And, Gio can always get trunks at Target if he wants to swim."

"Well, I'm not swimming 'cause I just got my hair did," Brook said. Her mother turned around and looked at her like she was crazy with her grammar. Brook just smiled at her and gave her a 'that's my lick back for the surprise family barbecue' smirk.

"Good night, family. I'll see you all in the morning."

Gio gave her mom a good night kiss on the cheek, shook her dad's and Brandon's hand, and gave Phyllis a hug. "Good night. I'll see y'all tomorrow." Brook saw her mom notice Gio's use of the word y'all. Such a school teacher.

CHAPTER 49

The house smelled great. Gio was in the backyard with Brook's dad while he barbecued and gave him the tips of how to have the best barbecue. Brook was in the kitchen talking to her mom while she baked her fabulous brownies and her famous, homemade chocolate chip cookies. Her mom was a wonderful baker. Brook could hold her own in the cooking department, but she never could get the hang of homemade desserts, so she did store bought and enjoyed her mom's homemade desserts.

"He seems like a very nice young man," her mom was saying. She had been grilling Brook all morning. She said she didn't know what to expect since he was famous.

"I told you, Ma, he's really down to earth. We're going to visit his folks next weekend."

"I just can't believe you never even mentioned you two were dating, and a celebrity at that. You never were into the celebrity thing."

"I know. And that's why I didn't mention him, because he's a celebrity. I was just making sure everything was everything. That just goes to show you can't pick who you fall in love with. We actually met while he was here doing one of our parties. Then, I ran into him again in Atlanta last year. I didn't tell you because I was just going with the flow. I knew we were in love, I just didn't know he was going to propose, especially on national television. Plus, I haven't introduced you to every guy I've dated."

"I know. I guess it just seems so sudden. You're not pregnant, are you?"

"What!? Of course I'm not pregnant! And, people don't get married because they're pregnant anymore, they co-parent."

"Co-parent! They have a new name for it now? It's called out of wedlock! There's no way to fancy up having a baby and a baby daddy."

Brook cracked up laughing. "Ma, what the heck do you know about a baby daddy?"

"I'm a retired schoolteacher, I've heard it all. Just because I don't agree with it doesn't mean I don't know about it," she said.

Brook could hear people talking and her dad laughing.

"Brooklyn, you'd better come out here and get this man before I put him in my purse and take him home with me," Brook's Aunt Bonnie said.

Aunt Bonita was hilarious. She was her mom's older sister and had never met a stranger. Her dimples were just as deep as Brook's moms, and everyone loved her Aunt Bonnie. Her husband, Uncle Kyle, was the total opposite. He was very serious, laid back, and quiet. They never had any children and had been married since before Brook was born. Aunt Bonnie was also a retired school teacher who taught elementary school, and they were very involved in their church. Uncle Kyle was a Deacon and Aunt Bonnie was a Sunday School Teacher. Aunt Bonnie made the best chess pie. Brook went to open the back door for them.

"Hey, Aunt Bonnie, Uncle Kyle," Brook greeted. Uncle Kyle was carrying the chess pies.

"Hey, baby," Aunt Bonnie greeted, and gave Brook a hug. Uncle Kyle gave her a kiss on the cheek as he walked by to bring the pies in the kitchen.

"Okay, make room for the pies," Brook teased. "And, what's that you're out there talking about taking my man?"

"Oh, he is such a sweetheart. Very nice young man. And, those eyes. Yes, indeed, I'm gonna have me some pretty, brown-eyed great nieces and nephews."

"What is it with you Henderson sisters and trying to get me pregnant," Brook joked. Henderson was their maiden name. "I'm not even married yet. And, I'm not in a rush to have a bunch of babies."

Aunt Bonnie sat down at the table as Uncle Kyle headed back outside with the guys. "What? You're not going to have any babies?" Aunt Bonnie said.

"Of course I will, just not yet. I'm not in a big rush. Maybe in a year or so."

Brook couldn't mention that it was really a taboo subject for them. "I know he wants kids because he loves his twin nieces to death. Let's get me married first is all I'm saying."

"So when is the wedding?" she asked.

"Six months and two weeks," Brook answered with a smile. "We're getting married at the church. In fact, Gio and I are meeting with Reverend Coleman tomorrow afternoon. I'm just hoping we don't have paparazzi problems."

"Paparazzi! Oh yeah, he probably has them hounding him a lot."

Brook told Aunt Bonnie about the episode of them at her job. "You know, they can take pictures or whatever, just not of me. He's the star. I want them to leave me out of it!"

"Well, baby, now you're news, too, because you're marrying him, so you just have to get used to all of that," Aunt Bonnie said.

"I know. I just don't want them coming and messing up the wedding. I'm hoping since it's here, they won't bother. It has gotten worse since he won an Oscar. They're everywhere! I'm surprised they're not here. I think they have a locator embedded in us! They even took pictures of me at the grocery store... the grocery store! Who the heck cares what groceries I buy?"

Brook heard more commotion in the backyard and heard her Aunt Camille, her mom's younger sister, and her cousins Timon, Brieonna, and Kenitra. She grew up with them. Timon was Brandon's age, and she was a year older than Brieonna, and five years older than Kenitra. They used to have a great time when they were kids, trying to hide from Kenitra, who always wanted to follow them everywhere. It was so funny when the animated movie *Lion King* came out and the meerkat's name was Timon. Luckily, he was grown, but they still teased him about it.

"Let me head out to the backyard. I hear Brie and Nitra. Ma, you sure you don't need me to do anything?" Brook asked.

"No, sweetie. In fact, we'll be right out there," she answered.

"Whad'up, cuz," Kenitra yelled with arms outstretched in the air. Kenitra was definitely the ghetto one of the family. It was just something about that younger age group that missed a gene or something. She was over talking to Gio and Brandon. Brieonna just gave a little screech and ran to give her a big hug.

"Let me see that ring, girl," Brie said, and whispered, "Girl, damn, he looks better than he does on television, and I didn't think that could be possible."

Brook just smiled. "You know I want you to be a bridesmaid."

Brieonna gave Brook another big hug. "Cousin, I would be honored. We'll definitely have to catch up. That proposal was beautiful. Girl, Mama was watching the awards show and almost had a heart attack when it happened. Kenitra said she was screaming, 'Oh My God, Oh My God, it's Brook, Oh My God.'" Brieonna laughed. "Nitra came running in the room thinking something bad had happened and there you were, on television, getting proposed to by that fine ass man. I missed it when it happened. Nitra called me but by the time I turned it on, it was over. But, of course I saw it on every show that replayed it, over and over again." She giggled.

"I know when I talked to you on the phone, you sounded like your mama," Brook teased. "Oh my God, Brook, oh my God."

The girls shared a laugh as Kenitra came over. "Yo, cuz, Gio is cool peoples. He's fam now," Kenitra said.

Brieonna just shook her head. Kenitra was only twenty two years old, that crazy age where she was an adult kid, trying to fit into both places.

"What's up, boo," Brook greeted Kenitra with a hug.

"Congrats, cuz. That was mad cool the way he popped that question."

"Yeah, you shoulda been there. I know I showed my tonsils my mouth fell open so wide."

They all laughed.

"Did somebody say Brian was on the grill? That's what I wanna know, is Brian Bridges on the grill?" Brook's Uncle Stefan shouted. Brook loved her Uncle Stephan. He was always the life of the party. He was her dad's younger brother and always reminded her of Jay Anthony Brown, the comedian. Not really in the looks department because her Uncle Stefan was tall and skinny with freckles, it was more of the way he acted. He and her Aunt Sherry were hilarious together.

"Hey, Unc, hey, Aunt Sherry," Brook greeted with hugs. "Let me introduce you to Gio. Hey, babe, this is my crazy Uncle Stefan, my daddy's brother, and my crazier Aunt Sherry."

Gio shook Uncle Stefan's hand and Aunt Sherry gave him a big hug.

"How you doing, baby. Welcome to the family."

"Thank you, Aunt Sherry," Gio answered, causing Aunt Sherry to smile at him for calling her Aunt.

"Is that Damon and Dameon, getting all big?" Brook asked.

Those were Aunt Sherry and Uncle Stephen's grandsons, and they were running around, ready to get into the pool.

"Double Ds, y'all better get over here and give me some love," Brook shouted. They came running over to give Brook hugs. "Where's Andrea?" Brook asked. She was the boys' mother.

"She's at work. She'll be here when she gets off. You know she's a manager at Blockbuster now, so she works a lot," said Aunt Sherry.

"That's great news. I can't wait to see her. I haven't even seen her in probably over a year. The last time we were at your house, she was at work then too. She's getting her hustle on. Good for her," Brook said.

"Yes, she is. I'm just so happy she's settling down into a stable job. You know that girl changed jobs more times since Big D got locked up. So, we try to help as much as possible with the boys. She finally has a job that she likes, so that's a plus."

"I sure wish London could've made it. I miss her so much," Brook said.

"Yeah, me too. But, she and Malik are doing their thing in Florida. We went out to visit them a few months ago. She's settling into that television station that she works for. And Malik is a pharmacist at Publix, the grocery store there," Aunt Sherry said. "She really seems happy."

Hmm, Brook noted. Aunt Sherry said *seems* happy not *was* happy. *Did she see Malik like her dad and Brandon did?* She wondered. His family was really weird. She made a mental note to call London when she got back to Atlanta to check on her. The boys were bugging to get into the pool. They were four and five years old and could swim like little fish. They had gotten lessons when they were babies. Uncle Stefan and Aunt Sherry had a swimming pool at their house, too. They had a huge house, more like a ranch out in Shelbyville, Kentucky on a few acre of land. And, those boys had every toy known to man.

"Let me get these boys in this pool before they drive me crazy. I'll talk to you later, sweetie, and congratulations on your wonderful engagement."

"Thank you, Aunt Sherry. I'm sure Mama told you it was going to be at the church."

"Yes ma'am. The family is so excited. We haven't had a wedding since London and Malik got married. So, we're looking forward to it."

The backyard barbecue was in full effect. The kids were in the pool. Her daddy, Uncle Stefan, Gio, and her cousin, Iman, were playing dominoes, another table had a spades game going, which was where Brandon and his partner in crime were sitting, talking smack. Him and Timon were always partners and talked more mess. Brook and Brieonna swore they cheated. Her mama, Aunt Bonnie, Aunt Sherry, and Debra's mom, Ms. Ava, were all talking about who knows what, but there was a lot of laughter coming from their table. Brook was just getting ready to go call Debra again when she and Glenn finally got there.

"Well, about time," Brook said, going over and giving them a hug.

"We hit a lot of traffic," Debra said.

"There was an accident in Murfreesboro. It was a mess and it took us about two hours to get through it," Glenn said.

"I know y'all are hungry. Debra, go introduce your man around first. There's your mama over there," Brook pointed with a smirk.

Debra sighed. Debra loved her mother, however, they still had an unresolved issue between them. Debra's mom had slept with one of Debra's boyfriends. It was a really bad time for Debra and they hadn't ever quite gotten past it. Debra couldn't believe her mom could do something like that. And, while her mom was really sorry, she didn't understand why Debra was so upset because she didn't really even like the guy. So, Debra never introduced her mom to another boyfriend, and that happened back when they were in college.

"Let's get this over with. I'm starving so you're going to get the quick introduction." Debra laughed.

"Cool. In fact, why don't we just start running and give people five as we run past them and go straight to that food table. I'm starving, too," Glenn joked.

They all laughed, and Debra and Glenn headed for the table with the mamas. Brook headed over to Gio to see how their game was going.

"Hey, boo," Brook greeted and sat next to Gio. Gio grinned and pulled Brook over to give her a forehead kiss.

"Look at 'em. Young love at its best. Hey, Sherry, get on over here and me give me some sugar, woman," Uncle Stefan yelled.

Aunt Sherry just waved him off and finished talking. She was used to his craziness.

"I see Debra and Glenn finally made it," Gio said.

"What! Debra got a man? Man, you'd better run from that girl. She crazy," Uncle Stefan joked.

"Shut up, Stefan, before you make me come over there," Ms. Ava said.

"You hush up, Ava, before I have to sic my wife on you. Handle that, Sherry," Uncle Stefan said.

"Yep, and I'm gonna help her whoop your behind," Aunt Sherry said as they all fell out laughing.

"See, Gio, remember, women always stick together. You gotta watch out for them," Uncle Stefan said.

"I'll do that, Uncle Stefan," Gio agreed and high fived Uncle Stefan and gave Brook a wink.

CHAPTER 50

Everything had gone well at Brook's parents'. They all had a great time and Gio fit right in. He couldn't stop laughing about Uncle Stefan and something crazy he had said, and her dad and he were going golfing the next time they came home. It was time to go to visit Gio's parents and she was nervous. She had never been nervous about meeting anyone's parents before. She just loved Gio so much that she wanted it to go well. They flew into Savannah and were at the car rental counter getting their car when it started. The girl behind the counter saw the proposal and said congratulations. The people in line behind them asked for an autograph and everyone joined in. So, they stood around for another half hour while Gio gave autographs and Brook smiled. She took a couple of pictures for people, declining to be in the pictures, yet happy to snap them. She really had to get over being so uncomfortable about being in the pictures. She didn't sing or act, and she didn't want to steal any of Gio's sunshine, but she knew she'd have to get used to it eventually. She just never understood why they would want a picture of her. She was just Brook. Fly, yes, celebrity, heckie naw!

The drive to Midway, Georgia took about an hour. They pulled up to Gio's parents' house and it looked like the whole town was there. He wasn't kidding when he said it was a small town. They had a lot of land, and Brook loved their home. It reminded her of an old country ranch. Everyone started gathering together when they pulled up. Considering Gio rented another Benz, they knew it was them. Everyone was yelling, hugging, and patting Gio on the back. As they made their way to the house, Gio's parents were standing on the porch and Brook knew instantly that she was going to be okay. His mom had the happiest look on her face. Brook went right up to her and gave her a hug. She hugged Brook and whispered in her ear, "Welcome to the family, sweetie. I'm so glad to finally meet you." Brook almost felt like crying because it was so sincere. Gio's mother was a small woman, barely standing five feet tall with a beautiful chocolate complexion. She was thick, not fat, like she was used to those country meals, and she had the most peaceful face Brook had ever seen. She was one of those people that was a shoo-in for Heaven, like she never did any wrong to anybody. Brook went to shake his dad's hand and he grabbed her in a big bear hug. He was a big man, probably standing six feet or so and around two hundred and fifty pounds. You could tell he liked to laugh because he had laugh lines in his face. Gio said his parents were opposites, his dad was loud and crazy and his mom was really laid back and loved her church. The twins were absolutely adorable. They hung all over Gio while smiling shyly at Brook.

"What did you bring us, Uncle Gio?" Kendyl, the outspoken one, asked.

"Hmmm, did I bring you anything? What do you think, Brook? Did I bring them anything?"

"Of course, you did," Brook said. "And, guess what, I bought you something, too."

The girls squealed, jumping up and down ready for their gifts. Brook had gotten them the cutest earring and necklace set. The necklace spelled their name with a little tiara above it. The earrings were little dangling tiaras. To top it off, she found cute little pink purses that said princess, so she used that as the gift bag.

"I'll tell you what. We'll give you your gifts later after everyone goes home because we didn't bring anything for the other kids, and it wouldn't be fair for us to give you gifts and not everyone else."

"But, you're not their uncle," said Kennedy, the rational one.

"I know, but I'm their big cousin, and it wouldn't be nice. Look at Aliya over there. Do you want her to be sad because I didn't bring her a gift?

"No, sir," the girls said sadly.

So, we'll do it later, okay," Gio said with finality, giving the girls hugs.

"Okay, Uncle Gio," the girls answered.

"Don't worry," Brook said with a wink, "it's going to be worth the wait." That got smiles out of them as they skipped off.

Brook met so many people she couldn't get the names straight. She remembered his two sisters, Natalie and Monica, their husbands, Donald and Michael, and his younger brother, Patrick. That was about it. There were about five generations of family there, and they had a great time. There were games for the kids and a moonwalk, and of course dominoes and spades, some bid whist, and horseshoes. There was so much food. Brook didn't think she would ever be hungry again. She saw what they meant by country cooking. Gio's family was definitely down to earth, and they welcomed her right in. But, Gio's mom was special, she truly felt love from the woman, she just had an aura about her. Brook found herself drawn to her.

"Ms. Gabrielle, you have to give me that recipe for your sweet potato casserole. That was delicious," Brook said to Gio's mom.

"Of course I will, sweetie. I'm glad you enjoyed it," Ms. Gabrielle said.

"I've enjoyed everything. Everyone is so warm and welcoming," Brook said.

"That's because Gio has never brought anyone home. And not only is he bringing you home, he's bringing you home as his fiancée, which says a lot. Gio is very selective and we thought he'd never settle down. I knew you had to be special for my son to propose, especially on television." Ms. Gabrielle laughed.

"No one was more surprised than I was." Brook laughed, too.

"So tomorrow, we'll have time to ourselves and you can tell me all about your plans. Gio only told me it would be at your church in Kentucky, so you'll have to fill me in on the rest."

"That sounds like a plan to me. And any input you have, please feel free to let me know. This is your son getting married, too."

"Whatever you decide is fine with me. You tell me when, where, and what you need me to do and it's done. Now, I know it's old fashioned, but we're from the south and still do things the old fashioned way, so we'd be honored to host the rehearsal dinner. Just let me know where and we want to take care of it. We know Gio can afford it, but it's the groom's parents' responsibility to take care of the rehearsal dinner."

Brook smiled and told her it would be no problem at all. There was absolutely no way Brook could tell the woman no.

CHAPTER 51

Things were going smoothly with the wedding plans, Debra was helping out a lot, and it was wonderful living with Gio. Brook was a few blocks away from work when her phone rang and she saw it was Gio. Totally confused, Brook answered the phone. He was in a deep sleep when she had left about a half hour prior.

"Hey, babe, what in the world are you doing awake?" Brook answered.

"Baby, I need you to come home. We have a small problem. Don't even go to work, just come back home," Gio said.

Brook's heart dropped. "Oh my gosh! Is it my parents? Your parents? What's wrong?" Brook asked nervously.

"Everyone is fine, babe. But, there's been a leak. They found out about the abortion," Gio said.

Brook was totally confused for about five seconds because she had pushed it so far back in her memory. When it dawned on her what he was talking about, her heart sank. "What do you mean they found out? Who found out?" Brook questioned sadly.

"The tabloids, babe, I'm so sorry. Jamar just called me. I'm sure the paparazzi are at the radio station. I didn't want you to be ambushed. Just come back home and we'll figure this out," Gio said calmly.

Brook just said softly, "I'm on my way," and hung up.

She rode past her job to see if there were any paparazzi out there and sure enough, they were. Brook felt like she was going to throw up. Her stomach was doing flip flops. Gio's voice just kept going through her head, 'they found out'. Would her parents read about it? What about his parents? Tears flowed down Brooks face. She picked up the phone and called her best friend. She needed her right now.

"Whaddup, boo," Debra answered happily.

"They found out," was all Brook could say.

"Huh, who found out and what did they find out?" Debra said, totally confused.

"The tabloids, they found out about the abortion," Brook wailed.

There was total silence on the phone. "Oh shit! Are you okay? How do you know they found out? Where are you?"

"Gio just called me. His manager, Jamar, called and told him. Girl, what am I going to do? Everyone's gonna know. My parents, his parents, everybody," Brook cried.

"You're going to get through this. Don't worry. I'll meet you at the house," Debra said.

"But you have to get to work."

"My girl needs me and that's the most important thing. We're going to get through this, you'll see. Just hang in there, boo."

"Okay," Brook sniffled and hung up the phone. Brook called her sales manager and left a message on his voice mail that she wouldn't be in and left it at that.

Brook rode past the paparazzi as she turned into their subdivision, glad that the gates kept them out. As she got to the house, she saw there were a lot of cars in their driveway. She walked in the house and followed the voices.

They were all there, Jamar, and Randy, and a few other people. They all stopped talking and looked at her when she walked in the room. Tha Dogg smiled at her, but looked like he was ready to go kill somebody. Gio jumped up and came over to her.

"Excuse me, fellas," he said as they left the room and went to their bedroom.

As soon as Gio shut the door, Brook broke down. She cried harder than she had ever cried in her life. All the hurt feelings of guilt that she had buried resurfaced and she cried from the bottom of her heart. Gio held her and rubbed her back, telling her it would be okay while tears slowly rolled down his face. He hated to see her in pain, and her wailing was cutting him deep. He blamed himself for her getting the abortion. Brook cried until she had no more tears. She just kept doing the hiccup breaths like she did when she was a kid and her cat, Mittens, had gotten hit by a car and died.

"Babe, we're going to get through this. It will blow over. There will be some other tragedy they can focus on," Gio said.

"But my parents, your parents, our family and friends, they're all gonna know," Brook wailed and started crying again. "Your mom loved me. I felt it. What is she going to think about me now? And, my daddy! Oh my gosh, my daddy! My mom will be understanding, hurt, but understanding. I don't know how my dad is going to react," Brook cried.

"Sweetheart, we are grown. Yes, we want to please our parents, but ultimately, we have to do what is best for us. My mom is not a judgmental person. She won't have much to say at all and will quiet anyone who does. So, put my parents right out of your head," Gio said reasonably. "I'll talk to my parents and your parents, too, but really, those are the only people whose opinion really matter." Brook and Gio held each other.

"I know, babe. You're right. We'll get through this, together. Let me go wash my face," Brook said and headed to the bathroom.

Gio and Brook headed down to the basement where everyone was sitting around talking about everything but what was going on. Debra jumped up and came over and gave her a hug.

"We're going to get through this, boo," she said, eyes red from crying. Brook just nodded her head. The lump was back in her throat. She loved her girl. That was how close they were. If Brook was going through something, Debra was, too. "The little fuckers are all out front. I started to give them the finger as I drove in, but I figured that wouldn't help anything," Debra said, totally pissed.

For the first time since that morning, Brook laughed. She could see her girl flipping them the bird as she flew past them.

"So, I'm thinking we'll just ignore this and it will blow over. Brook, this is the best thing to do, just ignore it," Jamar said.

Brook simply nodded her head, hoping they were right. "How did they even find out?" Brook asked no one in particular.

"That would be easy, Brook. Someone at the clinic may have recognized you and called it in. Unfortunately, it's easy enough to get private documents," Jamar said.

"What are you going to do about work? Are you going to be okay with going?" Debra asked.

Brook got wide eyed, clearly not thinking of all the repercussions of it going public.

"I think I'll take some time off," Brook said, looking at Gio. He came over to her and rubbed her back.

"Of course you should take some time off. You don't ever have to go back if you don't want to. Just think it over," Gio said.

Brook simply nodded again. Words seemed to be leaving her. "Debra, go to work. You don't have to stay. I'm going to call my parents and prepare them and then I think I'll take a nap," Brook said. She felt totally drained.

"Girl, I ain't going *no* damn where. I'm straight. You go call your parents and I'll make you some coffee. Are you hungry? I'll make breakfast. And, before you answer that, hungry or not, you need to eat," Debra said with finality. "You guys hungry? We'll all feel better with a full stomach. Now, I'll be right back. I'm going to run to the grocery and pick up some stuff. You all handle your business and help get my girl through this," Debra said.

"Debra, there is plenty of food in there. You don't need to go to the grocery. Brook shops in bulk," Gio joked, getting a small smile out of Brook.

"Well, I'm going to the room to call the station and then my parents. I'll see you all in a few," Brook said and headed to their bedroom, her head hung low.

Her job was the easier of the two, so she called Jeremy. "Jeremy," he answered.

"Hey, Jer. It's Brook."

"Hey, Brook. Are you okay? I got your message."

"Well, Jeremy, things aren't okay. I'm having some personal problems that are going to require me to take some time off work. It shouldn't be longer than two weeks, and I'm really sorry. Come tomorrow, you'll understand why I have to take time off."

"Are you okay? Is there anything I can do? I saw the paparazzi out front again," Jeremy said, concerned.

"Just don't judge me, okay. I'll give you a call in a week or so. I'm sorry to dump on you like this," Brook sniffled, near tears again.

"Don't worry about it. You just get you together. Your job will be here."

"Thanks for being so understanding, Jeremy. Talk to you soon," Brook said and hung up. Brook headed to the kitchen that had started to smell delicious.

"You done, already?" Debra asked when Brook came in.

"No, I just talked with Jeremy, and he was completely, understanding. I figured I'd need a cup of coffee before I call home," Brook said as she headed over to make a cup. "You need some help?"

"Girl, boo. Stop trying to put it off and go call your parents. It's not going to be as bad as you think. You'll see."

Brook just nodded and headed to the bedroom with her mug of coffee. She took a couple of deep breaths before she picked up the phone and called the number that was instilled in her heart, the first phone number she had learned as a child.

Her mom answered, sounding chipper that early in the morning. "Hey, Ma," Brook said.

"Hey, daughter, I wondered who in the world was calling me this early. Your daddy and I are sitting here having breakfast looking over some brochures for Costa Rica. How's your morning going?" Brook's mom asked.

"Not too good, Ma," Brook said and burst into tears.

"Sweetie, what's wrong? Brook, is it Gio, is he okay?" Brook's mom asked. Brook heard her mom say to her dad, "It's Brook, she crying and upset." Brook gathered her composure. She had to get through this and the faster she could get it out, the faster it would be over with.

"Mommy, I need you and daddy to go to the speaker phone so I can talk to you both at the same time."

She could hear her mom repeating it to her dad as they headed to their bedroom where they had a speaker phone. Her mom knew something was wrong, because Brook only reverted to calling her Mommy when she was really upset.

"Hey, pumpkin, we're here. And no matter what, you will get through this," her dad said.

Brook started crying again. Her parents offered consoling words, thinking that maybe Brook and Gio must have broken up. "What I'm going to tell you is probably the hardest thing I'll ever have to tell you in my life. I am so sorry. I never wanted to disappoint you two. And, I'm so sorry I'm bringing shame to you. You don't deserve this," Brook said tearfully.

At that point, her parents were looking at each other, totally confused. "Baby, we are very proud of you. And, there is nothing in this world that you can do to disappoint us. You've been a wonderful daughter," Brook's mom said.

"Well, you may want to hold off on all that praise. There's a problem." Brook slowly and clearly said, "When Gio and I were together for only a few months, we had a slip up and I got pregnant. We then had a falling out and I got an abortion. The paparazzi found out about it and it will be all over the news tomorrow." She said it slowly and clearly because she didn't want to have to repeat anything. There was total silence on the phone. "I'm so sorry. I know you're so ashamed of me. I'm sorry for causing you this embarrassment," Brook said, crying.

"Oh, baby, I'm so sorry. I'm sorry you had to go through that alone. Of course we're not disappointed in you. You did what you felt you had to do. You get that right out of your head. I just wish I was there for you when you were going through your time. Do you need us to come out there? We can be on the next flight," Brook's mom said. Brook just wept softly.

"Babygirl, you are a grown woman and we respect whatever decisions you felt you had to make. We will not judge you because we love you unconditionally," her dad said.

"You don't know how much this means to me. This has been my biggest worry. I'm so glad you don't hate me," Brook said again, and started right back crying. Her parents were giving her words of encouragement while offering her their love and support. "With all of this love surrounding me, we'll get through this. And don't worry about coming here. You know Debra is here, ready to beat up the paparazzi," Brook said. That got a chuckle out of her parents. "And, Gio is being very supportive. His manager has decided that we'll just ignore it because it will blow over. I just hope it will blow over fast. I took off work for a couple of weeks because the paparazzi are there ready to pounce. So, I'm just going to lay low. Heck, if it gets too crazy, I may come home for a few days," Brook said.

"Whenever you want, you come on home. I wish the paparazzi would come to my house," said Brook's dad, ready to do damage to the people who hurt his princess.

"Now, Brian, don't go threatening to beat up anybody. That will only land you in jail," said Brook's mom reasonably.

"Not if somebody is on my property. So, just let us know if you need a break and want to get away from the craziness. We'll be here," her dad said.

"Thank you for being such great parents. I love you two so much," Brook said, getting teary again.

"We love you, too," they said.

Brook washed her face again and lay across the bed. She felt like she deserved what was happening to her because she believed when she had gotten the abortion that it was a sin. She had taken the easy way out and now these were the consequences. She dozed off and had a horrible nightmare. The paparazzi had her surrounded and were screaming questions at her while flashbulbs flashed in her face. She kept calling for Gio, but he wasn't there, he was gone to make a movie. Then, they pushed a baby in the circle with her. The baby was a newborn, yet was walking, face angry, flashing flashbulbs in Brook's face. Brook awoke with a start. She had been asleep for two hours. She went and washed her face again and reapplied her makeup. Her eyes were puffy. She went out looking to see where Gio and Debra were.

The guys were playing pool. Gio came over and gave her a hug and asked how she was feeling. She told him she felt better, asked where Debra was and was told she was in the theater. Brook headed in and saw Debra lay back watching their favorite love story, *Love & Basketball.*

"Hey, boo," Brook greeted.

Debra popped up. "Hey, sleepyhead, did you get a nice nap?" she asked.

"Not really. Had the worst nightmare that I don't even want to remember," Brook answered.

"You hungry? I can warm you up some breakfast. There's plenty left. I thought those negroes had a real appetite. Girl, they barely scratched the surface."

"Or, it could be that you still cook when you're upset, like I do, and you fixed enough to feed the whole neighborhood," Brook joked.

"Oh, you got jokes, huh? You must be feeling better. How'd it go with your parents?"

"Totally awesome! Girl, my parents are a blessing. Not only were they not judgmental, they offered to come here to help me through this and Daddy wants to fight the paparazzi!"

Debra burst out laughing. "Girl, Mr. Brian is no joke. Don't mess with his baby girl," Debra teased.

"They were very understanding. I hope this doesn't turn out bad for them with their friends and at church."

"Your parents are tough, so don't sweat it. Did Gio call his parents yet?"

"I'm not sure. I didn't ask him, just asked where you were," Brook answered.

"Remember the first time we saw this movie? We were so in love with Omar Epps," Brook said, thinking of easier times.

"Then we went back with Shandrea to see it again. I remember I looked at my ticket stub and it said another movie. I didn't know any better at the time. I just thought they were out of tickets for *Love & Basketball*. I know now it's how they count how many people go to see a movie. They definitely got over on that movie. They did the same thing with *Set It Off*. Everyone we knew saw that movie at least twice, but you won't be able to tell by the ticket sales. I'm so glad Tyler Perry hip'd us to that."

Silence came upon them as they watched Omar Epps and Sanaa Latham play strip basketball. They sat back, relaxed and watched the movie for probably the tenth time.

Brook and Gio lay in bed talking about the day and what to expect for the next day. "You know, this just reminds me that I was the worse jerk that I've ever been in my life. I've never let this life get to me or change who I am. Never! And, look what happens when I do. I am so sorry, baby. This is all, my fault! If I wasn't an ass, we wouldn't be going through this right now," he said.

"Don't even go there. I didn't have to do what I did, either. We can play the blame game all night long and it's not going to change anything. This happened, period. God forgives me, you forgive me, and our parents forgive me. That is all that matters. We just have to see how bad it will get. Like Jamar said, if we ignore it, it will go away. They'll pounce on someone else's misery," she reasoned.

"You're right. We don't even know if anyone else will see it. It will probably only run in a rag or two. And, you know my moms wants to talk to you," he said.

"I know. I'll call her tomorrow. I know you said she understands, but I'm still so ashamed," she confessed.

"My moms' is the fairest woman I know. She said that what happened between us was between us and it's no one's business. That's all she wants to tell you," he said.

"I'll call her tomorrow, I promise."

"I've been meaning to ask you something," Gio said.

"Hmm," she answered, getting comfortable.

"I was thinking that maybe you don't want to go back to work."

"Huh? Not go back to work. You mean ever?"

"Yeah, I mean, you already took off for two weeks because of this craziness. There will be times when they're gonna hound you and make it difficult for you to work, and you don't even have to go through that hassle. Babe, I can afford to take care of you. You know you don't have to work," he reasoned.

"I'm not the take care of kind of girl. I'm used to being independent. What in the world would I do, be a housewife?"

"You can do whatever you want to do. Haven't you ever wanted to own your own business?"

That got her attention. For the first time since they started the 'quit work' conversation, she felt a spark of interest. "But, babe, I just don't know. Let me think on it. I understand we're getting ready to get married, but I'm not trying to be totally dependent like that."

"And, you won't be if you start your own business. Maybe you can find us some more rental property. Then, the money you make from the rental property can be your spending money. Just think about it. Whatever you decide is fine by me. I just want to make you happy."

"Okay, babe, I'll think about it. I have the next two weeks to think about it."

"Well, that brings me to the next thing, your bills. I need you to give my accountant, Joseph, your statements and such so he can start paying them," Gio said matter of factly.

"Huh? Why does he need to pay my bills for me?"

"So he can pay them when he pays the rest of the bills. It makes no sense for you to pay them. I promise you, I can afford it." He chuckled.

"I can afford it, too," Brook said defensively.

"Brook, you have to understand that I make a lot more money than you. I'm asking you to quit your job, of course I'm going to make sure your bills are paid. You're over thinking this. It is not that serious! Do you actually think as my wife you'll be paying your own bills when I probably make more than ten times what you make?" he asked incredulously.

Brook really hadn't thought about it at all. She knew she was overreacting, but there was just too much going on for her at that moment. And, she knew she should be happy he even wanted to pay her bills. It was taking time for her to go from the independent woman she was used to being to moving in and quitting her job and getting her bills paid.

"I know, babe. I'm trippin'. You just have to be patient with me. I know it sounds crazy, but it took twenty-seven years to develop into me, it's gonna take a minute for me to bring it down a notch or two."

"Babe, you definitely are a needle in a haystack," Gio laughed, pulling her closer as they dozed off to sleep.

CHAPTER 52

It was bad, worse than they thought. Evidently, no one else had any other drama going on in their life because every rag, newspaper, and entertainment show talked about it. She finally turned off her phone because it kept ringing. There she was, on the front cover of the *Inquisitive* with a frown on her face. *When in the world did they take a picture of me with a frown*, she wondered. And, she was looking especially frumpy. *Gio Lay's New Fiancée Aborted His Child* the headline screamed. The next one, *The Exclusive, We're Breaking The News to Gio Lay. He Didn't Know Fiancée Was Pregnant, Wedding Plans Are Off!* And, another screamed that she had been pregnant by Gio's best friend. She didn't even watch the shows on television and didn't want to see any more articles. Jamar thought it best to see what everyone was saying. She called her parents to make sure they were okay and they said they weren't even reading any of it, but everyone had been calling. She talked with Gio's mom, who was really understanding, made her feel a lot better. She told Brook that there were times in everyone's life that they made decisions for themselves. And when they did, then it meant it was no one else's business, so to hold her head up. Brook really did love that woman. She spoke with Debra briefly, who told her she was just a phone call away.

Brook spent most of the day in the theater watching her favorite movies. She watched everything from *Daddy's Little Girls* to all four Terminator movies, which she loved. Gio was talking with a little bit of everybody who came by the house for damage control. Brook felt uncomfortable being around them, she felt like they were blaming her for hurting Gio's career. Heck, she blamed herself. She couldn't wait for the day to be over and went to bed early, taking a Tylenol PM to get to sleep. She didn't even feel Gio when he got in bed.

The next few days, Brook hardly ate and didn't want to be bothered with anyone. She only came out to fix her a light snack. Every night, she turned in early, taking a Tylenol PM to help her sleep. It had been almost a week and the stories weren't going away. She was losing weight and had dark circles under her eyes. Brook knew she needed to get away. She didn't like the fact that every night she was taking something to help her sleep, and, she hardly ever even talked to Gio. They hadn't even made love since the story came out. It was affecting her too deeply. She told Gio she was going home for a few days and he agreed. Brook figured he wanted her to go away because of all the problems she was causing. She was falling into a bad depression. She called her parents to let them know she was driving home for a few days. Her mom told her they would be waiting for her, which made her feel better.

"Gio, I'm really sorry about all of this. I know you all have to do a lot of damage control," Brook said sadly.

"Babe, this is not your fault. Will you quit blaming yourself? That's why I think it's a great idea for you to go home and see your parents. You need a break from all of this. I tried to give you your space because I thought you needed space, but don't go reading anything into it. Just have a safe trip and enjoy being with your parents. And quit worrying, this will blow over," he said. "I love you, baby. You just finish planning our wedding, okay?" Gio said.

Brook kissed him softly on the lips and got in the car, thinking about running over some of those meddling paparazzi.

Gio was pissed. He was ready to do damage to somebody, so went in his gym and hit the gym bag. He hated to see Brook cry. It tore at his heart. And, it was all his fault. Had he not been so damn full of himself, she never would have had to get the abortion. It was all thrown back in his face. And, now everyone knew she had an abortion and they were crucifying her for it. He wanted to shield her from it all. She hardly ever smiled, she was losing weight, and he knew she was taking something at night to sleep. When he came to bed, she was knocked out. And, she didn't even want to make love anymore.

So, when she said she wanted to go home for a few days, he gladly agreed. He knew being with her parents would be just what she needed. She came from a close-knit family and family is what would build her back up because he couldn't seem to do it. All she felt she got from him was blame, and he wasn't blaming her at all. But, she wasn't hearing that, only looked at him with sad eyes. Damn, he was such a fool! But, he couldn't continue with the woulda, coulda, shoulda scenario, he just had to roll with the punches and be strong for Brook. It would blow over eventually. He just hoped he still had a woman and a career when it did.

CHAPTER 53

Being home was just what the doctor ordered, and Brook began to heal immediately. No one knew she was in town, not even her brother. She had spoken to him briefly after the story broke and apologized for any turmoil her actions caused him. He told her to forget about it and to know he had her back, always.

Her mom gave her that mother's love that she needed to get through it, and her daddy was her strength. She talked to Gio a couple of times a day. She told him she was going to stay a few more days and then she'd be home, and he told her to take her time and that he missed her terribly. She had not picked up a paper or looked at television except for *Wheel of Fortune*. And, the good news was she didn't need anything to help her sleep. She helped her mom redecorate one of the guest bedrooms. They painted the walls and changed the curtains and bedding. It was nice to do something normal. Brook told her mom about Gio asking her if she wanted to invest in rental properties. Her mom thought it was a great idea.

"Baby, there is nothing like owning your own. Gio is right. You already have two properties, why not get more? Do you really love your job that much that you'd consider passing up being an entrepreneur?" her mom asked.

"I like my job well enough, although not as much as when I first started. My sales have tripled, but that's mainly because of Gio. Everybody wants me to have Gio do something for them and I politely decline, but it was starting to bother me. It's gotten so weird since we got engaged. I feel like it's not my skills that is selling, but the fact that I'm Gio's fiancée. I've really been thinking about what he said, and I've been looking at properties online in Atlanta as well. The good, yet sad part is, this really is a great time to invest in property. People's homes are foreclosing left and right and you can buy them dirt cheap. Debra said that I should consider renting as Section 8 housing."

"What! Section 8 housing! And have them tear up your property! Not a good idea," Brook's mom said.

"Ma, everyone on Section 8 won't tear up your property. Those are the people that won't tear up your property. Secondly, Section 8 screens them, and covers all kinds of costs if anything does happen to your property. I'm going to look into it more."

"Well, it sounds like you've made up your mind about the real estate thing," Brook's mom said with a chuckle.

"Hmm, I think you're right," Brook answered with her own chuckle.

Brook stayed at her parents' for almost two weeks and knew it was time to go home. She missed Gio badly! She hugged her parents goodbye and headed on back down the road. She played her CDs and sang loudly, feeling better than she had since the news broke. She was going to talk to Gio about the real estate thing and planned on calling Jeremy and letting him know she wasn't returning. Brook was feeling optimistic for the first time in over two weeks. She called Debra to let her know she was on her way home.

"Whatsup, girlie. I'm on my way back, I know you missed me," Brook greeted when Debra answered the phone.

"Well, about damn time," Debra said. "Are you on the road now? I'll come over after I get off work."

"Yeah, I left out about two hours ago, and you come over tomorrow. I gotta get some quality time in with my man." Brook laughed.

"You ain't *never* lied! Well, if you need me, you call me. I don't care what time it is," Debra said.

"Woooow, you really did miss me. I was only gone a week or so," Brook teased.

"Whateva, heiffa. Just know that if you need me, I'm here."

Brook saw that the paparazzi were still in front of their subdivision, and she couldn't believe it. She thought for sure this would be over by now. In fact, she wasn't even sweating coming back because she just knew they would be onto something else. She hated to think it but hoped it was someone else's misery they were exploiting. Brook had been sheltered for the past two weeks. She hadn't looked at the newspaper or pretty much any television, so since she hadn't seen anything, she assumed no one else had either. Gio greeted her at the door with a big hug, picking her up and spinning her around. Brook squealed.

"Hey, babe, I missed you," he said.

"I missed you, too," Brook said giving him a big kiss. "I can't believe the paparazzi are still here. I haven't looked at a paper or at television since I've been gone, well, with the exception of *Wheel of Fortune*," Brook said. "Is that still for us?"

"Yeah, they're still hounding us," Gio said. Brook noticed he looked tired.

"Are you okay?" she asked.

"Yes, I'm fine now that you're home. I've gotten too used to sleeping with you so I haven't been sleeping well," he answered. But, Brook knew something wasn't right.

"Let me go tell the guys hello," she said as they walked to the basement. Brook went in and they all got silent. That's when Brook knew something was definitely up.

"Hello, fellas," she greeted.

"Hey, Brook," everyone greeted back.

"What's going on?" she asked. She thought about Debra telling her to call if she needed her and knew something wasn't quite right.

They all looked at Gio. "Uhh, nothing much, just getting ready to shoot some pool," Tha Dogg said while Gio was saying they were just chilling. Brook held up her hand and everyone just stopped with the excuses. She turned and looked at Gio.

"What is going on?" she asked.

"Nothing for you to worry about," he said.

"Just tell her the truth, Gio," Jamar said.

"Just shut up, Jamar," Gio said angrily.

Brook looked at Jamar and said, "You tell me the truth, Jamar. Keep it 100! I'm a big girl, I can handle it."

Gio cleared his throat. "Babe, I just don't want you to worry. This thing is just lingering on longer than we thought, that's all."

"I know I've been gone almost two weeks and I have not picked up a paper or looked at television, and I don't know what's going on. So, will someone please enlighten me?" Brook said, getting agitated.

"They're now blaming Gio. They're saying he made you get an abortion because kids would mess up his career and that is the only reason he asked you to marry him," Jamar blurted.

Brook's eyes got huge. She never thought they'd blame Gio. It hurt her when they blamed her and called her all kinds of names, but she hadn't expected them to turn on him. She didn't care what they said about her, but this was his career and he couldn't afford that kind of press.

"Who's saying this?" she asked, getting upset.

"Everybody! The tides have turned. They even canceled his appearance at the American Music Awards," Jamar said.

"That's enough, Jamar," Gio said sharply. He didn't want Brook to have a setback and start worrying again. His job was to protect her.

"What? No! Unt uh! I am not going to allow that to happen," Brook said while shaking her head. "This was my decision, not Gio's. He didn't even know I did it. I want to talk to someone," Brook said firmly, arms folded.

"Now, babe, there is no need for you to do that. They will just try to upset you. We just have to wait this thing out," Gio said.

"I think she's right, Gio," Jamar said. "But we need it to be someone that is going to reach the masses, a one shot thing." Jamar snapped his finger and said one word... "Oprah."

The room got silent as everyone digested what he said.

"Yeah, right! Like Oprah is going to have us on her show," Brook said.

"Oh, you really haven't been reading any papers lately. It's everywhere. This is perfect. Oprah will hear you out and let you explain what happened. You can tell your story once and be done with it," Jamar said.

"Set it up," Brook said.

"Babe...," Gio started, but Brook stopped him.

"Gio, I'm going to do whatever I can to make this right. And, if that means being on Oprah to tell our story, then so be it. I am not going to sit back and let this affect you negatively. I don't give a damn what they say about me, but you, they're your fans and this is your career you've worked too hard to build. It's settled. If Oprah will have us, then that's what we'll do," Brook said and walked out of the room with determination. She wasn't feeling sad anymore, she was pissed.

CHAPTER 54

It only took a week for them to appear on Oprah. Oprah cleared someone off and they were in, so one week to the day that she got back from visiting her parents, they were in Chicago getting ready to appear on the *Oprah Winfrey Show*, and Brook was nervous. She and Gio had talked about what they would say and decided to just be honest. That was the only way to get it all out and over with and for nothing to come back and bite them in the butt. They got an itinerary of how the show would go. First, they would talk about how they met and their engagement, then they'd talk about what led up to the abortion.

"You okay?" Gio asked her for the tenth time.

"Not if you keep asking me that," Brook said with a laugh.

"We're ready for you on the set," the man in the headphones said to them. Brook took a deep breath as they followed the man.

"We need to wait here until Oprah introduces you," he said.

She heard them countdown coming back from the commercial and then she heard Oprah.

"You've seen all the tabloids about Giovanni Lay and his beautiful fiancée, Brooklyn Bridges. You've heard the stories. Well, we have them here today to set the record straight. Giovanni Lay and Brooklyn Bridges, come on out."

Gio and Brook walked to the sofa on stage that headphone man told them they'd be sitting on. Gio wanted her to sit at the end closest to Oprah, but she moved to the side so he could sit there. They both shook her hand.

"So, you two have been put through the ringer," Oprah started. They both nodded.

"You are absolutely right about that," Gio said.

"Why don't we start at the beginning? How did the two of you meet?" Gio ran down how they met at her event back home and how they ran into each other in Atlanta. They hung out and ended up falling in love. "Was it that easy?" Oprah asked Brook.

"No, it wasn't. In my mind, I was always conscious of not being a groupie. I always held back because I didn't want him to think I was trying to be with Gio the star. So, I was always thinking too hard in the beginning," Brook confessed.

"I knew she was special. We just clicked. And, we also have something else in common," Gio said.

"Really, what's that?" Oprah asked. The audience was listening closely, ready to hear some juicy gossip.

"We both love *Wheel of Fortune.*" Gio laughed, and Brook laughed as well.

"*Wheel of Fortune*! I didn't even know Black folks watched that game show," Oprah joked.

"Not only do we watch it, we have the home version and play it all the time. We're very competitive," Gio chuckled.

"That is funny. So who wins the most?" Oprah asked, and both of them answered, "Me," causing everyone to laugh. And, then Oprah got serious. "So when did you find out you were pregnant? Did you all not use protection?" she asked.

"Yes, we always used protection, except for one time. We got a little carried away and didn't use a condom. I assumed she was on the pill, so I really wasn't worried about it," Gio answered.

"But, I wasn't on the pill. The condom *was* my form of birth control because I didn't believe in having unprotected sex. It's too dangerous. So, when it happened, I was more concerned with getting checked than getting pregnant," Brook said.

"Hey!" Gio said with a chuckle.

"Not that I really thought you were carrying a disease or anything like that, but we had always used condoms, and we had not established what our relationship was. We had never even said we were exclusive."

"And, the even crazier part is for round two, she made me use a condom," Gio said.

"Wow, round two, huh?" Oprah joked as the audience roared with laughter and Brook blushed. She gave Gio a little nudge with her elbow. "When we come back, Brook will tell us what happened from that point on. We'll be right back," Oprah said.

You two switch seats. I noticed you wanted Gio to sit here. You're okay sitting next to me, aren't you?" Oprah teased.

"No problem. It's just that he's the star and he should sit next to you, not me," Brook explained.

"Wow, a woman who isn't trying to steal her man's star, she *is* a keeper," Oprah told Gio. Gio smiled the biggest smile. Brook took a sip of water as they counted down out of the break. "We're back with Giovanni Lay and Brooklyn Bridges. You all remember Gio proposed to Brooklyn as he accepted his Oscar award." A few clips showed Gio excitedly proposing. Then the headlines went from good to horrible.

Brook had looked online to see what they were saying about Gio after she had gotten back from her parents' to catch up on what was being said. It was ugly, real ugly. They went from loving poor Gio and calling her a conniving bitch, to absolutely hating him. Brook shook her head.

"What happened, Brook?" Oprah asked solemnly.

"Well, sure enough, a few weeks after our slip up, I didn't get my monthly visitor," Brook started.

"Aunt Flo," Gio said proudly, happy he got the name right and causing Oprah and the audience to laugh.

"Of course, I was really upset when I found out I was pregnant," Brook continued. "Sure, I was a grown woman, but I still believed in getting married before having children. My parents have been married for thirty-five years and are still in love. So, that's what I hoped to have when I got pregnant. After denial and about ten pregnancy tests, I realized I may really be pregnant and went to my doctor to confirm it. Gio was away filming so I had to tell him on the phone. He was very supportive and said he'd be there for me. I had only told my best friend, Debra, and was still a little nervous about telling my parents. And then, Gio got back from filming and everything had changed."

Brook took another sip of water and Gio said, "I turned into a first class jerk," he confessed.

"I knew things had changed because he was calling less and less. When he got back, he called me after he had already been home most of the day, which was definitely different. I knew something was up, so I went over to see him and things got ugly," Brook said.

"I accused her of trying to trap me," Gio said and hung his head. The audience gasped.

"He even said he didn't know if he was the father," Brook said sadly. The audience gasped again.

Oprah took that moment to announce another commercial break. Brook could hear everyone whispering in the audience. Brook and Gio both drank water, their throats becoming very dry.

"We're almost through the rough part, you're doing fine," Oprah said understandingly.

In no time, they were back from break and Brook had to tell the hardest story of her life.

"He's right. He accused me of trying to trap him by getting pregnant. Now, that is pretty much the worse thing someone can say to me. I've always been an independent woman. I've worked since high school. I make decent money, maybe not as much as he does, but I do okay. I own my own home, actually two homes, and have a nice little portfolio. I pride myself on not being that type of woman. So, for him to say that stung deeply. And then to say he didn't even know if he was the father, like I was some type of groupie, that was unforgivable," Brook said, beginning to tear up. Gio rubbed her back, sadness written all over his face. "I left out of there that night with two things on my mind, and that was that I never wanted to see him again and I no longer wanted to have his baby," Brook said.

"And me in my crazy guy-thinking mind, I thought she'd cool off, and when I decided to call her, she'd come running back. Man, was I in for a surprise. I didn't hear from her again... period!" The audience started clapping. Gio just nodded his head in agreement, "I know. I deserved it. She didn't answer or return my calls. I called her at work and she wouldn't accept my calls. So I just figured, she'd eventually have to call me. She was carrying my child, even though I stupidly told her I didn't know if it was mine. That was anger talking."

"…Except he didn't know that I went and terminated the pregnancy the very next weekend after we fell out. And then, I just laid low and buried myself in work. I didn't even see Gio until almost two months later when we ran into each other at a party."

"And when I saw her, I knew instantly that I loved her, I missed her and I had to get her back in my life. I noticed she still wasn't showing, but I just thought she was one of those women who showed later in her pregnancy. I had no idea that she wasn't pregnant," Gio said.

"He *didn't* know!" Brook confirmed. "And that's why I'm here today spilling out all of my business. People are accusing him of all types of things and it's simply not true. I did what I felt I needed to do at the time. Do I feel guilty? Of course! But, you know what, God forgave me, so I forgave me. And, Gio forgave me. My parents and his parents forgave me. So, I'm going to be okay, but I cannot allow all of these lies about Gio to keep happening. He had nothing to do with it. We had an argument, and yes, he was a jerk. That was his sin, he was a jerk. I decided to end the pregnancy. He found out almost two months later and he was totally surprised," Brook said.

"The fact that she wasn't pregnant anymore hadn't even crossed my mind. I just assumed she'd get over our argument and we'd be back together. I've since learned that is not how Brooklyn Bridges rolls. She's my needle in a haystack, and I have to give respect if I want respect. And, I respect this woman," Gio said.

The audience 'ahhhed' and clapped.

"So did your parents know about it beforehand?" Oprah asked.

"No. No one did, with the exception of my best friend, Gio's manager, and Tha Dogg, Gio's body guard," Brook said.

"Okay, so you run into each other at a party. How did you get from there to a proposal at the Oscars?" Oprah asked.

"Gio cornered me at the party and told me I didn't look pregnant and I told him I wasn't. I left him standing right there, totally in shock. I left the party and Gio came to my house later that night, roaring drunk," Brook said.

"Yeah, I was drunk and I embarrassed myself," Gio said bashfully.

"Of course, I couldn't talk to him like that, so I put him on my sofa and let him sleep it off," Brook said.

"You drove while you were that drunk?" Oprah asked.

"Of course not! Tha Dogg dropped me off," Gio answered.

"I woke up after a horrible night of tossing and turning and cooked breakfast because I needed something to do while he snored on my sofa. I always cook when I'm nervous," Brook explained.

"And, I woke up to the smells of my mama's house," Gio joked.

"We ate, and we talked and decided to be friends. Because more than anything, we really had been great friends," Brook said.

"And after that, we were just friends for a loooonnnng time," Gio said. The audience started laughing. "Then, I got the call that I had been nominated. I was with Brook at the time. We got caught up in the excitement and one thing led to the next. I was so afraid she'd reject me. I knew I didn't even deserve her love, but I wanted it so bad," Gio said.

"Yeah, he had definitely been courting me, as my Grammie would've said," Brook joked. "And, that leads us to now. I thought no one knew my dirty little secret, our dirty little secret, until it was displayed on all of the newspapers. We had to tell my parents, his parents, our church family now knows. It has been a really difficult time for us." The audience 'ahhhed'. "And the negativity was directed at me at first. But, when they started on Gio, I was not having it," Brook said.

"Protective, huh?" Oprah said.

"Very," Brook replied seriously. "So, that is our story. Please, don't blame Gio. He didn't make me do anything. He didn't even know," Brook reiterated.

"One more question," Oprah said. "Gio said that this was the second time he was proposing to you and you turned him down the first time. Now, what was that about?" and the audience agreed. You could hear 'yeah' and 'what happened' mumbled throughout.

"Well, that would be that drunken night he showed up at my door after I broke the news to him about no longer being pregnant. He drunkenly asked me to marry him that night. Of course I said no! Wouldn't you?" The audience clapped again.

"I'm so glad you set the record straight. I think we'll all come away with a better understanding of what happened and why. Everyone has been fascinated with you Brook. You're the woman that stole this man's heart. Why don't you tell us a little about yourself, for instance, how did the name Brooklyn Bridges come about?" Oprah asked with a laugh.

"That would be my crazy parents, and there's not a lot to tell. Gio's more interesting. He's the star in our family," Brook dimpled.

"I noticed you said that when you wanted him to sit in the seat next to me. And the thing is, you really are being sincere. Are you shy or just not want to spotlight?" Oprah asked.

"Oh no, I'm not shy at all" Brook laughed as Gio shook his head in agreement and the audience laughed. "I just don't feel I deserve the spotlight. I haven't done anything spectacular for people to want to know who I am. Gio is the star. I'm the woman who loves him. I understand there are some things I'll have to deal with by being with him, like the paparazzi, but I don't understand the paparazzi wanting pictures of me when I'm not with him. I was Brooklyn Bridges, Radio Account Executive when we started dating. I was Brooklyn Bridges, Radio Account Executive when we fell in love. And I'm still the same Brooklyn Bridges. Gio is an amazing singer and a wonderful actor. On top of that, he's hella sexy. Don't you all agree?" Brook asked the audience with a grin, dimples deepening her cheeks. The audience clapped vigorously as Gio blushed. "So, while I'll go along with what comes with my role in our relationship, I still don't understand it."

"Well, America does want to know more about you. You've intrigued us all. So tell us, who is Brooklyn Bridges?" Oprah asked.

"I'm just a down-to-earth girl. I graduated from the University of Louisville. I work in Advertising Sales at a popular radio station in Atlanta. Well, at least I did until this madness started. I go to church, and I love *Wheel of Fortune*. I have a brother and parents, and soon will have a niece or nephew. I grew up in a normal, middle class home. I'm your average American woman who was blessed enough to find the man of her dreams," Brook answered with a smile.

"And, what is it you want people to get from this story?" Oprah asked.

"I want people to not blame Gio and to not judge me. I made a very hard and painful decision that I thought I needed to make at the time I made it. It's over. We have to move on from that. Gio and I are planning our wedding and we can't do that with this looming over us. The AMAs even canceled Gio's performance. That is just unfair," Brook stated.

"They canceled his performance! Well, we'll just see about that," Oprah threatened. The audience roared and clapped loudly.

"So, audience, what do we now think of America's sweethearts?" Oprah said, and the audience went wild with applause and gave them a standing ovation.

Brook's dimples deepened with her first genuine smile in over a month as she blew everyone kisses.

Epilogue

Oprah was IT! Ever since they were on her show, they became America's new "it" couple. The paparazzi went from calling them murderers to trying to find out about the details of their wedding. Brook became America's sweetheart and even learned to pose for the cameras. The only downfall was the paparazzi really began swarming them. The great part was they met Will and Jada, a really fun and comical couple. Brook was already impressed with them before she knew them, but once she met them, she really loved them. Will was all jokes and crazy, but in a classy sort of way, and Jada was crazy fool from the hood. Brook had not laughed that hard in forever. They went to a party and every A-lister was there from Jay-Z and Beyonce, T.I. and Tiny, and Tyler Perry. Jermaine Dupri was there and told Brook he knew she was the one when Gio brought her to the studio because Gio never bought women to the studio. And, Gio did perform at the American Music Awards. Oprah was the bizness! Gio had so many more movie offers, it was crazy cool. Even Brook got a few movie offers, which she quickly declined. They even asked if she'd be interested on being one of the *Housewives of Atlanta*.

"Not even an option," she had told Jamar. Yep, Oprah was definitely the woman. But best of all, Oprah had managed to get them on the *Wheel of Fortune*! Brook couldn't believe it. They were actually going to be contestants on the *Wheel of Fortune*! Her parents were flying in to attend the show live in the audience since they were huge fans. Brandon and Phyllis couldn't make it as she was ready to have the baby any day now, she just hoped her and Gio didn't blow it and freeze up. They were on the celebrity couple edition. Brook and Gio took their places behind the red podium area and got ready. They heard the introduction, and Brook was really nervous. She was squeezing Gio's hand hard. He gave her a smile and the light hit them.

"...And we have Giovanna Lay and fiancée Brooklyn Bridges, playing for their charity, The Study of Alzheimer's and Dementia."

Brook and Gio grinned, ready to spin that wheel, happy that things were finally falling into place. They were to be married soon, Gio's career was going great, and his new single that he played for Brook forever ago had dropped and debuted at number one. Brook had rented out her house and bought two more pieces of property and was preparing them for rental. She found that she loved fixing the houses up for families to enjoy. And, America no longer hated them. Brook and Gio were truly America's new sweethearts. And, they were ready to kick butt on their favorite game show, *Wheel of Fortune*.

THE END

CPSIA information can be obtained at www.ICGtesting.com
Printed in the USA
LVOW121616230212

270120LV00003B/99/P